10TH ANNIVERSARY

Special thanks to our well-wishers, who have contributed their congratulations and support.

"The best historicals, the best romances. Simply the best!"
—Dallas Schulze

"Bronwyn Williams was born and raised at Harlequin Historicals. We couldn't have asked for a better home or a more supportive family."
—Dixie Browning and Mary Williams,
w/a Bronwyn Williams

"I can't believe it's been ten years since *Private Treaty,* my first historical novel, helped launch the Harlequin Historicals line. What a thrill that was! And the beat goes on...with timeless stories about men and women in love."
—Kathleen Eagle

"Nothing satisfies me as much as writing or reading a Harlequin Historical novel. For me, Harlequin Historicals are the ultimate escape from the problems of everyday life."
—Ruth Ryan Langan

"As a writer and reader, I feel that the Harlequin Historicals line always celebrates a perfect blend of history and romance, adventure and passion, humor and sheer magic."
—Theresa Michaels

"Thank you, Harlequin Historicals, for opening up a 'window into the past' for so many happy readers."
—Suzanne Barclay

"As a one-time 'slush pile' foundling at Harlequin Historicals, I'll be forever grateful for having been rescued and published as one of the first 'March Madness' authors. Harlequin Historicals has always been *the* place for special stories, ones that blend the magic of the past with the rare miracle of love for books that readers never forget."
—Miranda Jarrett

"A rainy evening. A cup of hot chocolate. A stack of Harlequin Historicals. Absolute bliss! Happy 10th Anniversary and continued success."
—Cheryl Reavis

"Happy birthday, Harlequin Historicals! I'm proud to have been a part of your ten years of exciting historical romance."
—Elaine Barbieri

"Harlequin Historical novels are charming or disarming with dashes and clashes. These past times are fast times, the gems of romances!"
—Karen Harper

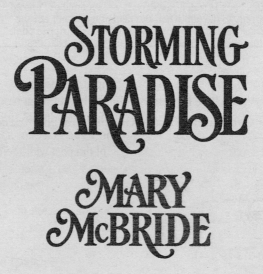

STORMING PARADISE

MARY McBRIDE

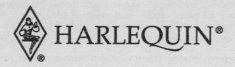

HARLEQUIN®

TORONTO • NEW YORK • LONDON
AMSTERDAM • PARIS • SYDNEY • HAMBURG
STOCKHOLM • ATHENS • TOKYO • MILAN • MADRID
PRAGUE • WARSAW • BUDAPEST • AUCKLAND

For Cynthia MacDonald Gamblin, my gold friend

ISBN 0-373-29024-1

STORMING PARADISE

Copyright © 1998 by Mary Myers

"We were discussing your dismissal, I believe,"

Libby said.

"All right." Shad crossed his arms over his chest. "Go ahead."

"I want you to leave."

"You already said that."

Libby crossed her arms now. "Well?"

"Well what?"

"Go." She angled her head toward the door. Once he was gone, she thought, she'd be able to breathe normally. However did he manage to suck up all the air in a room, leaving only scraps for everybody else to breathe?

But he wasn't going. He seemed stuck to that backward chair as if he were glued to it by the seat of his pants. The pants—she couldn't help but notice—that were pulled so taut across his thighs. She could actually see the power in those hard curves, could almost feel... Her eyes snapped back to his face, only to discover the most irritating grin she'd ever seen.

"You've got a lot to learn about firing, Miss Libby...."

Prologue

Dear Daughters, Amos Kingsland wrote.

And then, because he was a blunt man, never known to hold his temper or his tongue, he continued. *I'm dying.*

As if to underscore the words he wrote, pain shot through his belly just then. Amos closed his eyes. The doctors in Corpus Christi wanted to slice him open and poke around inside, but he'd told them to ply their lily-fingered trade on somebody else. He'd already been cut twice—once by a blind-drunk Cajun in New Orleans, and once—worse—by a woman in Matamoros who didn't like the word *adios.* Any more scars, he figured, and Saint Peter wouldn't recognize him when he knocked on the pearly gates. Or Lucifer, when he pounded on the blazing portals of perdition.

He was sixty-two years old and didn't particularly want to die, but—damn!—when the pain grabbed at his gut, he didn't take much pleasure in living.

Not that his pleasures had ever come easy. He'd worked hard creating Paradise—battling Mexicans and Indians and wrong-headed whites, wrestling long-horns and mustangs and Mother Earth herself until he'd built the biggest, most prosperous ranch in Texas.

He'd lost a partner along the way. Good riddance. Hoyt Backus had taken his profits in cash and had set himself up on an adjoining spread that he'd named Hellfire just for spite.

And Amos had lost a wife and two daughters, as well. He'd barely flinched fifteen years ago when Ellen had taken their two little girls to Saint Louis. Good riddance on that count, too. He hadn't missed them. A man didn't miss what he didn't need.

Until now.

He picked up the pen again.

I want you to come to Texas.

Dammit! What he wanted—what he needed—was a son. If he regretted anything, it was that. After Ellen walked out, he'd considered marrying again. But he'd found matrimony to be more hellish than holy. God knows, and the devil, too, that he hadn't done right by his wife. He was too hot tempered, too set in his ways, too hard. All the qualities that had allowed him to wrest Paradise out of a harsh land didn't add up to good husband material. Truth to tell, Amos just didn't like women very much.

Only now he was dying, and everything he'd worked so hard for was going to die with him because there wasn't anybody to take over. Somebody to keep the damn rustlers from chipping away at the stock. Somebody to oversee the breeding, to see that the cattle survived parched summers and harsh winters, then made it to the railhead without losing half their lives and most of their weight. Somebody to carry on.

A son. He needed a son and all he had were two daughters he hadn't even seen in fifteen years. Two women, fragile as their mother, no doubt, who'd spent their lives in the prim parlors and on the paved avenues of Saint Louis, who just might recognize beef on a plate in a fancy restaurant, but wouldn't know a steer on the hoof from a damn dairy cow if their lives depended on it.

Now Amos's life—his life's work—depended on them. Paradise depended on them.

Please, he wrote, grimacing, galled as much by that plea as by the pain in his midsection.

But then Amos heard the soft jingle of spurs in the vestibule outside his office door. A smile hitched up one corner of his mouth as he put down the pen and called out.

"That you, Shad? Come on in."

The heavily paneled door swung in, and Shadrach Jones stood in the doorway. Big as life, Amos thought. Barely tame. Tall and trim and tough as the land itself. A man nobody tangled with. Nobody with any sense anyway. Hell, he wished he'd had a son. A son like Shadrach Jones.

The man didn't so much enter a room as take possession of it. His gaze encompassed it first before his body even moved. Then he eased forward, boot heels hitting the floor with a slow certainty, as if the man were branding it, making it his own somehow. The ease of his stride belied the fact that every muscle and sinew was forever primed to react. Whenever possible, he would straddle a chair, subduing it with his size and weight. Right now, he lowered his big body into one of Amos's leather armchairs, scraped his hat off and balanced it on his knee.

Suddenly Amos became aware of a difference in the room. It seemed to grow warmer. It smelled of

healthy animals, both man and beast; of sunbaked
flesh, dust-caked denim and a hard day's work. It
reeked of vitality. Paradise. These days every room
Amos inhabited took on the stench of a sickroom, the
miasma of death. Shadrach Jones had changed all by
his mere presence.

"Hand me that bottle." Amos pointed to the whiskey on a shelf of the bookcase. He poured them each
a couple fingers and proceeded to ask his foreman
about the strays by Caliente Creek and the Brahma
bull that had arrived from Shreveport earlier that
week.

Judging from Jones's replies, all was well at Paradise. Almost all.

"I'm sending for my daughters," Amos said,
glancing down at the sheet of vellum on his desktop.

"All right." Shadrach Jones's tone was low and
somber, and his level gaze acknowledged the unspo-
ken—that he knew his boss was dying. His ensuing
silence said more—that the man had seen death before, many times, and accepted it. It simply was.

"I want you to see this letter gets mailed, Shad.
And when they arrive in Corpus Christi, I want you
to see they get to Paradise in one piece."

Jones nodded.

Silently then, Amos studied his face. Easy enough
tasks for such a man. Mail a letter. Bring two women
forty miles. What about the other? *Be my son,* Amos
longed to say.

He was a fool even to consider leaving Paradise to
a man whose mother was a Comanche and whose
father was anybody's guess, to a man whose past was
more shadow than sunlight. Hell, Hoyt Backus would
get himself a smart lawyer and take this place away

in a matter of weeks. His daughters were his legal, rock-solid heirs. No question about that. Hoyt could get all the lawyers in Texas then and Paradise would still elude him.

With a sigh, Amos drained his glass then leaned back in his chair. ''Do you remember those daughters of mine, Shad?''

A sudden grin split the big man's unshaven face. ''I remember a little redhead chasing the ninth life out of a barn cat.''

Amos nodded. ''That'd be Shulamith. Do you remember the other one?''

Shad resettled his hat on his knee, twisting the brim in his fingers. His grin disappeared. What he recalled was a little girl crying when her mama took her away. He'd been nineteen or twenty then, and hadn't known squat about little girls. But leaving he knew. He remembered his heart hurting for that skinny, dark-haired child.

''No,'' he told the old man. ''Can't say as I do.''

''Elizabeth,'' Amos murmured. ''We called her Libby.''

Shad nodded again. When he rose, the armchair creaked like saddle leather. ''Well, I'll be saying good-night now, Amos, unless there's anything else you need.''

A son. Amos almost said it. ''No. Nothing. Good night, Shad.''

Chapter One

Bill collectors! They were all overgrown, beady-eyed bullies in cheap serge suits and scuffed shoes. Shula Kingsland fully expected to see one of them right this minute, oozing out of the carriage that had just pulled up on Newstead Avenue in front of the house she shared with her sister.

Crouching behind the velvet overdrapes, Shula eased the lace sheers back a fraction. Her heart was pressing into her throat as she watched the cabbie extend a hand into the closed coach to help his passenger out.

"I'm not home," the redhead muttered into the dark folds of the drapes. "I simply won't answer the door. I won't. Let him knock till his knuckles bleed. Till dooms—"

The cabbie handed a woman down from the coach. A child scrambled after her.

Shula yanked back the sheers. "Oh, for heaven's sake." Her relief was sweet, although brief. She wasn't going to be forced, after all, to wheedle more time from some fool the bank had sent. But here came her sister with that ragamuffin again.

Shula stomped to the door, flinging it open just as the two of them were coming up the walk. Her bracelets jangled as she shook her fist and her rings glittered in the sunlight.

"Libby Kingsland," she called, "if you want to be a mother so badly why don't you marry and have babies of your own instead of dragging other people's children home?"

The two sisters faced off in the arched oak doorway—Libby in her stiff-boned, grosgrain walking suit and Shula, still ruffled in her morning wrapper despite the fact that it was late afternoon. Both women had fire in their eyes, unlike the child who cowered now, caught between the Kingsland sisters' silk flounces and sharp pleats.

In rough wool trousers and muddy brogans, and with her cropped blond hair, nine-year-old Amanda Rowan looked exactly like a boy. And it exasperated Shula Kingsland no end.

"Why can't you leave him…I mean…her with the Sisters of Charity where she belongs?" Shula hissed at her sister now.

Libby's gloved hand cupped the child's ear as she brought her close against her hip. "Because they're letting a certain someone out of jail today, Shula. And I'll be damned if he's going to hurt this little girl any more than he already has."

"Oh." Shula's mouth closed with a smart little snap and her ringed fingers fluttered at the frilled throat of her gown as she dropped an almost sympathetic look on the child half-hidden in Libby's skirt.

Gently Libby urged the little girl across the threshold and into the vestibule. "Go on up to the spare room, Andy. I'll be up soon to get you settled."

When the child nodded, blond hair straggled across her forehead. The sight provoked an instant cluck from Shula, whose hand whisked out to push the stray locks back.

She sighed wistfully. "Maybe while you're here, Miss Amanda Rowan," she said, emphasizing the feminine first name, "I'll take my curling iron to that haystack on your pretty head."

The child shot her a wounded look before turning to flee up the stairs. Shula winced at the sound of the big brogans thudding on each step.

"And maybe I'll take that same curling iron to your tongue, Shulamith Kingsland." Libby pulled the front door closed and turned the bolt. "There. Her father will have to crack through that to lay a finger on her now."

As her older sister strode down the hallway toward the kitchen, Shula regarded the locked door. Lord, how she hated being cooped up in this dismal little house. First with her tight-lipped, stiff-boned sister, and now with a little girl who was trying with all her might to be a boy. Still, she thought, it didn't hurt one bit that Libby was now as reluctant as she was to open the front door.

Libby! She was in the kitchen where Shula had tossed the unopened mail when she'd heard the carriage pulling up. The mail these days consisted mainly of overdue bills and disgusting letters from rude and impatient creditors, none of which she was anxious for her skinflint of a sister to see. Shula grabbed up her ruffled gown and rushed down the hall in Libby's wake.

As she pulled the pins from her hat, Libby scowled at the stack of dishes in the dry sink, noting that it had grown considerably since she'd rushed out of the house this morning. Princess Shula, no doubt, had used a clean plate every time she passed through the kitchen. Of course, it had never occurred to her to do up any of them.

Still, fair was fair, and the dishes were Libby's domain. They had agreed to that when they decided to use part of their small inheritance from their mother to buy and share a house. Shula, because she cared about money, would see to the bills and their investments. Libby would see to everything else, which meant she was cook, laundress, parlor maid and—judging now from the tower of dirty dishes in the dry sink—scullery maid.

Right this minute it felt closer to slavery, Libby thought as she tossed her hat onto the table before sagging into a chair. She tugged off her gloves and tossed those, too, onto the stack of mail that Shula hadn't bothered to open. Probably too busy taking clean plates from the cupboard and putting dirty ones in the sink.

Well, she didn't have time to worry about Shula's laziness right now. And she wasn't going to let her sister's comment about frustrated maternal instincts bother her, either. Amanda Rowan needed her help. Desperately. It was as simple as that.

A constable had brought the battered child to the Sisters of Charity on Christmas Eve, the same night they had locked John Rowan up for "doing his daughter wrong," as the grim-faced policeman had explained. The extent of that abuse was obvious, even to the sheltered Sisters of Charity who ran the orphanage, when they saw the bruises on young

Amanda's body. And when the child took a pair of scissors and chopped off her long blond curls; when she refused to wear anything but trousers and ungainly shirts and big, clumsy shoes; when she refused to respond to any name but Andy, it became obvious that, since being a little girl had only brought her pain, Amanda Rowan was determined to change that sad fact of her brutal, young life.

Libby, who spent time with the children at the orphanage, had been drawn to the battered child immediately. Out of compassion, certainly. Out of her need to help and comfort the bruised waif. And, perhaps as Shula continually accused, out of some frustrated maternal inclinations. She was a woman, after all. At the age of twenty-five it was only natural that she would feel such stirrings. But since she had no intention of marrying—ever—those instincts would remain just that. Vague stirrings.

As always, the thought of marriage made Libby's mouth crimp slightly. Her smooth brow furrowed. The very idea of marrying caused her stomach to tighten and twist into a hard little knot. She was unlike her sister, who reveled in the notion and seemed to consider marriage her very reason for being. Well, a profitable marriage, anyway.

Shula had already tried it once—unsuccessfully— by running off with the Van de Voort boy when she was eighteen. They had spent, according to the bride anyway, a grand and glorious time in Rome until young Charles Van de Voort had succumbed to a fever, leaving Shula a widow before her nineteenth birthday. She couldn't even claim widowhood, however, because the groom's family had had the marriage annulled, along with seeing that their former daughter-in-law was persona non grata in the finer drawing rooms in Saint Louis.

As a result, Shula was having a devil of a time trying to find a wealthy beau. And she spent the major portion of that time carping about her trials and tribulations, sighing and whining and generally making Libby's existence miserable.

"And here you sit, Libby Kingsland," she admonished herself now in a disgusted tone of voice, "stewing about your sister who's twenty years old and perfectly capable of taking care of herself when you ought to be worrying about a nine-year-old who can't and whose monster of a father means to snatch her back."

Shula wafted into the kitchen, plopping herself down in a chair directly across the table. "And if you don't stop talking to yourself, Libby Kingsland, people are going to start looking at you peculiarly and thinking you're an addle-brained old maid." The redhead gave her sister a satisfied little smile as she fussed with the ruffles at her neckline.

Libby's nose twitched. "What's that smell?"

"My new perfume." Shula gave her lush auburn curls a tender pat. "It's from Paris, France. Isn't it heavenly?"

Heavenly? It struck Libby more as something dredged up from the gutter—wet sycamore leaves, perhaps—but she knew from long experience that an honest reply would send Shula into a royal snit for the rest of the day.

"It's fine," she offered. Then, seeing Shula's mouth begin to curl down at the corners, Libby added, "It smells good."

While Shula fashioned a smile and lifted a wrist to

sniff the foul fragrance, Libby once again berated herself for even considering her baby sister's outsized, overwrought sensibilities when she had much more pressing problems. One anyway. The brutal John Rowan was getting out of jail. Today.

"I don't know what I'm going to do about Andy," she murmured.

Shula made a noncommittal little noise, extending an arm casually across the table, then reaching beneath one of Libby's gloves to extract the pile of mail. There were three envelopes, two of which she immediately recognized—another notice from the bank and another "polite but firm" note from the dressmaker. She slid them toward her and surreptitiously tucked those two into the folds of her gown, all the while studying the unfamiliar envelope postmarked Texas.

"I don't suppose you have any suggestions," Libby said.

"About what?" And who the devil was writing them from Texas? Shula wondered now, frowning as she slid a fingernail underneath the flap then slipped out a single sheet of vellum.

"About what!" Libby's fist hit the table. "Haven't you been listening to a word I've been saying, Shulamith Kingsland? Don't you care one whit what happens to that poor little—"

"Oh, my Lord!"

"What?"

Her sister's face had gone white as the cloth that covered the table except for the dabs of rouge on each of her cheeks.

"Shula," Libby insisted, "what in the world is the matter?"

"It's from him," Shula breathed, still staring at the paper in her hands.

"Him?" A score of young men's names flitted through Libby's brain. Shula was forever mentioning this one or that one. None of them, though, struck Libby as capable of shaking the stuffing from her sister or taking the color right out of her face. "Him who?" she demanded.

In a whisper that was more breath than voice, Shula replied, "Him. Our father."

Libby felt her own cheeks paling. "Give me that." She grabbed at the letter, but her sister immediately clasped it to her bosom and sighed dramatically.

"He begins it *Dear Daughters,*" Shula said.

Libby snorted. "That's probably because he can't remember either of our names." Angling back in her chair now, she crossed both arms. "Well, what else does the old goat have to say after fifteen years of utter silence?"

Shula's lips trembled. "He says he's dying, Libby."

"Dying?" The older sister repeated the word as if it were incomprehensible, as if she hadn't enough breath to clearly speak it nor enough sense to understand it. The Amos Kingsland she remembered was an enormous and vital man. He couldn't be dying. Every muscle in her body, every ounce of her being seized tight, rejecting the notion. "I don't believe it."

"He wants us to come to Texas. To Paradise."

"Paradise." Libby's head was swamped with images, not of angels in long, flowing robes or billowy white clouds, but of huge, dusty cowhands in leather chaps, of wild dark clouds rushing across a shadowed landscape. The music she heard suddenly wasn't com-

prised of heavenly harps or choirs of angels, but
rather the bawling of hundreds of cattle, the thunder
of thousands of hooves. She shivered and blinked,
then stared at her sister as if suddenly realizing she
wasn't alone.

Shula was smiling not so much at Libby but at the
world in general. The color had returned to her face.
It was flushed now, and her eyes were bright. Fever-
ishly so. "I knew it," she exclaimed, waving the letter aloft. "Didn't I tell you? Well, I probably didn't
since you close your ears whenever the man's name
is mentioned. But I always knew he'd send for us."

After pushing away from the table, Shula began
fluttering around the small kitchen. "Paradise. Don't
you just adore the sound of it. It's bigger than the
whole state of Rhode Island. Did you realize that,
Libby? Bigger than an entire state." Shula sucked in
a breath. "I guess that makes our father about as important as a governor. Do you recollect the house? I
confess I haven't any memory of it. Of course, I was
only five when we left. But it must be grand. Was it
grand, Libby?"

Her silk gown swished as Shula turned to her sister,
who sat rigid and silent. "Libby?"

"I won't go." Libby's lips barely moved when she
spoke. "I'm sorry he's dying, but I will not go. Not
ever."

Shula sniffed, resuming her circuit of the room.
"Don't be silly," she said dismissively. "Of course
you'll go. Our father's dying and he wants us. Good
Lord, Libby! Think what that means."

It meant trouble, Libby decided, or worse. Unable
to bear a second more of her sister's outlandish ex-

uberance, she had left the kitchen and had gone up to the spare room to check on the child, whom she found smack in the middle of the big four-poster bed, fast asleep. As gently as she could, Libby unlaced and removed the dreadful brogans from the little girl's feet.

How fortunate Andy was, Libby had thought, to be able to escape all her trials and terrors in such deep and innocent sleep. For a moment, as she had stood gazing down at her, Libby had envied the child for that. She was sleeping like an angel. Libby couldn't even remember the last time she'd had such an angelic rest.

But—dammit—yes, she could. It had been at Paradise with the white curtains billowing in, with South Texas sunshine buttering the walls of her room, with the lullaby of cattle and the sweet, sweet smells of hay and mock orange and jasmine.

So long ago.

Libby sat for a long time, keeping watch over the sleeping child, letting her mind drift back to a time and a place she had tried for fifteen years to erase from her memory.

Paradise! Lord, how she'd loved it. Every inch of the place from Caliente Creek where the mesquite tangled to the southernmost pastures where the air was heavy with salt from the gulf. The images—all the sights and sounds—came back so quickly and with such intensity now, it nearly took Libby's breath away. As if having been locked away for so many years, they were rushing and spilling over one another to make themselves seen and heard. Fast. Bursting its banks like a creek after a summer storm. A flash flood. Or—Libby smiled softly at the notion—as they said in Texas, a real gully-washer.

So many memories. And superimposed on them all was the image of Amos Kingsland. His glossy black boots. His enormous, work-roughened hands. His deep auburn hair and the scratchy beard that bristled from his chin. That beard was what Libby remembered best.

Her father had been a steamboat captain in the Gulf of Mexico before venturing inland to raise cattle. The salt breezes of the gulf seemed to have permeated his beard and to have given it a permanent thrust so that, even in the house, it was as if the wind were tugging at his chin.

Or so his little girl had imagined. It hadn't been wind at all, Libby thought now, but pure stubbornness, a will to succeed at any cost, and no qualms whatsoever about bending anyone to that will. As he had bent her mother. Bent and nearly broken the sweet, soft Ellen McCafferty Kingsland Carew.

Just then, as if the mere thought of her mother had somehow conjured up her form, Shula poked her curly head in the door.

Quickly Libby touched a finger to her lips, gesturing toward the sleeping child.

"You look so much like Mama sometimes, Shula, I find myself looking twice," she whispered.

The ruffled apparition rustled across the room and sought her image in the mirror over the dresser. "I do, don't I?" She rearranged a few curls, then leaned forward to more closely inspect her eyebrows. "Of course, Mama was a fool, bless her heart."

Libby opened her mouth to protest, then kept silent. Sadly enough, it was true. Their mother had been, if not a fool, then an exceptionally weak woman. Where she'd gotten the gumption to walk out on Amos Kingsland was a mystery. Even so, that strength had quickly deserted her once she had married that tight-fisted mercantilist and bully, Edgar Carew.

Thoughts of her poor mother prompted Libby to whisper, "What would you do, Shula, if a man ever lifted a hand to you?"

Her sister snorted. "I'd slap him back." Her eyebrow arched in the mirror. "Or worse."

Libby sighed. "I wonder why Mama didn't."

Shula shrugged now. "She was afraid, I guess. Who knows? I can tell you I gave our dear stepfather the back of my hand on quite a few occasions, along with several pieces of my mind."

Libby's eyes widened in astonishment. "What did he do?"

"He just laughed. The pig! I hated losing Mama, Libby, but I have to say I didn't mind one little bit that that awful Edgar perished in that carriage accident, too."

Shula sighed softly at her reflection, then turned to face her sister, her hands lifting to fasten on her hips. "We need to start packing, Libby. Where's that old trunk of Mama's I took to Italy with me?"

"I have no idea." But what Libby knew was that she wasn't prepared to argue now, here, and possibly wake Andy, who needed all the peaceful sleep she could get. Once thwarted, Shula wouldn't be able to whisper, she would probably scream.

"Take a look up in the attic," she suggested, hoping to occupy Shula temporarily and thus forestall their confrontation.

"I hate it up there," Shula said. "It's dark as a

week of midnights, and all that dust gets into my pores and just takes up residence for days no matter how hard I scrub. I won't even mention the spiders." Shula shivered, sending her gown into a flurry. Then her expression brightened. "Maybe I could just order a new trunk. One with all those cute little drawers and..."

The heat of Libby's glare withered her sister's speech, as well as her enthusiasm.

"Well, they *are* cute," she finished glumly. "We don't want to look like two kitchen maids when we go to Texas, do we?"

As much as she felt like one sometimes, Libby thought there was nothing wrong in looking like one. But since she wasn't going to Texas anyway, it didn't make any difference. She continued to scorch her sister with her gaze, using her thumb now to indicate the door.

"All right. I'll go," complained Shula as she moved across the room. "But if I'm not back downstairs in fifteen minutes, Libby, it's because I'll have choked to death on all that dust."

"Maybe you'll be lucky, sister," Libby offered encouragingly as she bit back on a grin. "Maybe those big, hairy spiders will get you first."

With a shudder and a strangled little moan, Shula swept out of the room.

As soon as the door clicked closed, little Andy jerked upright in the center of the bed. She rubbed an eye with one grimy knuckle, then mumbled, "I heard about Texas. I heard it's real nice there."

Her comment, cool and disinterested as it sounded, didn't fool Libby for a moment. The child was terrified of being abandoned, or infinitely worse, of being returned to the clutches of her father. Libby left her chair and perched on the edge of the bed, reaching to smooth a pale hank of hair from the little girl's forehead.

"Texas is nice," she said, "but I'm not going there. I like it fine right here."

"I do, too," the child responded. "Especially when I'm with you." Andy scuttled across the mattress now and wrapped her arms around Libby, burying her face in the pleats of her bodice. "Don't let my papa take me back, Miss Libby. I want to stay here with you. Oh, please, don't let him take me back."

Libby hugged her tightly. "I won't, honey. I promise I won't let him get within a foot of you."

Fine words, she thought, as she sat and rocked the frightened little girl. The Sisters of Charity had cautioned her only this morning that John Rowan, once out of jail, had every legal right to reclaim his daughter.

"And he'll try," Sister Josepha had said. "Sure as the devil's prodding him from behind. They can't keep the man locked away forever. Once he's out, he'll be needing her for his cooking and his cleaning and whatever other despicable things the man has on his mind."

Libby's reply had been forceful. "I just won't let him."

Sister Josepha had merely shaken her head sadly, as if to say "How can you stop him?"

"I wish I knew," Libby murmured now. "Oh, Lord, I wish I knew."

The pounding on the door was enough to loosen the mortar from every brick in the two-story house.

By the time Libby got downstairs—after shoving Andy into a wardrobe and covering the child with a quilt—Shula was already there, leaning all her weight on one shoulder against the front door.

"Shh!" she hissed when Libby rushed to join her. "Just keep still and he'll think nobody's home."

"Miss Kingsland, I know you're in there," a voice boomed from outside while fists continued to batter the paneled oak.

When Libby opened her mouth to reply, Shula hissed again, menacingly this time, so Libby kept still. Maybe it wasn't such a bad idea, she thought, letting John Rowan believe the house was empty. Surely the man's fists couldn't keep up that pummeling indefinitely. From the sound of him, he was already getting hoarse.

The sisters stood there for what seemed like an hour, feeling the door tremble and quake, hearing the doorknob rattle again and again. When it stopped, and when there was only silence on the other side of the door, they waited another few minutes before they spoke.

"Andy's not safe here," Libby whispered. "Oh, Shula, what in the world am I going to do?"

Shula draped a comforting arm around her sister's shoulder. Certain as Shula was that their unwelcome visitor had been another bill collector—the most aggressive of them yet!—she was briefly tempted to allay Libby's fears and tell her the truth, that little Andy was plenty safe from creditors. It would have comforted Libby, no doubt, but then it wouldn't have done Shula herself the least bit of good.

So instead, she said quite somberly, "I only know one solution, Libby. We'll simply have to take the poor child with us when we go to Texas.'' She embellished her words with a lingering, sympathetic sigh. ''I believe we ought to leave as soon as possible, don't you? For little Andy's sake?''

Chapter Two

The big red-and-black Concord coach—its door branded with the famous *Circle P*—was a familiar sight on the streets of Corpus Christi. Amos Kingsland always came to town in style. He kept fresh teams at intervals along the forty-mile stretch. In the old days it guaranteed he could outrun whatever marauders lay in wait along the way. Now, with most of the rustlers and bandidos having been driven off, the coach's speed wasn't so much for safety as it was for its own sake and to let everyone in Corpus know that God, in the guise of Amos Kingsland, was down from Paradise.

Eb Talent was the reinsman. The grizzled sailor-turned-landlubber had been with Kingsland since the steamboat captain had moved inland nearly thirty years before. Eb hadn't been a young man then and the rigors of riding the range that first year had left him with what he called "permanent saddle sores," so he'd carved himself out an indispensable niche as cook and coachman. The red-and-black conveyance was his spit-shined pride and joy.

On this afternoon, though, it wasn't God who was

riding in the closed coach, but his foreman, Shadrach Jones.

With a blistering crack of his whip, Eb cut the corner onto Water Street, rocking the big coach and sending its dozing passenger sprawling onto the floor.

Once in the livery, the wiry man climbed down from the high seat, brushed the dirt from his britches and opened the door. His grin revealed an odd assortment of gaps and tobacco-stained teeth. "Six hours and thirty-eight minutes," he announced. "Only done it faster once, and that was back in '76 when we had that pair of quick-footed grays."

Shadrach Jones punched the crease back in the hat that had taken his whole weight when he slid from the seat. "You're a goddamn miracle, Eb." He slapped the black Stetson on his dark head before angling his long legs out of the coach, then stood a moment, gazing around the dim confines of the stable.

"Six and thirty-eight. Damn! I didn't know I had it in me," the driver exclaimed.

Shad's mouth slid into a grin—a flare of white against his deep bronzed skin—and he clapped the smaller man on the shoulder. "I wasn't surprised for a minute, hoss. You're still the best whip-cracker in Texas."

Of course, why the man had been in such a damn hurry was beyond Shad. It wouldn't have bothered him if the trip from Paradise had taken twice as long. He was about that eager to meet up with Amos's two daughters and escort them back to the ranch.

He'd tried to get out of it, coming up with at least half-a-dozen crises that required his immediate attention, but Amos would have none of it. "You're the only man I'd trust my daughters to, Shad,'' the old man had said. ''Do this for me, son.''

Hell. How could anybody deny what might be a dying man's last request? And when that man called you son...well, it wasn't in Shad to say no. He'd killed men for Amos Kingsland; the least he could do now was round up the two stray heifers and cart them back to Paradise. If only they were heifers, he thought. He knew how to handle those. But ladies...

The quiet of the stable was suddenly broken by the sound of female laughter and the swish of skirts.

Eb shook his head. ''What do they do, smell you?'' he muttered as three young women paraded across the hay-strewn floor, each trying to elbow the others out of her way, each flashing her petticoats in order to outdo the others.

Shad would have replied, but his arms were quickly filled with women. Rosa clasped her arms around his waist. Nona plastered herself against his hip. Carmela—bless her—fit herself like a favorite saddle to his backside.

''We saw the coach,'' Nona cried, her face tipped up, her breath catching. ''We ran. Come see us.''

''Come now.'' Rosa pulled seductively at his gun belt.

While the prostitutes continued to press against Shad, Eb Talent stood nearby, poking a chew into his cheek. ''Beats me, Jones,'' he mumbled, ''how a fella who claims he don't care for ladies can draw 'em like flies on dead meat.''

Shad lifted his head from Nona's ardent kiss. ''I said I didn't care for *ladies,* Eb. I never said anything about real women.''

The girls giggled and squirmed all the more in light

of the compliment, until Shad was forced to peel them away, one by one. They refused to leave until he had promised to spend the night—upstairs—at the Steamboat Saloon. It wasn't a difficult promise as that had been Shad's intention all along after he had paid a dutiful call on the Misses Kingsland to inform them that they would be leaving for Paradise bright and early the following morning.

Eb turned from watching the prostitutes as they sashayed out of the stable. He cast his cohort a look that told him he was one lucky son of a bitch, then spat out of one corner of his mouth.

"Don't s'pose Amos's daughters will be half so taken with all that road dust, though." The driver grinned. "Guess they're used to fancy fellas who smell more like hair tonic than Texas dirt."

As he realigned the gun belt that Nona had nearly undone, Shad grumbled, "Some women like it fine."

"Yup," mused Eb, "I 'spect it depends some who it's on." He bent then to pick up a bucket and rag, and began to wash down the dusty red-and-black coach. "Still, you best wash some of that dirt off, Shad, afore you pay your respects to the Captain's daughters. Can't walk through the door of a fancy eating establishment looking like a man who works for a living, I hear."

Grumbling under his breath and rolling up his sleeves, Shad ambled toward the washbowl on a bench. "Doesn't make much difference since I'll be taking my supper at the saloon," he called over his shoulder.

"Not tonight, you ain't," Eb called back.

"What do you mean?" Shad dipped his hands into the soapy gray water and splashed it on his face. "I always eat and bed down at the Steamboat when I'm in Corpus.''

"Bed down maybe, but tonight you're eating with the Captain's daughters at a fancy restaurant.''

The big man shook his wet head, sending beads of water in a wide spray. He pulled the towel roll till he found a dry spot. "Says who?" he asked.

"Says Amos.'' Eb put down his bucket and rag, then fished in his pants pocket a moment before producing two gold coins. "He gimme these here double eagles to give you. Said you're to see those females have a proper meal. I'm surprised he didn't tell you hisself.''

Actually Eb Talent wasn't at all surprised. When the boss had handed him the money and had instructed him in how it was to be spent, Amos had laughed as he added, "Shad'll tell me no to my face, Eb, but once he's in Corpus he can't do that, now, can he?''

When it came to getting his way, the Captain didn't miss a trick. And nobody knew that better than Shadrach Jones. Given half a chance, Shad could usually outfox the old man, too. The two of them were so much alike that some of the hands at Paradise had speculated over the years that the Captain might even be Shad's natural father. Eb knew different, though. He and Amos had still been steaming back and forth across the Gulf of Mexico when Jones had been born some thirty-four or thirty-five years ago.

There was a lot about Shadrach Jones that Eb didn't know, including his sire, but he did know right that moment in the livery stable that the man was about to explode. The former sailor was tempted to haul himself up into the coach as fast as his old legs could move in order to avoid the fireworks.

But Shad didn't explode. He laughed instead, shook his damp head and muttered, "That old fox. I'm telling you, Eb, I don't envy the Almighty once Amos Kingsland starts staking his claim on the real Paradise." He jerked a thumb heavenward, then extended his hand toward Eb. "Gimme the damn money."

Eb did as he was told, saying, "I sure wouldn't mind being a fly on the wall when you're having supper with those gals."

Shad jammed the coins into his back pocket. "Come on along then. Only don't expect to linger over coffee and prissy little desserts. Fancy or not, this is going to be one quick meal." Shad sighed. "I don't get to town so often that I intend to waste my time with a couple of thin-lipped, bony-assed Eastern ladies when there's all those willing women down the street."

For a moment, the notion had a certain appeal for Eb. "Maybe I could get a couple new recipes. Fancy stuff, you know, to fix up for the Captain."

"Sure," Shad agreed.

Then the old man glanced back at the big coach, still covered with dust. He shrugged. "Nah. Guess I'll stay right here. Anyway, fancy eats might not sit right with the Captain what with his aching stomach."

"Suit yourself." Shad planted his black Stetson on his damp hair and turned for the stable door. "I won't be long, hoss. You can count on that."

The second floor, corner room in the Excelsior Hotel was pleasant but small, made smaller still by a cot and a huge assortment of trunks, handbags and hat-boxes. The room was so crammed that Shula Kingsland could barely pace. She kept tripping over luggage.

"Damnation," she howled, grabbing onto the iron footboard to keep from pitching forward onto the floor. "Well, I don't know why I bother holding on, really. A person couldn't possibly fall *down* in here. All this junk would keep a body propped up indefinitely."

Libby was tempted to remind her sister that most of the junk was hers. Instead, she remained silent and continued to press a cool cloth to the forehead of the little girl lying on the cot. The long trip from Saint Louis—by train and finally by steamship—had taken a toll on Andy. She'd been seasick on the steamship from Mobile and what little she had eaten had promptly come back up. Shula, too, had claimed to be deathly ill while they were on *The Belle of the Gulf,* but it hadn't stopped her from taking a seat at the captain's table or consuming copious quantities of oysters and champagne.

"Lord, it's hot in here," Shula said now, fanning herself with her hand as she picked her way toward the window. "I'm fairly dripping, Libby. I don't remember Texas being so hellishly hot, do you?"

"It's no worse than Saint Louis," Libby said softly. Andy seemed to have drifted off to sleep and she didn't want to wake her. She angled off the cot as delicately as she could. "If you'd sit a minute, Shula, maybe you'd cool off."

Shula was peering out the window now. "I can see the gulf."

"Well, that should make you feel cooler."

"No," Shula said with a sniff. "Looks to me like it's boiling."

Libby sighed. It would be a miracle, she thought, if she survived this day, let alone the several weeks she planned to remain in Texas. It wasn't a trip she wanted to make, but all her resolve had evaporated that afternoon last week when John Rowan had nearly broken down their front door in his attempt to get his daughter back. Damn that man anyway. Libby had felt she'd had no choice but to spirit the child away— far away—for a while at least. With any luck, the man would commit other crimes for which the police could successfully put him away permanently.

In the meantime, she merely hoped she could endure her sister's theatrics. Sharing such close quarters with Shula was like being strapped to a front-row seat at a melodrama. The woman could go on for hours about everything and nothing. Complaining, it seemed, had become Shula's favorite pastime. And she never just talked. She exclaimed!

At the moment she was flapping her arms in an effort to dry the damp fabric of her dress. "I'll be dehydrated in a few hours," Shula muttered now. "How can anybody stand this? It's like a steam bath."

Libby went to the window and gazed out at the sparkling gulf. Funny she didn't recall it, she thought. Her memories of Texas were land, not water. Land and nothing else, as far as the eye could see. Her father's land. Paradise. She wondered if it would seem as vast, as purely magical now that she was grown.

When she turned from the window, she was greeted

with the sight of Shula's draped and ruffled backside as she bent to rummage through a valise.

"Aha!" Shula straightened up, holding a tin of talc. "Help me undo my dress, will you, Libby?"

Libby sighed and crossed the little room to assist her, more aware than ever that her own dress felt clammy and uncomfortable. After unfastening a myriad of tiny buttons, she went back to the window while Shula slapped powder under her arms.

"I want to look good for Daddy," Shula proclaimed. "What if he's disappointed, Libby? What if he just plain doesn't like us?"

"If he doesn't, he doesn't." Libby shrugged, continuing to gaze out at the water.

"Well, that's a fine attitude. Are you telling me it makes no difference to you whether you wind up filthy rich or as poor as a piddling church mouse?"

"We're not poor, Shula." Libby turned to discover her sister wreathed in a cloud of talcum powder, waving a ringed hand to clear the air. Shula appeared flustered by more than mere talc dust, however.

"We're not poor, Shula," Libby said again.

"I meant relatively speaking," Shula insisted.

Libby angled one hip onto the windowsill now and crossed her arms. Her lips firmed as her gaze narrowed on her sister. "Sometimes I think money's all you care about."

"It isn't *all*."

"Name something else then." Libby's chin lifted and her arms crossed tighter. "I dare you."

Shula's brow wrinkled a moment, then she made a little clucking sound and bent to brush powder from the drapes of her overskirt. "I care about how I'm going to keep from looking like a dowdy catfish in all this humidity.''

"Ah," crowed Libby. "Money and appearances."

Shula glared at her. "I'm sure our daddy doesn't want two ragtag, mop-headed women descending on the ranch. Gracious! I want to look nice for him, that's all. Who knows? We might be the last human beings he'll ever see. It's our duty to make his final moments as pleasurable as possible."

"Foolish," Libby muttered under her breath.

"I heard that," her sister shot back. "It's all right with me if you want to look like a frump. But men take great pleasure in the way a woman presents herself. And maybe if you spent a little more time worrying about your appearance, you might not be Miss Kingsland all your life, *Miss* Kingsland."

It was an ancient argument. Their surroundings may have changed, but their differences remained. And it was an argument that Libby knew she would never win, so she was relieved when a soft knock sounded on their door.

"Now who do you suppose that is?" Shula did up a few fast buttons, then bustled to the door. She opened it a fraction.

Libby could hear a deep Texas drawl coming from the opposite side of the door. In a flash, it brought back the music of Paradise. A shiver rippled up and down the length of her spine.

Then, a moment later, Shula closed the door and just stood there, looking a little addled, breathing as if she had only just mastered that most difficult task.

"Who was it?" Libby inquired.

Shula sucked in a full breath then, and waved a dismissive hand. "Oh, I don't know. Just some big, dirty cowboy who says he's supposed to take us to supper. I told him we had made other arrangements.''

''Shula!'' Libby strode through the trunks, kicked a hat box out of her path and opened the door herself. Then, like her sister, she suddenly couldn't remember how to breathe. And when she did remember, Libby was overwhelmed.

The big, dusty cowboy was halfway down the hall, but still the fragrance of Paradise lingered where he had stood. Leather and lye soap and dust. Sunshine and something more. Something purely and gloriously male. Libby cleared her throat and called out to him.

''Sir. Just a moment, please.''

Hell and damnation. Shadrach Jones stopped dead in his tracks. Another couple yards of carpet and he would have been trotting down the stairs, whistling, then pushing through the hotel's fancy front door toward freedom. And Rosa and Nona and—bless her— Carmela.

Now he shook his head slightly, then scraped off his hat again and pressed it over his heart as he turned to get a look at the lady who'd just put the capper on his escape.

This one looked every bit the lady, too. The redheaded sister who had answered his knock on the door had been as painted and powdered as any whore he'd ever seen. This one, though, had *lady* written on every stiff pleat, every rigid bone, and every square inch of her prim little face. Tiny, this one. Pretty, too. For a lady.

''Ma'am,'' he drawled, moving toward her.

She reached out a small, pale hand. "I'm Elizabeth Kingsland."

Even though he'd just washed up and his hands were probably cleaner than they'd been in weeks, Shad still felt compelled to run his palm along his pant leg before he took her hand. Her grip was firmer than he anticipated. Even so, her bones felt delicate and breakable as a newborn kitten in the depths of his hand. He let her go after one quick pump.

"I'm your father's foreman, ma'am. Shadrach Jones." He shifted his weight onto one hip and held his hat in both hands now, dragging the brim through his fingers, wishing like hell this little lady would slam the door in his face the way the other one had.

"My sister said you had mentioned supper?" She tipped her heart-shaped face up.

Well, hell. There went half his evening. He was doomed, but for Amos's sake he figured he'd just have to smile and take it like a man. "Yes, ma'am."

His sudden, slantways grin did the oddest, most unexpected thing to Libby's stomach. It quivered and then drew taut, like a reticule whose strings had been pulled tight. Or perhaps it wasn't the grin at all, she thought fleetingly. Perhaps it was as simple as hunger. Still, almost before she knew it, Libby was accepting the huge cowboy's invitation.

"I can't speak for my sister, Mr. Jones, but I'd be happy to accompany you. If you'd like to wait downstairs, I'll join you in a few moments."

"Yes, ma'am."

She closed the door on that engaging grin.

"Well? What did he say?" Shula was reclining atop the bed now, with a damp cloth covering her eyes.

Libby smiled. "'Yes, ma'am,' mostly."

"He didn't happen to say what time he'll be calling for us tomorrow, did he?" Shula whined. "I hope it's not before ten o'clock. You know how I am in the morning."

"He didn't say." Libby was gazing in the mirror now, frowning. All of a sudden her hair seemed wrong—too curly, not curly enough, just wrong somehow—and she wasn't quite sure why that bothered her. She picked up her hat and jammed in the pins. "I'll ask him at supper."

Shula swiped the cloth from her eyes. "You're not actually considering going with him, are you?"

"I'm not considering it, Shula." Libby turned and faced her sister. "I'm doing it. One of us ought to go since the man was kind enough to ask. If you'd like to go yourself, I'll stay here and watch over Andy."

Shula lay back on the pillows and returned the cloth to her eyes. "I can think of a million things I'd rather do than suffer through a meal with some big, dumb ranch hand who only says 'yes, ma'am' and 'no, ma'am.'" With a little sigh, she added, "Even if he is handsomer than sin."

"Really?" Libby shrugged as she pulled on her gloves. "I hadn't noticed."

Shula yawned. "Now why doesn't that surprise me one little bit?" She flounced onto her side and scrunched a pillow beneath her cheek. "Try not to wake me when you come back, Libby. I'm sure we'll have to be up before the damn chickens tomorrow."

Libby didn't know how handsome sin was, but she had to admit, seeing the tall cowboy spilling out of the dainty chair in the hotel lobby, he was a very nice looking man. All of him. From his wide shoulders to his trim waist and on down the endless length of his denim-clad legs.

His hair was dark and longer than she was accustomed to seeing on gentlemen. She thought she liked the way the raven waves brushed his collar and framed his angular face. That face wasn't tan so much as it was bronze, and not all of that deep color had come from long hours under a hot Texas sun, she was sure. Judging from his cheekbones, the strong flare of his nose and the flint in his dark eyes, Libby assumed her father's foreman was more Indian than Jones.

Funny, she thought as she crossed the Persian-carpeted lobby while scrutinizing the man in the chair. She felt an overwhelming sense of recognition, yet she doubted that Shadrach Jones had been at Paradise fifteen years ago. He didn't look like the type to stay in a place fifteen minutes, let alone fifteen years. He looked wild somehow—dark and shiny as a mustang stallion she remembered from years before.

The thought brought instant color to her cheeks. Stallions, indeed, Libby admonished herself, straightening her shoulders and firming her mouth as she proceeded toward him.

When he caught sight of her, he unwound from the little chair and rose with what Libby could only define as a casual grace. The way smoke rises on a windless day. He was, she thought suddenly, handsomer than sin.

"Mr. Jones." She extended a gloved hand.

Damnation! There she went again, putting that little paw out for him to crush. He could feel the kitten warmth even through the thin fabric of her glove.

And, as before, he had intended to let go immediately when it struck him like a lightning bolt that this lady was the dark-haired, skinny little girl who'd been crying all those years ago. Elizabeth? No...Libby. Sad little Libby.

She was looking up at him now, dry-eyed, even a trifle confused. He wondered all of a sudden if he had said her name out loud.

"Miss Kingsland," Shad said now, letting go of her hand, trying to clear his head of visions from half a lifetime ago.

"It was kind of you to ask us to supper, Mr. Jones."

"It's not exactly me, ma'am. Your father—"

"I realize that," she said, cutting off what was probably going to be a pretty muddled, bush-beaten excuse anyway.

"My sister has decided not to join us, I'm afraid."

Shad didn't know if he was glad about that or not. Was one lady worse than two? Especially when the one was prim little Miss Libby? He shrugged slightly as he planted his hat on his head.

"Well, let's get going then," he drawled as he gestured toward the hotel's front door.

It wasn't exactly an enthusiastic invitation, Libby thought. More like a man on his way to the gallows than one preparing to dine. The man had all but admitted he was just doing his job and following her father's orders. Still, he offered her another of those sunny Texas grins as he was waving her toward the door.

"Yes, let's," she said with as much brightness as she could muster, once again aware of that peculiar thread tightening in her stomach.

Libby sniffed garlic as she stepped into the foyer of the restaurant. She sniffed trouble, too, the minute she caught a glimpse of the crystal sconces and the silk-swagged windows. It was a very elegant establishment. Much too elegant for a big dusty cowboy and a woman in a wilted traveling suit.

Behind her, Shadrach Jones muttered a grim little oath as his hand pressed into the small of her back to urge her forward toward a mustachioed little man in a black cutaway coat whose expression was hovering between panic and disgust.

The maître d' dismissed her with a quick *"Bon soir, madame,"* then slid his gaze to her companion. "I am sorry, *monsieur,* but gentlemen are not permitted to dine without the appropriate neckwear."

There was a sudden change in the temperature of the room. It had seemed merely warm before, but now Libby noticed that it had become distinctly hot. And she realized that the source of that heat was the man standing behind her. Shadrach Jones was giving off heat like a blast furnace.

"Appropriate neckwear," he muttered now from between clenched teeth, making the phrase sound like an oath.

"Oui, monsieur." The little man gave his mustache a quick twist. His eyes flicked toward the door, as if inviting them to use it.

Libby would have, too, only her father's foreman was bolted to the floor like a big, hot stove behind her.

"You mean like a tie?" he drawled now.

The little man lofted his gaze heavenward as if to seek patience and deliverance from ill-dressed, persistent fools. *"Oui, monsieur,"* he said with a sigh.

"Kinda like the one you're wearing?"

The question seemed innocent enough, but Jones's tone—much to Libby's horror—was what a snake might use if snakes could speak. Its lethal quality seemed lost on the officious little man, however, who lifted a finely manicured hand to touch his black cravat.

"*Oui, monsieur. Comme ça.*"

The words were barely out of the Frenchman's mouth when a dark hand flashed out and, in what seemed like a single movement, flicked loose the bow and whipped the tie from beneath the starched white collar with such incredible speed that Libby thought she caught a whiff of smoke from rope-burned skin.

A second after that, Shadrach Jones was looping the black silk around his own neck and grinning down on the stupefied maître d'.

"We'd like a table for two," he drawled.

The little man swallowed audibly. "*Oui, monsieur.*"

Chapter Three

You wanted fancy, Amos? Here's your goddamn fancy. Shad yanked at the silk noose around his neck and let his gaze travel around the room as he forced himself to cool off. Actually, he thought, he'd acted with considerable restraint in just relieving that snooty horse's ass of his necktie when what he'd really wanted to do was take the man's life for looking at little Miss Libby like she wasn't good enough to shine his shoes. Prissy, pointy-toed French shoes, too. Good thing he—

"Mr. Jones?"

His eyes flicked back to the lady across the table. Hell, he'd been so steamed up he'd almost forgotten she was there. And what the hell was she smiling about?

"Ma'am?"

"You're either grinning or you're grumbling, Mr. Jones." She cocked her head to one side, causing the silk flowers on her hat to sway. "Do you have any neutral expressions?"

Shad laughed, and he felt the heat of his temper

dissipate and his whole body relax. "I guess not. I apologize, ma'am."

"There's no need. But thank you. I suspect it's something you don't do too often." She tilted her head the other way now and the silk posies followed along while her smooth brow wrinkled and her fine eyebrows pulled together. "You remind me of my father, Mr. Jones."

From her tone, Shad couldn't tell if she meant that as a compliment or not. He didn't know how to respond, so he just kept looking at her. He caught himself wondering what she'd look like without that silly garden of a hat, then dismissed the thought. What did he care anyway?

"How is my father?" she asked him now. "Is he truly dying, or was that just a ruse to draw us to Texas?"

"He's dying."

She winced and sucked in a quick little breath, making Shad immediately sorry he'd been so blunt. But, hell, she'd asked, hadn't she? He sighed roughly.

"Your father's had a good life, Miss Kingsland. A long one, too. I don't know for a fact, but I think he's ready to go."

"I imagine he's in a great deal of pain." Her lips drew together, wavering just a bit.

"It's tolerable," he replied.

She nodded, letting her gaze fall to her clasped hands. Damnation! She wasn't going to cry, was she? Shad felt a fine film of sweat glaze his skin now. *Oh, hell. Don't cry, lady. Please.*

He was almost relieved when the snooty little Frenchman appeared at the table just then and distracted her by putting a menu into her hands. When she thanked him, her voice was solid and her eyes were dry. Lord! Thank you.

Along with sweet relief, Shad suddenly felt hungry enough to stick a fork right into a steer. He reminded himself he needed to keep his strength up for the night ahead, too, once he ditched Miss Libby. He opened his own menu, muttered a gruff curse when he saw that it was written in French or some prissy language, then closed it and slapped it on the table. ''I'll have whatever you're having,'' he told the lady glumly.

Her sister hadn't been entirely wrong, Libby thought. Mr. Jones's conversation during dinner had been largely limited to ''Yes, ma'am'' and ''No, ma'am.'' Of course, she didn't suppose her own was any more scintillating, unaccustomed as she was to dining with men.

She had ordered two thick steaks, and when he was finished, she offered Jones what was left of her own. As they exchanged plates, their hands touched. Just a touch. It barely lasted a second, and yet it had such an immediate and potent effect on Libby that she nearly dropped the plate. She could feel the color rise in her face until her cheeks were burning. And her stomach once again began that infernal fluttering.

Touching her wrist to her forehead, she wondered if she wasn't coming down with a fever of some sort. But her skin was cool, or relatively so considering it was summertime in Texas. Her water goblet was empty, so she took a healthy sip of the champagne she had ignored earlier.

Her dark companion winked at her now, which didn't do a thing to dispel the butterflies inside her.

"Go easy on that, Miss Kingsland. I wouldn't want your daddy to think I'd gotten his daughter drunk."

She had felt a little drunk even before swallowing the pale champagne, Libby thought. Shula ought to be the one sitting here, sipping the bubbly liquid. She was the one who loved fine wines and elegant settings, who conversed easily and thrived on the warm attentions of the opposite sex.

What in the world was she doing even thinking about a man's warm attention? Her father's foreman had paid more attention to his steak than he had to her. But that was just the way Libby wanted it. Didn't she always dress in dowdy, dull-colored clothes specifically to avoid such attentions? And wasn't she always secretly glad to hide in Shula's gaudy shadow?

You best remember just who and what you are, Libby Kingsland, she reprimanded herself sharply. Then, deciding her cheeks had cooled off sufficiently, she raised her face to meet the dark eyes of Shadrach Jones.

"What time will we be leaving for Paradise, Mr. Jones?"

"Oh, about eight o'clock." Shad was making some quick mental calculations, beginning with the wee hour he'd finally get to sleep tonight upstairs at the Steamboat. "Best make that nine."

She nodded. "We have a great deal of luggage. I hope that won't be a problem." She paused then— just long enough, Shad noticed, for her little pink tongue to make an appealing pass over her lower lip. "Also, I believe I forgot to mention that I have a child traveling with me."

Shad blinked. She had a child? Little Miss Libby didn't look as if she'd ever been within spitting distance of a man, let alone close enough to make a baby. He narrowed his eyes now, seeing her suddenly in a whole new light. "Yours?" he asked.

"Well, yes. In a way."

He leaned back and crossed his arms. Hard to imagine such a prim little lady rolling in the arms of a man, he thought. And that thought nettled him for some reason. Irked the daylights out of him. "I didn't realize you'd ever been married," he said almost gruffly.

She looked surprised. Even the posies on her bonnet looked wide-eyed now. "Oh, no. I've never been married," she said.

Now both her little hands flew up to her face like sparrows flushed from cover. "Oh, no. I didn't mean...not that. Not ever." Her face got about as red as a sunset. "What I mean is..."

Shad would have liked to find out exactly what it was she meant, but just then a hand gripped his shoulder and a big voice boomed, "Shadrach Jones! As I live and breathe. And this must be one of Amos's pretty daughters. How do, honey. I'm Hoyt Backus. Just call me Hoyt."

The man was burly as a bear. And, if bears smoked fat cigars and drank rye whiskey, Hoyt Backus smelled like one, too. A gray-haired grizzly with a roar like a wounded bull. A big arm that finished off with a meaty paw angled across the table now, scooping up Miss Libby's little birdlike hand.

While that arm was working Miss Libby's like a pump handle, Shad pushed his chair back and rose. "You're a long way from Hellfire, Hoyt." What was the old coyote up to? he wondered.

"Aw, hell. I come to Corpus to meet with my law-

yers a couple times a year." He had released Miss
Libby's hand by now, freeing his paw to clap Shad
on the shoulder. "I like to keep them on their toes."

Shad eased away from the man's grasp. "And you
just happened to do it on the same day Amos's daughters got to town, I guess."

"Pure coincidence," Hoyt boomed. He threw
Libby a wink. "Ain't that something?"

"That's something, all right," Shad said through
clenched teeth as he reached across the table and
jerked Libby up and out of her chair, then brought
her into the protective curve of his arm. "Too bad
we're just leaving, Hoyt. Nice seeing you though."

"Now wait just a damn minute, Jones." The burly
man got hold of Libby's hand again. "I'm only being
neighborly here."

Shad laughed. "That's what a fox claims when he
sneaks into the chicken coop, you old devil." He
tossed two gold coins onto the table, then tightened
his arm around Libby. "Come on, Miss Kingsland.
Let's go while you still have a few feathers left to
pluck."

Outside the restaurant Libby dug her heels into the
planked sidewalk. The big cowboy was sweeping her
along like a broom, as if she were some inanimate
object he could just push this way and that. "Stop
it," she hissed.

He stopped walking, but his arm was still wrapped
around her like a boa constrictor, and he continued to
curse under his breath. It seemed to be a perpetual
thing with him—like a dark melody twisting through
an opera.

She wriggled out of his grasp, and stood there trying to repair some of the damage he'd inflicted on her. Her hat was askew; one glove was on while the other dangled from her bare hand. Her corset felt as if it were climbing up her neck.

Worse, now she found that she was muttering, too. Words like "rude" and "insufferable." Even a few choice curses of her own. Shadrach Jones, she decided, was definitely bringing out the worst in her.

"You know who that fella was, don't you?" he growled at her now.

"Of course I do," Libby snapped back. "Hoyt Backus. He and my father used to be partners until they had some kind of falling-out." She lifted her chin to glare at him. "That's no excuse to be rude to him. Or," she added hotly, "to manhandle me."

"Manhandle!" He swiped his hat off and slapped it against his leg, then shouted the word once more, nearly choking on it. "Manhandle!"

Libby stiffened her spine, as much to demonstrate her outrage as to reposition her errant corset stays. Then she sniffed indignantly. "Well, your ears work, Mr. Jones." She graced him with a tight little smile. "Now why don't we see if your feet do as well? Would you mind escorting me back to the hotel?"

"Glad to, ma'am." The statement might as well have been another oath, the way he swore it.

"Fine, then."

"Fine," he snarled, slapping his hat back on his head, gesturing down the street. "After you."

She took off like a jackrabbit in a silly hat. Shad stalked behind her, gritting his teeth, trying not to step on the damn drag of her dress, then thinking maybe he would. That would bring her to a right quick stop. Then he could take her by the shoulders and shake a little sense into whatever lay beneath that milliner's nightmare. Hoyt Backus hadn't come to Corpus today to keep tabs on any lawyers, and it was no coincidence he'd just happened into them at the restaurant. The man was getting a reckoning on his competition for Paradise.

It didn't take a lawyer to figure it out. With Amos on his deathbed, the ranch would soon belong to his daughters. And if they decided to sell the place, Hoyt intended to be first in line, his big fist stuffed with cash. If the Kingsland sisters decided to keep it…hell, who knew what that wily old fox would do then? Who cared? Shad wasn't going to be around once Amos was dead and buried.

He'd been walking—head down and his hands jammed into his back pockets—thinking so hard about Hoyt that he didn't notice when Libby stopped in front of the hotel. He rammed right into her. Then he blistered the air with curses as he wrapped his arms around her before she hit the sidewalk. Tiny. God, she was just a little bit of a thing under all those pleats and puffs. Well, most of her, he thought, vaguely aware that his hand was curved around a firm, fine breast.

Shad couldn't let go fast enough. Good thing, too, because he needed both hands to deflect her flying little fists.

"Whoa now, Miss Kingsland."

The prim little lady was suddenly a hellcat, hissing. And turning him into a howling fool when her foot slammed into his shinbone. What the hell was wrong with her? When he turned his head to see the little crowd that was gathering around them, her palm connected with his cheek. If word got back to Paradise that the foreman couldn't control five feet two inches of female, he'd be trying to live this incident down much longer than he cared to imagine.

A little fist caught him in the rib cage now.

"That's it, honey," somebody cheered. "Use your knee now and give that big lug something to really remember."

Her knee came up.

"Dammit, Miss Libby." Shad yanked her toward him and wrapped his arms around her, crushing her against him in a defensive embrace.

She squirmed like an eel. "Let me go," she demanded into his shirtfront.

"No, ma'am. Not till you calm down."

"I *am* calm."

"Like the eye of a hurricane," he said through clenched teeth, then he lowered his head to whisper roughly, "There are about two dozen folks standing around us, taking great delight in watching just how calm you are, lady."

Libby opened one eye just wide enough to glimpse a greasy smile centered in a bystander's greasy beard.

"Atta, girl, honey," the beard called. "You give that fella of yours what for."

Dear God! What had she done? For a bleak moment Libby wasn't even sure who she was. Certainly not the woman who never lost her temper, the one who used reason and good sense no matter how angry or vexed, the one who used well-chosen words to express herself rather than her fists. She'd gone from articulate lady to street brawler in the course of an evening. It had to be the champagne. Liquor was poison. She'd always known that.

But she hadn't even felt its effects until Shadrach

Jones had manhandled her. Which he was still doing now, she realized. She couldn't move at all. It was like being bound to an enormous oak. Then the tree leaned back a fraction and scowled down at her.

"Go on. Kiss her," somebody called out.

"Yeah. Kiss and make up, you two," another voice urged.

The crowd took up the chant.

The tree cursed once more—rough as bark—and then a firm hand curved to Libby's chin, lifted it, and a warm, wet mouth slanted over hers. She was vaguely aware of cheers and a sprinkling of applause at her back. Most of her senses, however, were magnetized by her first real kiss. By soft lips. By a tingling scrape of whiskers. By a faint taste of champagne and the slow, seductive touch of a tongue.

Shad was about to lift his head, thought better of it—or worse, didn't think at all—and kept kissing her. Kept losing himself in the prim little mouth that had melted like sunstruck butter beneath his own. Kept telling himself the unexpected kiss was only to convince the crowd their "lovers' quarrel" was over. It was just for show and he shouldn't be feeling anything. Especially not the hammering in his chest and the hot surge of blood through every inch of him. She was a lady, for God's sake. Ladies were poison. Sweet, warm, succulent poison. And nobody knew that better than Shadrach Jones.

He broke the kiss, literally ripped his mouth from hers, and stepped back so abruptly that Libby nearly fell. Then he was growling—at her, at the several curious spectators who remained on the sidewalk, at the world in general—as he gripped her elbow and propelled her through the hotel door and across the lobby.

At the foot of the staircase, he halted and drew himself up like that towering oak again. "Good night, Miss Kingsland. I'll be seeing you about nine tomorrow." Then he turned on his heel and strode toward the door.

Shad slammed through the side door of the livery stable. He wasn't worried about waking Eb Talent; once the old salt strung up his hammock and settled in, not even the devil could wake him. He was snoring like a band saw now in a back stall. The big red-and-black coach was still parked in the center of the stable. Shad climbed in and closed the door.

He slumped back against a tufted leather cushion, then slammed a foot against the edge of the opposite seat, shifting his shoulders and rolling his neck to ease the knots of tension there. He'd stroll on down to the Steamboat, he told himself, as soon as he got his head back on straight. As soon as he had cursed himself sufficiently for losing that head a moment ago with Amos's daughter.

What the hell had he been thinking, to kiss her like that? There had to have been a dozen other ways to settle her down and keep her from making a spectacle of herself. He could have said good-night right there on the sidewalk and walked away. He could have slung her over his shoulder and carried her inside. He probably should have just drawn his gun and shot her right then and there. The prospect of spending the next twenty years in jail didn't strike him as half so bad as getting tangled up with a lady.

A lady! He slammed his other foot into the carriage

seat and crossed his arms. Hadn't he vowed never to
get within spitting distance of one of those again?
Once was enough. Hell, his once had been way too
much.

No, thank you. Shad scowled into the darkness inside the big coach. It felt less like a coach than a cage
now.

Well, he'd get the job done, he thought. He owed
Amos that. "Here're your daughters, Amos," he'd
say as he dropped them off at Paradise then continued
on his way. Here're your daughters, Amos. The fetch-
ing redhead and the other one. The lady. The prim,
stiff-backed little priss. Sad little Libby. The one with
the mouth the devil made for kissing.

He hadn't had the dream in years, and now in the
cramped interior of the coach it was rolling over him
like a hot tidal wave, pulling him deeper into the
bloodred dark, drowning him. Somewhere in his
brain, Shad was aware that it was a dream. He kept
telling himself to wake up, to get the hell away. But
he couldn't. He couldn't. Just as twenty years before—when the dream was real—he hadn't been able
to get away. From *her*.

She was rubbing up against him now in the dreamy,
dizzy dark, the way she always did when they were
alone. She was whispering—words he didn't want to
hear—words that stirred him nevertheless. Her dainty
hands moved over him like feathers at first, then like
flames, making his fourteen-year-old body stiffen and
his tongue stammer and his heart nearly explode with
desire and dread.

"Yes," she whispered. "There. That's right." He
knew it wasn't right, but what he knew and what he

felt bore no relation to each other. The lady made sure of that.

Shad groaned now in his sleep as he had groaned years before, with a mixture of pleasure and anguish.

Wake, he warned himself. Before she laughs. Before the door downstairs clicks open and the footsteps come. Before…wake up!

He couldn't. Then she was pushing him away. Those dainty hands were slapping at him now. ''Get off me, you clumsy little half-breed.'' Laughter twisted her lips.

Wake up before the door clicks open and the footsteps echo, deafening, down the hall. Please. Before her laughter turns to a sickening scream. Wake up, goddamn you!

He did. Cold with sweat, sick, shaking uncontrollably as he stared into a dark corner of the coach. Seeing nothing. Seeing everything all over again. Remembering.

He'd made two vows that terrible night twenty years ago. The first was to get so good at loving that no woman would ever laugh at him again. By God, he'd done that. He'd done that, even though there was always that moment afterward, that single icy heartbeat when he was glazed with sweat as salty as tears, when he was gripped with fear and his chilled blood shunted to his limbs, priming him to run.

He'd made two vows that terrible night. And Shadrach Jones renewed the second one now—never, ever to touch a lady again.

Chapter Four

At nine o'clock the next morning Libby followed Shula, Andy, and a swaying mountain of luggage down the hotel stairs. As she descended, she was making mental notes of all the things she would not do to Shadrach Jones, including hitting, kicking and scratching. Her list of commandments was not only longer than the Lord's mere ten, it was more specific, and it concluded with an adamant "Thou shalt not kiss him."

As angry as Libby had been all night long—tossing and turning on the scrap of mattress Shula hadn't claimed—she hadn't been able to forget that kiss. Lord, how she had tried, thinking of a hundred reasons why she detested her father's foreman. He was crude. A rude and impudent man. A bully who insisted on his own way and used his inordinate strength to get it, whether it was snatching neckties or hauling a woman out of a restaurant. He was exactly like her father during those final, violent years before her mother had taken her away from Paradise.

Worse, the big cowboy seemed to ignite some explosive part of her nature that Libby never wanted to experience again. "Thou shalt not scream or bellow like a fishwife." "Thou shalt not slap, slug or sink your teeth into another human being."

"Thou shalt not, shalt not, shalt not kiss him."

She followed the luggage through the hotel door, out to the street where a big red-and-black coach was waiting. And leaning against it, like a leering footman, was Shadrach Jones. Libby's breath hitched in her throat.

"Lord Almighty!" a voice exclaimed. "If it isn't Miss Libby, all growed up."

She turned to watch a wiry older man clamber down from the front of the coach, relieved to see a familiar, safe face. Suddenly she was able to breathe again.

"Eb, is that you? Oh, it's good to see you." Libby extended her hand.

Her father's longtime employee spat out of the side of his mouth, grinned, then grabbed her hand and shook it with gusto. "Miss Libby. My, my. Don't it just beat all how you've growed up."

"You look the same, Eb. The years have treated you well."

"Oh, I don't know about that," the old man said. "It's prob'ly all the salt water I swallowed those years at sea with your pa. I'm just pickled, is all. Tickled to see you, too, Miss Libby. Now where's that cute little redheaded sister of yours?"

"Right over there." Libby pointed to where Shula was instructing one of the hotel porters in the proper handling of expensive luggage. Haranguing the poor boy, actually. Libby was surprised Eb Talent hadn't noticed her first with all those red curls gleaming in the morning sunshine and her lilac dress ruffling in the gulf breeze.

When he did notice her, though, he said almost wistfully, "Ain't she something?"

She was something, all right, Libby thought, as the old man moved toward Shula like a moth to a flame. Before Eb reached her, though, a second moth appeared. Hoyt Backus brushed past Libby with a brisk "'Morning, Miss Kingsland," then swooped down on her sister, and shouted, "By golly, if you're not the prettiest thing I've seen in Texas since the day your mama left."

It was no surprise when Shula went from stern luggage monitor to simpering princess in the next instant. And no surprise when she paused from basking in Hoyt Backus's warm attention just long enough to call, "Oh, Libby, honey, as long as you're just standing around, you'll keep an eye on these hatboxes for me, won't you?"

Libby sighed and added one more commandment to her growing list. "Thou shalt not think unkind thoughts about thy sister."

At the sight of Hoyt Backus, Shad straightened up and pushed back the hat that had been shading his eyes. The fox was sniffing around the chickens again, and the foreman of Paradise didn't like it one bit. He was briefly tempted to insert himself between predator and prey, but then—seeing the redhead's slick smile and her long red claws—Shad decided he wasn't exactly sure which was which. Anyway, he was in no mood to tangle with another Kingsland sister right now, so he yanked down the brim of his hat and glared at Miss Libby.

She looked like a dove this morning in her prim, dull-colored clothes. Except for the damn hat. Even that, though, paled in comparison to her sister's. Lord, what a pair. He'd be glad when this day was over.

He was glad last night was over, that was for sure. It had been one of the worst nights of his life, sitting in a corner of the cramped coach, wet with sweat and shivering like a newborn calf, unable to shake off the dream that had seemed so real, unable to wake from the nightmare that had driven him from home twenty years ago.

If he'd slept even a wink, Shad wasn't sure. His eyes felt like he'd spent the whole night riding drag in a dust storm. He hadn't spent it upstairs at the Steamboat. That he knew for certain. Not with Rosa, or Nona or—dammit—Carmela.

And it was all Miss Libby's fault. Miss Libby, who looked this morning as if she'd spent a prim and dreamless night between starched sheets. With her damn hat on.

He dragged his gaze to the kid who was standing close beside her. At least she didn't dress him in fancy little French suits and pointy-toed shoes. Just the opposite, in fact. The youngster had a slightly unkempt look about him, especially the tousled hair that fell across his forehead. He would have expected Miss Libby's boy to look polished, from his slicked-down hair to his spit-shined brogans.

Shad sighed. He didn't know why that surprised him. Nothing a lady did should ever surprise him. They were never what they seemed, those fine-spoken, delicate, devious creatures. They could be all thin lipped, cool and demure one minute, then the next they were hot as whores. He liked whores better.

They were honest. A man knew where he stood, or lay as the case may be.

Or didn't lie, as was the case with him. But not for long. Six or seven hours by coach to Paradise, provided he could hustle these ladies along. Here're your daughters, Amos. Then five or six hours back to Corpus on a fast horse. Back to Rosa, Nona and—Shad sighed again—Carmela.

Libby tapped a foot on the sidewalk. Their luggage was loaded now—most of it strapped to the top of the coach—but Shula was still batting her eyes and playing flame to that burly behemoth, Hoyt Backus.

She had expected any second that Shadrach Jones would be wrenching Shula away from her father's former partner as he had done with her the night before, but the man was still slouched against the coach, apparently unconcerned. Possibly asleep for all she could see of his eyes beneath the low brim of his hat. His mouth she saw quite plainly, and that had a lazy slant to it, which brought to mind his kiss. Which set off the butterflies in Libby's stomach once again.

"Why are we all just standing around here when the coach is ready to go?" she said with more than a little irritation, directing her gaze toward her sister. "Shula? I said..."

The redhead waved her off, continuing her animated conversation with Backus.

"Shula!" Libby snapped.

"Oh, all right, Libby. For heaven's sake. Did you check inside the lobby to see that all of our bags were put outside?"

"No, I didn't," Libby said. She didn't intend to,

either. Let Shula do without one or two of the twenty outfits she had brought.

"I'll go," Andy offered.

Libby instinctively reached out to stop her but then drew back. It was the first time since they'd left Saint Louis that Andy had seemed willing to be more than a few feet away from her. Taking that for a healthy sign, Libby nodded her assent. "Come right back, though," she cautioned the child. With any other nine-year-old she might have added a warning not to speak to strangers, but considering that Andy hardly spoke to friends, she didn't think it necessary.

She had barely turned toward the street, intending to tell her sister to stop her infernal chattering and get into the coach, when Andy was suddenly back, clinging to her skirt.

"I saw him," the little girl sobbed. "I saw my papa. Don't let him take me, Miss Libby."

Libby knelt down and took the child into her arms. "Hush, now, Andy. Shh. You're getting all worked up over nothing, honey."

"I saw him."

Shula's perfume swirled around them. "What in the world's going on, Libby? What in heaven's name are you doing down on that dirty sidewalk?"

"Andy says she saw her father." Libby's worried eyes flicked up to her sister. "Just now. In the lobby."

"That's ridiculous," Shula said with a snort.

Glancing toward the hotel's front door now, Libby frowned. It wasn't possible, was it? As far as she knew, John Rowan didn't have the wherewithall to buy a ticket to the Saint Louis levee on a horse-drawn tram much less one all the way to Texas.

"I'm sure it was just somebody who resembled your father," she told the little girl as she brushed hair from her forehead. "Your eyes were probably just playing tricks on you."

"Little wonder, with all that hair falling over them," Shula said. "Well, it's time to go to Paradise. Libby, if you'd get up off the sidewalk, we could be on our way."

Libby closed her eyes, seething as her sister flounced off to bid farewell to Hoyt Backus. She struggled up.

"Ma'am."

A hand gripped her arm and suddenly Libby was on her feet, standing in the shadow of Shadrach Jones. His dark eyes scanned her face then lowered to Andy.

"Everything all right with your boy now?" he asked.

Libby blinked. "With my...?" He meant Andy, of course. And if she even began to explain, Libby realized, they'd be standing here till the sun came up tomorrow. "Everything's fine now, Mr. Jones. Shall we go?"

A moment later his hands were on her again. He was lifting her like a piece of baggage into the coach.

"Up you go, sonny."

The cowboy lofted Andy like a feather, before the child could even squeak. He followed then, and the roomy coach seemed suddenly small. Libby's breath was failing her again, so she fussed with her gloves and her skirt before settling back with a sigh.

Shula's head poked in the door. "Well, this won't do at all, Mr. Jones."

"Ma'am?"

"I'm afraid you'll have to move. I can't ride backward. It makes me deathly ill. Tell him, Libby."

Libby didn't say a word. She was listening to the blood boiling in Shadrach Jones's veins. Or was it her own? There was a brief moment of hard-bitten silence then, after which they all got up and exchanged seats.

Halfway to Paradise, Shad found himself praying—something he hadn't done since he'd lived under the roof of his adoptive father, the Reverend Jones. Dear Lord, deliver me. From redheads who couldn't ride backwards, couldn't tolerate heat or dust or apparently silence. From the mute little boy who was stabbing him with his eyes whenever he thought Shad wasn't looking. From the prim and quiet Miss Libby directly across from him.

He would have ridden on top with Eb, but he thought he could catch a few much needed winks inside the coach. Every time he drifted off, though, he'd jerk awake to another complaint from Miss Shula, to the boy's gaze slicing away, to his boot heels hooked in Miss Libby's dove-colored skirt.

When Eb pulled the horses up at the twenty-mile relay station, Shad opened the door and shot outside. Lord, it felt good to stretch. To breathe air that wasn't scented with a perfume that reminded him of sodden leaves. To get away from them. All of them. Her.

He couldn't stop thinking of the way she'd felt in his arms, of the way her stunned little mouth melted under his. As if she'd never been kissed before. As if he'd been the first. Which made no sense at all, considering the kid.

Shad scraped off his hat and slapped it against his leg. The hell with her. The hell with them all. "You got that lunch basket stowed up there, Eb?'' he called to the driver.

"Right here." Eb tossed the heavy basket down. "Don't look like I'll be breaking any records today, does it, what with the Captain's daughters lollygagging so?'' The old man clambered down to stand beside Shad. "Been so long since I've been around women, I'd pretty near forgotten just how dawdling they can be." The old man shrugged then sauntered toward the men who were unhitching the horses from the coach.

"That wouldn't be a lunch basket, would it, Mr. Jones?'' Her voice came from just behind him. A soft, musical tone in contrast to her sister's strident dramatics. Shad turned slowly and lowered his gaze to Miss Libby's upturned face.

About to give her one more "yes, ma'am," he suddenly changed his mind. "Hungry?" he asked.

Her eyes widened in surprise, as if he had asked her for her measurements instead. "No," she said. "Not really. But I imagine Andy is. The poor child's hardly eaten a thing in the last two days."

"Andy. I expect that's short for Andrew."

Again she blinked. Anybody'd think he was mouthing indecent proposals, the way she kept being taken aback. All he'd done was ask a friendly question.

Her prim little mouth quirked into an unexpected grin. "Actually, Mr. Jones, it's short for…"

Libby's next words were drowned out by Shula's screams as she came running, her lilac skirt rucked up about her knees. She pushed Libby aside in order to yank open the door of the coach and, without ceremony or dignity, hauled herself inside.

"Snakes," she screeched. "If there's anything I hate worse than spiders, it's snakes."

"Where's Andy?" Libby asked frantically.

Shula aimed her chin out the coach window toward a nearby mesquite bush. "Back there." She shivered. "I told the child to run. Especially when I heard that horrible rattle."

Libby gasped and pulled up her skirt, ready to run.

Shad grabbed a handful of bustle and dove-gray dress. "Stay here," he growled, tacking on an oath for emphasis before he strode to where the boy was standing. Still as a statue. Staring.

The snake was about as big as they came—seven feet of coiled muscle with a death rattle at one end and just plain death at the other. Death for a boy who didn't weigh much more than a fifty-pound sack of grain.

"Don't move, kid." Shad's voice was low and calm, unlike his mind, which was scrambling over options. Ordinarily he would have drawn his gun and put a bullet right between the rattler's eyes. But he couldn't trust the kid to stay still a second longer. He looked about ready to bolt right now.

Shad's eyes swept the ground. He needed a pitchfork or a sturdy limb, but there was nothing within reach. Nothing but one of his own limbs. Well, hell. It had to be him or the kid. If he was lucky, the fangs would catch him on the boot. If he wasn't...

Libby rounded the corner of the mesquite bush. The stillness of the scene was chilling. Andy like a tiny statue. Jones like a massive oak. The gray diamond-patterned snake rattling ominously and poised to strike.

"Do something." She wasn't sure if she had

screeched the words or merely felt them searing across her brain, but a second later there was a flash of denim, a sweep of arms lifting Andy up and out of harm's way as the snake snapped from its coil, struck, then went slithering away.

Libby struggled to release the breath she'd been holding. Andy was safe. She was safe. The big cowboy had her planted on his hip, holding her against him with one big, bronze hand splayed across her chest. But by the time that pose fully registered on Libby, it was already too late. Andy had already begun screaming in Jones's arms—kicking, hitting, scratching, fighting for her very life. No longer afraid of the snake, the little girl was terrified of her rescuer.

"She's asleep now," Libby whispered inside the dim interior of the coach. They had pulled the side curtains down in the hope of calming the hysterical little girl. Finally, over Libby's strong objections, Shula had poured a liberal dose of laudanum down Andy's throat.

"I told you that would do the trick," Shula said with a little cluck of her tongue.

Libby edged away from the sleeping child now, inching back one of the canvas side curtains to peer outside. "Where do you suppose everybody went?"

"Probably in the shade," Shula said, lifting her damp hair from her neck, "trying to stay cool in all this heat." She flicked her gaze toward Andy, then lifted her shoulders in a shrug. "Not to mention trying to get away from all the crying and fussing."

"She was terrified, Shula. Andy thought—"

"I know what she thought," Shula snapped, "but it doesn't make any sense. First she's making up stories about seeing her father in the hotel. Then she's convinced he's way out here in the middle of nowhere, attacking her.''

"She's confused,'' Libby said.

"Obviously.''

"You're a heartless person, Shula Kingsland.''

"No, Libby. I'm a hot person. And I want to get on to our father's ranch. Why don't you go find our driver.'' She closed her eyes. "I'd go myself but that snake might still be lurking out there.''

If it was, Libby thought as she climbed out of the coach, she was going to catch it and then wrap it around her sister's neck. She lifted a hand to shade her eyes against the bright noon sun. Eb Talent was stretched out in one of the few patches of shade the relay station had to offer. He got to his feet with some difficulty as Libby approached.

"You got that little one all settled down now, Miss Libby?'' he asked.

"I believe so, Eb. We're ready to continue on to Paradise if you are.'' Libby's gaze drifted around the relay station. "Where's Mr. Jones?''

"Down by the creek.'' The old man turned his head and spat into the dust. "We didn't know, Miss Libby. Why, that little girl coulda fooled anybody. She don't care much for men, I take it.''

"She's had some rather nasty experiences.'' Libby looked around again, noticing a thin line of cottonwoods against the intense blue of the sky. "Where is the creek? Over there? Shall I inform Mr. Jones that we're ready to leave?''

"That'd be fine, ma'am. Save me some walking and some shouting. I'll go on and make sure the horses are all set.''

On her way to the creek, Libby ran her fingers through the damp curls at the nape of her neck. She had taken off her hat, or rather Andy had knocked it off during her hysterics earlier, and at the moment Libby had to admit it felt good to be bareheaded and ungloved beneath the sweltering sun. There wasn't a breath of breeze, still the leaves of the cottonwoods were shimmying up ahead. She could hear a faint ripple of water running over rocks as she approached, and she could see the long dark hair skimming the broad shoulders of Shadrach Jones as he sat, his back to her, on the bank of the creek.

"We're getting ready to leave, Mr. Jones," she said as she neared. "Before we do, however, I wanted to thank you and tell you how much I appreciate what you did for Andy."

He angled around, cocking his head, squinting against the sunlight. One leg was bent, its denim covering rolled up past his knee. Two bright, bloodred lines were streaming down his calf.

Libby gulped in air, then let it out in a rush. "Good Lord! You're bleeding," she exclaimed as she sank down on her knees beside him. "Is it…was it the snake?"

He laughed. "He just clipped me a little. I did most of that damage myself just making sure all the poison's out. It looks a lot worse than it is, believe me."

She didn't believe a word of that casual denial. On her knees, Libby edged closer to him. "We need to get that bleeding stopped," she said firmly. "Do you have a clean handkerchief, Mr. Jones?"

"No, ma'am." He pointed to the blood-soaked bandanna now lying in the dust.

Then Shad narrowed his gaze on her worried face.

If she bit any harder on that lower lip, he thought, pretty soon she'd be bleeding, too. It dawned on him suddenly that she wasn't wearing her hat, that her dark hair had a reddish cast out here in the sunlight. He didn't know why that pleased him or sent a quick jolt of desire through him. The lady could be bald for all it mattered to him. What mattered, after all, was the fact that she was a lady. And he wanted no part of that.

"I'm fine," he told her gruffly. "Save your mothering for your daughter, Miss Kingsland. I don't need it."

"What you need is a clean bandage, Mr. Jones," she snapped, "and if you'll turn your back for a moment, I'll provide you with one."

The soft worry in her features had hardened to flint now, Shad noticed. Amos Kingsland's stubborn fire burned in her blue eyes. "Turn my back?"

"Please. I need to tear off a strip of my petticoat."

"Go ahead."

"I will," she said, "as soon as you redirect your gaze."

"I've seen petticoats before, ma'am."

"Not mine, Mr. Jones," she countered sternly.

Biting down on a curse, Shad turned and stared off across the creek while he listened to assorted rustlings and then to one quick, decisive rip.

He jerked slightly at the cool touch of her hand on his leg.

"Sorry. I didn't mean to hurt you," she murmured as she wound the torn cloth around him. "That was a very selfless gesture, Mr. Jones. What you did for little Andy. I'm grateful to you."

Shad didn't reply. He was trying to concentrate on

something else. Anything else. The way the creek ed-
died around the slant of a downed cottonwood branch.
A bluebottle fly edging along the pull-strap of his
discarded boot. Patterns of sun and shade. Anything
but the soft, almost dazzling drift of her fingertips.
Anything but those feathers and flames. He was thinking he much preferred the bite of a rattler. It did less
damage in the long run.

"There," she said, making a last little tear, giving
a last little tug as she tied the bandage. "That ought
to do, at least until we reach Paradise."

Hallelujah. He could feel the sweat trickling down
his side and he knew it had nothing to do with the
sun overhead. "Thank you, ma'am."

"You're quite welcome."

He heard the dovelike swish of her skirts—those
sacred, well-guarded petticoats—that meant she was
getting up. He could almost breathe again.

"Oh. One more thing, Mr. Jones." She was standing just behind him, her shadow spilling over him like
dark silk. "I hate to ask after what you did for Andy,
but I wonder if you'd mind riding the rest of the way
up front with Mr. Talent? The poor child's calmer
now, but..."

"Glad to," he answered quickly. God, how he was
glad.

Chapter Five

Libby lifted the side curtain to gaze out at the passing landscape. At the final relay stop, Shula had popped her head out of the coach and inquired—Princess fashion—about the time they'd be reaching Paradise. Eb Talent had slapped his knee and hooted with laughter.

"You hear that, boys?" he'd called to the men who were changing the horses. "This pretty lady wants to know when we'll be getting to Paradise."

"What's so funny about that?" Shula had demanded, her lips threatening a full-fledged pout.

"Well, nothing, ma'am," Eb had replied, "only we've been on your daddy's land for going on about two hours now. Right after we crossed Petronila Creek."

"Oh." Shula had sat back against the tufted leather seat a stunned moment. "Imagine that," she'd finally sighed.

Imagine that, Libby thought now as she looked out the window of the coach. But she didn't have to imagine it. She remembered it—nearly every square mile of it—so clearly. As if she'd left Texas only yesterday instead of fifteen years before.

Already she was feeling less city dweller than inhabitant of wide-open spaces. She drew in a deep and appreciative lungful of sweet, clean air. No cinder-laden smoke out here. No cobbled streets littered with paper scraps and sodden refuse. Just earth and sky, and between them only warm and glorious air.

When had she forgotten all the glory of Paradise? Libby wondered. When had the city and its grit worked their way into her heart, making her forget all this, convincing her she no longer cared?

She cared. Lord Almighty, how she cared. And she wasn't sure she wanted to feel anything as she continued to gaze out the window at the soft greens of prickly pear and mesquite, both so pretty from a distance and so dangerous up close. It was a deceptively thorny landscape with no tall trees to keep the sky from sweeping horizon to horizon, as far as the eye could see.

There were no tall trees because the sandy soil was like a sieve, letting all the water go. Little wonder they used to call this place the Wild Horse Desert. But that was before Amos Kingsland.

It occurred to Libby that her father was a lot like this land he'd claimed. Thorny. Tough. Dangerous. She supposed he'd had to be in order to wrest Paradise from such unpromising soil. It was probably a miracle he had survived this long, considering the harshness of the land he'd taken on and the vastness of his task.

"Good job, Amos," his daughter muttered, feeling a grudging pride in his accomplishments. Still, it was a pride colored by a profound sadness. She had loved this place so much so many years ago. Being yanked out of Paradise had hurt. Seeing it again hurt even more as Libby wondered what might have been.

She sighed then, directing her gaze inside the coach. Andy was still sleeping peacefully, her boyish body curled up on the seat. A few weeks in Paradise would do the little girl immeasurable good. A few weeks would even be good for Libby herself. Then they'd go back to Saint Louis. Back home.

For much as Libby had once loved it, she refused to think of Paradise as home. She wouldn't let herself.

The big white house—the place Libby had always considered the heart of Paradise—came into view. Years ago, for safety's sake, her father had chosen the highest point in the surrounding countryside for his residence. The elevation afforded him a sweeping view and prevented surprise attacks by Indians or marauding Mexicans. Those threats had subsided now, but the house still crested its hill like a great, white watchtower, its windows glinting in the late afternoon sun like dozens of watchful eyes.

Despite Shula's continual speculations about the baronial size of their father's residence, Libby had expected the house to seem smaller. After all, she'd been ten years old when her mother had taken her away, and the house had probably loomed outrageously large in her memories. But a single look at the place told her just how wrong she had been. The place was enormous, bigger than she recalled.

During the past fifteen years her father had added not only a gallery that spanned the entire second story of the white frame house, but he'd built on two large, single-story wings that gave the place a rambling, almost sprawling appearance. What it lacked in elegance, it made up for in sheer size.

Libby nudged her napping sister's foot, directing Shula's gaze outside the window.

Shula yawned. "What is it now, Libby?" she asked wearily. "More cows? I've already seen a thousand of those beasts, and that's about nine hundred ninety-nine more than I ever cared to see."

Again Libby nodded toward the window. "Take a look," she urged her sister, anticipating the expression on the Princess's face once she got a good view of the palace.

Shula eased up the side curtain a fraction and glared through the space, muttering "I don't know what you find so endlessly fascinating about beef on the hoof. Personally, I'd much prefer…"

"Welcome to Paradise, Princess," Libby inserted into her sister's stunned silence.

Eyes widening with sudden understanding, Shula lunged forward, wrenched the curtain out of her way, and gaped at the enormous house atop the grassy rise.

It was the first time in twenty years that Libby had seen her sister speechless.

The two sisters and the child stood in the large vestibule like three exhausted wayfarers in the lobby of a grand hotel. Italian marble gleamed beneath the hems of their wrinkled skirts. A chandelier of brass and Venetian glass winked above their heads.

It wasn't at all the way Libby remembered. The house where she'd spent her first ten years had been large, but comfortable rather than imposing. This was…

"Magnificent," Shula breathed.

Even the child, in her laudanum-induced stupor, seemed to be impressed. She rubbed her knuckles in her eyes and murmured, "It's like a palace in a storybook."

Just then, a heavily paneled door opened, revealing a dark-haired woman. She closed it quietly, then turned to rush across the glossy floor. In her loose blouse and long, gathered skirt, she seemed oddly inappropriate in such an elegant setting.

"*Señoritas!* You are here. I was so worried." The woman took possession of Shula's hands, then dropped them to capture Libby's. "Welcome. Welcome to Paradise."

Luggage thudded onto the marble floor behind them, followed by a muted curse. "Here they are, Antonia," a deep voice drawled. "Where's Amos?"

The woman let go of Libby's hands to touch a finger to her lips, then she angled her head toward the door she had closed a moment before. "He rests in his office, Señor Shad. He is in great pain." Tears muddled her dark brown eyes now. "The end," she whispered as she sketched a hasty cross over her bosom, "is near."

When a mournful little cry broke from Libby's throat, the woman grasped her hand again. "He wants to see you, *señorita,* both of you. He told me as soon as you arrived."

Libby nodded solemnly.

"That's impossible," Shula snapped. When Antonia looked at her in surprise, she waved a ringed hand. "Well, just look at us. We've been cooking in that oven of a coach all afternoon. We must look like a couple of immigrants."

"Shula," Libby hissed.

"You go on if you want, Libby," she said, then offered her sister a dismissive toss of her red curls. "But I don't care to have my father seeing me like this. Not after fifteen years of not seeing me at all."

To her surprise, even to her own dismay, Libby understood. Shula wanted very badly to please the father she hadn't seen since she was five years old. And according to the code of the Princess, being pretty was pleasing. "If that's what you want, Shula," she said. "Perhaps you could take Andy with you. Poor thing looks like she's about to fall asleep on her feet."

Bending down, Libby whispered in the little girl's ear. "You go with Shula, honey. I'll be along in a while."

Andy looked uncertainly at Shula, but when her gaze moved to the door and encountered the big cowboy who was standing there, she nodded her head in agreement, moving closer to Shula's lilac skirt.

"Fine, then." Shula smiled fetchingly down on the much-shorter Antonia. "If you'll show us the way, I'll just freshen up a bit."

The woman's brow furrowed, and she sought out Shadrach Jones's eyes.

"It's all right, Antonia," he drawled. Hell, he thought, Amos had just been spared spending a few of his remaining hours listening to the redhead's complaints.

She turned to him now, pointing a long red nail at the baggage he'd dropped at his feet. "I'll be needing that black satchel, Mr. Jones, if you don't mind."

"Not at all, ma'am." He enjoyed playing pack mule. He was even considering making a second career of it once he left Paradise. When he picked up the satchel, Miss Shula immediately concluded that she couldn't do without the alligator suitcase, either, so he sighed, hoisted both bags and started to follow her up the stairs.

"Shula, Mr. Jones has an injured leg," Libby called out. "Perhaps you could carry those yourself."

"It's just a few steps," Shula protested. "And those bags don't weigh a thing. Do they, Mr. Jones?"

"No, ma'am." He shot Miss Libby a grateful glance over his shoulder, as he continued up the stairs. If anybody looked like she needed a little help, he thought, it was Miss Libby—no longer prim, but just plain weary in her dove-colored dress.

Her little girl was keeping her distance, he noticed, watching her scuttle upstairs on the far side of her Aunt Shula's skirts. Fine. He wasn't going to be around all that much longer to terrorize her or to feel like a worm for doing it.

"You come right back down, Señor Shad," Antonia called to him now. "Señor Amos wants to see you, too."

Fine. Shad wanted to see him, too. He ran his speech through his head one more time.

Here're your daughters, Amos. One of them, anyway. The other's upstairs primping for you. I'll just be on my way, boss, if there's nothing else you need.

It was Antonia's firm hand on her back that finally sent Libby over the threshold of the dark office where the closed drapes let in only a few pink and gold threads of sunset.

"He longs to see you," the woman whispered, guiding her toward the large horsehair sofa against a far wall. "He does not have long to live, *señorita.*

Go.'' She gave Libby's arm an encouraging pat. "Go to him.''

Even in the dark and still at some distance, Libby could see how her father had changed. The prone body bore almost no resemblance to the massive man she remembered. As she stepped closer, she noticed that his beard—that stiff, windblown beard she remembered so clearly—was gone. It was as if she were paying a call on a sick stranger, a clean-shaven man she'd never seen before.

And then it occurred to her that Amos Kingsland himself was seeing a woman he'd never laid eyes on either. Did he still picture her as she'd been at ten, a dark-haired waif, thin as a stick and always trembling like a storm-tossed leaf whenever he was near?

"Come over here. Come closer, daughter.''

That voice! Like the deep rumble of distant thunder when you couldn't be sure if it was the last storm leaving or a new one rolling in. Her father's voice resounded inside her flesh and rattled her bones. She was ten again. And afraid.

She had to command her legs to keep moving toward him in the dark. The urge to run and hide was nearly overwhelming.

"Hello, Father.'' Libby laced her fingers together to still the trembling. She stopped, her skirt just brushing the edge of the sofa.

Amos's eyelids raised a fraction, seeking her face. "Which one are you?''

"Elizabeth,'' she whispered, meeting his gaze, allowing his pain-dulled eyes to track her features. His features, she thought. His own high forehead. His narrow nose. The same indentation that dimpled their chins.

"You don't look like your mother."

"No. I...I believe I favor the Kingslands," she said softly. *You.*

His gaze shunted away, searching. "Your sister? Where is she?"

"Shula wanted to freshen up some before paying her respects. She'll be—"

"Like Ellen," he snapped. "There's a bottle over on the desk. Are you a drinking woman, Elizabeth?" He lifted his head again, trying to take her in.

"Well, I..."

Before she could finish, he was waving her toward the desk. "Light that lamp, too," he told her.

Libby fumbled with the match and chimney lamp. *Yes, Amos. No, Amos.* Her mother's voice echoed in her head, pierced by the plaintive cry of a child. *Daddy, don't.*

The flame bit into her fingertips. She shook out the match, along with the memories, and reached for the whiskey bottle on a corner of the blotter just as footsteps sounded beyond the closed office door.

"That you, Shad?" her father called.

The door opened. Shadrach Jones stood framed in daylight pouring from the front hall. Libby felt that odd hitch in her breath again.

"Where will I find the glasses, Father?" she asked, turning back toward the sofa.

"Get them for her, will you, Shad? Get three."

His boot heels sounded as he crossed to the bookcase. It was the only sound in the room now. And the only air—the air Libby struggled to breathe—was suddenly permeated with leather, hot dust, Texas sunshine.

He dropped his hat onto a shelf, then gathered three

glasses in one hand. When he brought them back to the desk, there was only a hint of the limp she had noticed before.

"Miss Libby," he murmured as he put the glasses down.

"Thank you, Mr. Jones."

"Get on with it, girl," Amos ordered.

Libby lifted the bottle. It chattered against the lip of the glass, and she poured more whiskey onto the blotter than inside.

"Let me do that." Bronze fingers brushed hers as Shad took the bottle from her hand. A little white smile blazed across his face. "He won't bite, Miss Libby. Maybe years ago, but not anymore."

Chagrined that this big cowboy could read her emotions so plainly, Libby stiffened her spine. "If he does, Mr. Jones, I assure you I'll bite him back."

"I'm sure you would, ma'am," he drawled, smoothly filling the three glasses.

Shad moved two chairs close beside the sofa, then helped Amos so the man was half sitting, half reclining on a mass of pillows. As the three of them sipped their whiskey in silence, Libby felt awkward, as if her presence was preventing some male camaraderie, some routine exchange of gruff pleasantries and rough talk. Her father seemed to be more at ease now that his foreman was here.

For an instant, she resented that. There were things she had to say to Amos Kingsland now that she was here, she realized. There were questions—so many questions—only he could answer. Why had he allowed their mother to take them away? Why hadn't he contacted them for fifteen years? Why now, when there was no time left? And the most haunting question of them all—the question that suddenly threatened to overwhelm her with its sudden recognition—why hadn't he loved her?

He was looking at her now, over the rim of his whiskey glass, as if she were a sideshow exhibit. His deep voice rumbled. "Did Shad take you girls to dinner last night like I asked?"

Libby nearly choked on the thimbleful of whiskey halfway down her throat. "Yes." She ignored the pair of dark eyes she could feel scorching one side of her face. "Yes, he did. We had…we had a fine meal. Thank you, Father."

Amos shifted his gaze to the man straddling the chair beside hers. "That true, Shad?"

"Like the lady said, Amos, we had a fine meal."

Feeling like a conspirator all of a sudden, Libby squirmed in her chair. Their meal might have been fine, but everything else had been horrible. She didn't like lying to her father, especially now. Even less did she enjoy being in league with his bully of a foreman.

Her father was nodding now, his eyes closed and his lips tightened down with apparent pain. "Good," he mumbled. "That's good. Let me just rest a minute here."

Shad sighed softly and ambled over to the desk to pour himself another shot of whiskey, thinking maybe it would ease some of the throbbing in his leg. Maybe it would drown out the odor of the sickroom, or even blur his senses so he wouldn't be aware of sad little Libby.

Without her hat, she reminded him more than ever of the skinny, dark-haired child whose broken heart had left a jagged little scar on his. How Amos could have let those children go was beyond Shad's reckoning. He respected the tough rancher almost more than any man he knew, but he never claimed to understand how Amos could have ignored his own flesh and blood for fifteen years.

To send for them now that he was dying was fine, Shad supposed. To leave them Paradise and all its wealth was right and proper. But, Lord, what Amos must have missed along the way. If he ever had a daughter, Shad thought—a little dove-gray tintype like Miss Libby—he'd wrestle the devil himself in order to keep her.

He refilled his glass, thinking that since he never planned to marry, he wouldn't ever have a daughter who required him to face the devil or anybody else. And besides, it wasn't all Amos's fault. Miss Libby and her sister could have come back once they were grown-up. He doubted the redhead really required an engraved invitation.

But Amos and his lost girls weren't his problem. The major problem confronting him right now was how he was going to make it back to Corpus tonight with his leg aching the way it was. He hadn't expected Amos's condition to be quite so bad when he'd formed his plans to dump the two sisters and take off. It wouldn't have surprised him if wily old Amos had gotten worse on purpose just to wreck his plans.

He tossed back a hot swallow of whiskey. Damn his leg. Damn Amos's whole failing body. And damn Miss Libby, too. Mentally he slapped her stupid hat back on her head. It helped a little not to have to look at the soft dark spill of her hair, which he'd found himself doing ever since he'd walked into Amos's office. He didn't know why it tempted him so. It was just hair, after all. A lady's well-tended waves and artificial curls. He'd be better off not even looking at her after what she'd put him through last night, after all the dreams her delicate face had dredged up.

Well, he wouldn't be having those dreams tonight. Not at the Steamboat. His mouth tautened. He'd say what he'd planned to say. *Here're your daughters, Amos...*

There was a slight gurgling noise across the room. Shad swung his gaze toward the sofa just in time to see Amos's hand grow lax, letting go of the whiskey glass. It tumbled to the carpet below, thudded and rolled toward the hem of Miss Libby's skirt. She gasped.

"Amos?" Shad was across the room in three long strides. "Amos?" He knelt and pressed his fingers against the old man's throat, but there wasn't even the slightest surge of blood beneath his touch. "Oh, hell," he muttered from between clenched teeth. "Damn. Just damn."

He stared for a moment into Amos's pale and now unseeing eyes. The pain that had taken up residence there these past few months was absent. It was always like that. Death came more as friend than foe. He sighed and reached to close the lifeless eyes. "Your father's gone," he said softly. "I'm sorry, Miss Libby."

At his back, Shad heard a quick little intake of breath. For all that he told himself to turn and meet her mournful gaze, he couldn't. A kind of grim paralysis claimed him in spite of the instinct that prodded him to console and comfort the dead man's daughter.

She was so quiet, so still. Ladies, after all, were unaccustomed to the bitter realities of life, the harsh and irrevocable fact of death. Miss Libby—even though she'd seen what bad shape her father had been in—had had the stuffing knocked out of her momentarily, he supposed. In a minute, though, she'd be regaining her composure just long enough to lose it.

He needed to turn, he told himself. He probably ought to take the lady in his arms and let her cry her eyes out. For Amos's sake if not for hers. *Do it, damn you. It's only decent. Be a man.*

Her hands were fisted in the lap of her dress and she was staring down at them. Every inch of the lady's pose—from the slump of her shoulders, the slack of her spine, the tight, white-knuckled clench of her hands—was a portrait of grief.

Do it, damn you. Hold her. Give her whatever comfort a man can give.

"Miss Libby," he said uncertainly.

She lifted her eyes to his. Shad wasn't sure what he was seeing there. Grief that turned her pale blue eyes a pearly gray, or something else he couldn't even begin to comprehend. Or maybe it was the lady who couldn't comprehend.

"He's dead, Miss Libby." Shad swallowed hard. "I'm sorry." He was ready now to catch her if she pitched forward; ready to wrap his arms around her— skinny, dark-haired little Libby; fully prepared to embrace her and absorb her grief.

But he wasn't prepared for the sudden stiffening of her spine, or for the ghost of a smile that shaped her mouth, or the odd glimmer in her eyes when she looked at him head-on and said, "Well, that's that, I suppose."

Chapter Six

Libby left the dramatics to Shula. When she awoke the next morning to the news of their father's passing, Shula immediately turned on the waterworks, the hand-wringing and the loud recriminations.

"I should have gone to him as soon as we arrived last evening, regardless of the state of my appearance," she wailed at her own reflection as she tore a brush through her hair. "Oh, why didn't I?"

An arched eyebrow was Libby's sole reply as she perched on the windowsill, gazing out at a string of cattle that drifted across the horizon, brown against a bright blue sky. Closer, down below in the corral, horses lifted their big heads over fence po̶ nied and pawed at the dusty ground. Life at Paradise—going on despite her father's death. Why did that surprise her? Her stomach tugged into a tight knot, and she turned from the window to watch her sister's morning ritual of hair brushing.

Bent forward from the waist, spilling out of her snug corset, Shula dragged the brush through her red curls. "It's all my fault," she moaned.

"I hardly think so, Shula. Our father was very, very ill."

"Why didn't you wake me, Libby? The minute you suspected he was going, why didn't you send for me?" Shula straightened up, her hair billowing over the silk shoulders of her dressing gown.

Libby sighed. "There wasn't time."

Her sister gave her a disdainful little cluck as she began pinning up her hair.

"There wasn't time," Libby said again, more adamantly now, turning to gaze out the window once more.

There hadn't been time for anything, had there? Only hello after fifteen years. Hello—and a gruff one to boot. "Which one are you?" Not even a goodbye. No time to ask why, and certainly no opportunity once Mr. Shadrach Jones had established his presence in the room.

The questions she hadn't had time to ask rose like bile now in the back of Libby's throat. Why? Why did you let us go? Why did you wait so long to send word? The unasked questions threatened to choke her. Why? Why didn't you love me? Daddy, what did I do wrong?

Libby swallowed hard now and blinked back the film of tears in her eyes, wishing she could let them flow the way Shula did, wishing she could scream and wail and shake a fist toward heaven in her anger and her grief.

Last evening, the moment that glass had slipped from her father's hand as his life slipped from his body, Libby had felt a similar death inside herself. A death as cold and certain as Amos's own. Ice had shrouded her heart—a heart that continued to beat but seemed like a delicate, fan-tailed goldfish, twitching and skimming beneath the frozen surface of a pond. Ice—and death—had locked all the questions in her soul. There would never be answers now.

It was for those answers she had come back to Paradise. Not at first. At first it was simply for Andy's benefit, to get the child away from her father. But as they traveled—as they came closer and closer to the home she'd been wrenched from fifteen years before—something like hope took shape in Libby's heart. Something small and dull which, over the miles, grew and began to glisten. The questions formed even as she had been unaware of them. They begged answers. She had so hoped...

Her chin snapped up and her mouth tightened. It was too late. She hadn't wanted to come, she reminded herself. Her initial instincts had been right. She wasn't like Shula, who had no memory of this place or of their father. Shula, who hadn't borne the consequences of being ripped from Texas soil and transplanted in Missouri. Shula, who had no questions. Shula had come solely to claim the inheritance she felt was her rightful due as the daughter of Amos Kingsland.

Maybe it *was* her rightful due, Libby thought. She was welcome to it, too, as far as Libby was concerned. Paradise merely depressed her now with visions of lives and loves that might have been.

After a soft knock on the door, Antonia entered with a breakfast tray wedged into her hip. "You must eat, *señoritas,*" she said, lowering her burden upon a table.

No sooner were Antonia's arms free than Shula

was throwing herself in them, weeping and wailing upon the woman's ample bosom.

"Shula, for goodness' sake," Libby snapped. "You're going to drown the poor woman." Grimacing, she turned back toward the window, appalled by her sister's theatrical grief, but at the same time feeling something close to envy and wishing she could find such easy relief, could simply fling herself into someone's arms, soaking up comfort like a sponge.

There had been a moment last evening when the big cowboy had moved toward her, slowly, arms stiff but somehow willing, as if he considered it his duty to provide comfort. God! How she'd wanted that. How she'd needed to be surrounded by warm arms, to allow their heat to melt the ice that was gripping her heart. Instead, she had turned away.

Now, of course, she was glad that she had. There was no warm comfort in the arms of Shadrach Jones, a man so similar to her father. There was only ice. Hard, unyielding ice.

Antonia left them, having soothed Shula, having told them she would take care of the funeral arrangements, and having once more implored them to eat.

"I couldn't. I just couldn't. I'm much too distraught," Shula had proclaimed. But now, with Antonia gone, she was tearing off the corner of a piece of toast.

"This is nice, isn't it, Libby?" she murmured.

Libby studied her sister's dreamy expression. "What?" she asked.

Shula popped the toast into her mouth, then expanded her arms to encompass the room. "This. Being waited on. All of it.'' She sighed softly. ''It's what our lives should have been like all along.''

''We should have been loved.''

The bitter words left Libby's lips before she could stop them. Shula was drifting around the room now, oblivious of her sister's harsh statement. Her fingers skimmed a cut-glass vase, the carved walnut pull of a drawer, the gilded corner of a frame.

''It's ours now, I suppose. Well, maybe not officially.'' Her gaze flitted to Libby. ''When do you suppose they'll be reading the will?''

Libby shrugged. She didn't know and she didn't care. If Shula wanted all this, she was welcome to it. All Libby had wanted were answers, and none of those would be forthcoming now.

''After the funeral, probably,'' Shula said, providing her own answer. She began rummaging through one of her trunks. ''I wonder what I ought to wear.''

Teeth clenched, Libby trotted down the staircase. For all she cared, Shula could attend their father's funeral naked. She probably would, too, if she thought it would do her any good.

She glanced at the office door as she passed through the front hall, wondering if Amos's body still lay where she had last seen it. For a second she wanted to march inside and shriek at his cold, lifeless form. Scream so loud he'd hear her wherever he was.

Which one am I, Daddy? I'm Libby. The one who was crying so hard that day when Mama took us away that I could hardly see you. The one who longed to come home. Who used to look out her window at the paved streets of Saint Louis and pretend they were covered with dust and the people passing by were

wearing bright bandannas and broad-brimmed hats.
Who used to look up at the stars at night, wondering
if they were shining down on Paradise right then.
And, if they were the exact same stars, why did they
look so cold where I was?

Why didn't you love me? Why?

Without even realizing it, she had crossed the marble floor and was standing at the office door, her hand
clenched on the knob. She twisted it and stepped in.

Shad looked up from the ledger on the desk to see
her standing in the doorway, staring at him as if he
were a ghost. Judging from her pale complexion, the
lady could have been one herself.

"Miss Libby?"

Blinking, she leaned against the door frame. "I...I
thought..."

Damnation. The lady was going to faint. He shoved
the chair back and nearly vaulted over the desk to
grip her arms as she started slipping to the floor.

"Whoa now, Miss Libby. Here we go." He started
to lead her toward the sofa, thought twice about that
in light of Amos's demise, and instead directed her
toward the chair on the opposite side of the desk. She
sagged into it like a length of old, worn rope.

"Can I get you some water? Want a drink?" Shad
cast about in his brain. What the hell were you supposed to do when a lady got this way? His panicky
gaze traveled the room, lighting on the window. Fresh
air. Hell, it couldn't hurt.

He rammed his shoulders through the heavy drapes,
felt for the handle, then wrenched the window all the
way up in its frame. Sunlight poured into the office,
along with air that was as warm as it was fresh. Not
exactly what he'd had in mind, Shad thought, as he

turned back toward Miss Libby, who still looked as if she were ready to pitch onto the floor.

She looked the way he had expected her to look last night after Amos breathed his last. Only then she'd surprised him by being cool as a cucumber and not even half that pale. Ladies! Hell, who knew what to expect from one minute to the next.

Out of sheer frustration, he poured her a substantial jolt of whiskey and thrust it into her hand. "Drink that, Miss Libby."

Then she surprised him again by not arguing, but lifting the glass to her lips with trembling fingers and taking a good-size, even man-size swallow.

She made a strangling sound, then sputtered. "That wasn't necessary, Mr. Jones. That wasn't necessary at all."

It had brought the color back to her face, Shad noticed, not to mention a sheen of tears to her eyes. Damn if it hadn't brought her spirit back some, as well. She looked like she wanted to kill him.

"I thought it was water," she said accusingly now.

"No, ma'am. If I'd had water, I'd have tossed it in your face." He slid back into Amos's swivel chair on the other side of the desk, fairly assured that the lady would remain vertical now. Vertical as in ramrod stiff.

"I didn't expect to find anyone in here." Her Amos-blue eyes scanned the desktop, homing in on the open ledger. "Just what are you doing in here, Mr. Jones?"

From her suspicious tone, it was obvious she expected him to throw up his hands, confessing to embezzlement, to stealing Paradise blind now that Amos was gone. "I'm going over the books, Miss Kingsland. Your father's gone, but there are still seven thousand head of cattle, a couple hundred horses and forty-two men, all of whom need to be fed, watered and paid.''

She gnawed on her lower lip a minute. ''I wasn't implying...''

''Yes, you were.'' Shad leaned forward, planting his hands on the desk. ''I don't exactly blame you, either. Your father trusted me. But that doesn't mean that you have to, too.''

''Well, then.'' She shot up from her chair—bow taut, arrow straight, aiming for the door. ''I won't keep you from your business any longer. You haven't by any chance seen Andy, have you?''

''No, ma'am. I haven't.''

She paused in the doorway, hand lingering on the knob. Not going. Not staying exactly, either.

''Something else on your mind, ma'am?''

''I...I was just wondering. How is your leg to-day?''

''It's tolerable, Miss Libby. Thank you for ask-ing.'' Was it all that hard, lady?

Another one of those thin smiles edged her lips. ''I'm glad to hear that.'' She slipped out the door and closed it.

Libby hurried across the marble floor, this time keenly aware of her surroundings, all too aware that— for the second time since arriving in Texas—she had lost control of her emotions. In Corpus Christi she had abandoned all sense to a temper she barely knew she possessed. And just now she had seemed to have lost her grip on reality when she had found herself at the office door, confused and lost as a child.

It didn't help one bit that Shadrach Jones had witnessed both incidents, that he seemed to take her emotional disarray in stride as if he believed she was naturally that way.

She wasn't. It was Texas. It was old memories and ancient dreams working their way under her skin, prodding her to behave in such an uncharacteristic fashion. Texas. God! She couldn't wait to get away. What a fool she'd been to believe this was home.

Clinging now to her original and sensible reason for coming here—snatching Andy from the clutches of her dastardly parent—Libby pushed through the kitchen door to find the child laughing gaily as she handed Antonia a pitcher of milk.

For a bewildering moment, Libby heard her own laughter ringing off the whitewashed walls and the tiled floors. Then that laughter shattered like ice.

"I'm so sorry. I didn't do it on purpose," a small voice wailed.

"Can't you keep your children in line, woman?"

Her father's arm lashed out, the flat of his big hand branding her mother's cheek.

"I'm so sorry. I didn't do it on purpose."

Then Libby blinked, bringing the broken pitcher and its white pool of milk into focus.

Antonia was smiling at the disconsolate child. "It's all right, *niña*. Little ones spill. That is how you learn." She patted Andy's shorn hair while pressing a cloth into her hand. "Now you must learn to clean it up."

The little girl was instantly on her knees, picking up wet shards of crockery, sopping up the spilled milk.

"She is a sweet child, *señorita*," Antonia said. She

lowered her voice to a whisper then, glancing to make certain Andy was thoroughly occupied in her task. "What makes such a pretty little one want to look like her own brother?"

"Fear," Libby answered quietly. "I was hoping this trip would help her."

"She is not yours. I see no resemblance."

"No. Not mine. Although perhaps…"

Andy clambered up from the floor, looking enormously pleased with herself. Antonia took the dripping cloth from her hand and carried it to the sink.

Infected by the little girl's sudden happiness, Libby said brightly, "Let's go for a ride, Andy. Let's take a little look at this big place called Paradise."

Her black riding habit felt good, comfortably snug in all the right places. The handsome suit had been Libby's sole extravagance before leaving Saint Louis. You couldn't see the best of Paradise from a wagon seat, she'd reminded herself. And there was so much she longed to see.

With Andy by her side, she strode into the stable. Eb Talent was there, the way she always remembered him, scrubbing the coach wheels with a wire brush. The old man got to his feet immediately.

"I heard about the Captain, Miss Libby." He spat, first tobacco juice, then a small, soft oath. "I'll sure miss him."

Libby felt herself stiffen imperceptibly. She missed Amos, too, only…

"I'm sure you will, Eb," she said, trying to ease the old man's obvious distress. At the same time, she was aware of Andy's increasing discomfort as the child burrowed into her side. "Andy and I would like to go for a ride. Do you suppose you could find us two mounts gentle enough for city girls?''

Eb's face brightened. ''Sure enough, Miss Libby. You just come along with me and I'll get you all fixed up.''

He led them into a clean, well-tended tack room. ''Lookee there,'' he said, pointing to a far wall where two sidesaddles hung on hooks. ''Yours, Miss Libby. And your mama's. I've kept them all this time. Even dusted them, oh, maybe once or twice a year.''

The sight of those familiar objects—achingly familiar even after fifteen years—brought a lump into Libby's throat. She and her mother had ridden for miles and miles, enough miles that they could have crossed the country if they'd been going in a straight line rather than making circuits of Paradise. And she remembered how her mother would always sigh when it was time to turn back to the stable. As if she wanted to just keep going—away. Then she did. Libby hadn't been on a horse since then.

Once she was up, having teetered precariously on the step stool Eb had placed beside the full-chested roan mare, Libby felt as if she'd just ridden the day before, as if all those years had never intervened.

''You sure you want the little one to ride astride, Miss Libby?'' Eb asked her now.

''Yes. Of course.''

Andy had balked at the feminine sidesaddle, and Libby had given in immediately, asking Eb to put a regular saddle on the small dun mare. In all honesty, she wouldn't have minded going astride herself if it weren't for propriety and the skirt of her riding habit.

''Ready, Andy?'' She smiled warmly at the child, who was clinging to the saddle horn and holding the reins as if they were live snakes. "You'll be fine, honey. We'll go nice and slow."

Libby's riding crop hovered above the roan's flank. "What's her name, Eb? Or did my father stop naming horses once we were gone?"

The old man chortled. "Oh, no, Miss Libby. 'Cept I don't know if you'll care for this." Color flared from his neck to his cheeks. "Your daddy called this one...well...Miss Libby, ma'am...the Captain christened this mare Big Tits."

"I see." Libby bit down on a grin, feeling a blush steal across her own cheeks. "Well, perhaps I'll just call her by her first name. Let's go, Big."

When Libby tapped the horse's flank with the crop, the mare looked over her shoulder at the sideways woman, shook her head with a little snort, then trudged out into the sunlight.

After riding for nearly two hours, Libby decided it was time to stop. Andy appeared more comfortable on the dun; at least now she was letting go of her death grip on the saddle horn every once in a while. But her young muscles had to be protesting now. Libby knew hers were, and her muscles weren't all that young.

They had arrived at the bent elbow of Caliente Creek, the stretch where the water carved deeply into the earth when the spring rains came. The familiarity of the scene nearly overwhelmed Libby. It was as if she'd been there only a week or two before.

Amazing how it all came back—the way she'd once played in the twisted limbs of the mesquite, her own limbs twisting and her cotton dresses tearing on the rough bark and the sharp thorns. It hadn't bothered her a bit, though, even when her mother would chastise her later for her unladylike behavior. She'd been so high-spirited, so wild and free.

All that, of course, had been before her parents' difficulties. Those happy days had given way to dark and violent nights, subduing Libby's spirit while casting a pall over Paradise. She sighed now, remembering the welter of emotions she had felt at the time. The tangle of love and hate not unlike the twisted branches of a mesquite tree.

"Let's stop here awhile, Andy." Libby slid down from the big roan mare's back, then helped Andy down from her mount, steadying her until the child's wobbly legs recovered their strength.

Libby started walking toward the creek.

"Shouldn't we tie them up or something?" Andy asked, looking back at the two horses, who were now grazing.

"If they're proper Paradise horses," Libby told her, a distinct note of pride in her voice, "they won't stray but a foot or two from where we dropped their reins." She cast a worried glance over her shoulder just to reassure herself. It was a long walk back to the house, after all—but the big animals were right where they were supposed to be, so Libby continued to the creek.

They sat there for a long time, leaning back, looking at the nearly cloudless sky, listening to meadowlarks and the slow course of water over sticks and stones.

It occurred to Libby that Andy might not have been told of the death that had transpired the night before. Not knowing if it would upset her or not, Libby broached the subject cautiously. She plucked a weed, chewed its stem a moment, then asked, "I told you we were coming here because my father was very ill, didn't I, Andy?"

The child nodded and continued to watch the trickle of the narrow stream.

"He was even more ill than Shula or I had imagined. He passed away last evening shortly after our arrival." Libby was conscious of her own breathing as she waited for the child's reaction. When it came, it was probably what anyone might have expected from someone who'd had only horrible experiences where fathers were concerned.

Andy shrugged and glanced away, as if not knowing what to say. Then her gaze darted back to Libby's face. "Does that mean we're going right back to Saint Louis now?"

"Not immediately."

"I don't want to go back," the child insisted. "Ever."

Libby smiled softly, reaching out to adjust the little girl's upturned collar. "Is that because you like Texas so much, or is it because you hate Saint Louis?"

"Both." Andy jerked her collar upward once more then crossed her arms defensively. "I don't ever want to go back there, Miss Libby. I won't." Her mouth tightened in a hard, stubborn line.

It wasn't a confrontation Libby was prepared for. She had primed herself to answer a nine-year-old's questions about death, not the child's grave concerns for her future. Of course, they'd be going back to Saint Louis. Staying in Texas—remaining here at Paradise—was out of the question. Saint Louis, after all, was home.

"Let's not even think about Saint Louis now," she

said. "We'll be here a good, long while. Long enough to turn you into a fine rider, I expect. Are you rested enough to climb back on that big old horse again?"

"I suppose," Andy replied with a beleaguered sigh.

"Good." Libby got to her feet. "And who do you suppose will win if we race back to the horses?" The words were barely out of her mouth when she yanked up the long black skirt of her riding habit and took off.

Pretending to stumble over a mesquite root, Libby glanced back and was happy to see Andy scrambling after her, unburdened enough to sprint past her then with a victorious whoop. Maybe they couldn't stay in Texas, Libby thought, but at least while they were here she was determined to make Miss Amanda Rowan as strong and vigorous as possible. Who knew? She might even convince the little girl to dress like one. Which sounded like a fine idea then as Libby resumed the race. Skirt against skirt might have made it an even match.

Near the grazing horses, Andy was laughing, bending over to catch her breath, when Libby arrived, one hand pressed to the painful stitch in her side.

"I swear," Libby gasped, "I'll never do that again. I must be getting old as a—"

The crack of a rifle cut off her words. The horses jerked up their heads. When a second shot bit into the dust beside them, both animals bolted.

"Get down!" Libby dove for the ground, pulling Andy with her.

Chapter Seven

At the sound of the first shot, Shad reined in his horse. "What the hell?" he murmured. Amos had a standing rule at Paradise. No gunplay. Any shot fired on the ranch was a signal of distress. There had been few infractions over the years—only two or three incidents of unannounced target practice—and the guilty parties had been given their walking papers promptly for breaking that rule.

This morning, to Shad's knowledge, there were no hands working up by the big bend of Caliente Creek. If there was, and if that fella was getting off a few practice shots with Miss Libby and her daughter in the vicinity, the culprit would be gone from Paradise by sundown if not before.

As soon as the second shot sounded, Shad was digging his spurs into his stallion's hide.

Damn fool lady. Why didn't she ask him before she just took off on her own? Why didn't Eb come get him right away instead of waiting a full hour and then just happening to mention that Miss Libby and the little girl had ridden north "clinging to the saddle horns for their sweet young lives"?

Up ahead, not too far from the creek, he could see two riderless horses moving toward him at a good clip. Big Tits was tearing up the ground, and the little dun was trying to keep up. Shad cut between them, grabbing for the dun's bridle and lugging her to a halt. The roan, meanwhile, didn't even break her stride, but kept running flat-out.

Shad uttered a blistering curse. "What'd you do," he growled at the lathered dun, "just flick off Miss Libby and her daughter like they were fleas?"

With the small horse in tow, he headed for the creek where Miss Libby was standing now, slapping dust off her black dress and muttering what sounded for all the world like obscenities. The little girl scooted behind her mother's skirt when he dismounted and strode toward them.

His hands were balled into fists and his jaw was clenched so tight he could barely speak. But when he did, it came out in a shout. "This isn't some municipal park in Saint Louis, Miss Libby. What do you think you're doing, riding out here all alone like this?"

She gave one last, flat-handed slap to her skirt before raising her face to his. Her blue eyes burned dark, just like her daddy's always did. "I'll go where I please, Mr. Jones. When I please. We were doing fine until somebody decided to take a shot at us."

"I doubt that," he snarled, scanning the horizon for any sign of the rifleman.

When he returned his gaze to the lady, her face was still pointed up into his and her pink lips were taut as baling wire.

"You doubt that we were doing fine, Mr. Jones, or

you doubt that someone fired at us?" Her chin lifted a notch. "Which?"

"Both!"

He took his hat off and ran a sleeve across his wet brow. What was he doing, standing here arguing with her when whoever fired that shot—and he had a pretty good idea who it had been—might be drawing a bead on them right this minute?

"Let's go."

Before the little girl could even react, he swung her up on the dun's back. A moment later he had lofted himself onto his stallion and held a hand toward the lady in the preposterous skirt. "You'll have to ride with me, Miss Libby. Grab on and I'll lift you up."

With a single, searing blue look she told him he was as crazy as he was stupid.

"I'll walk, thank you."

She took two steps and then he scooped her up and plopped her sideways across his lap. "You'll ride," he told her, and set his horse off at such a clip that it knocked the wind—and the argument—right out of her.

Only temporarily, though. Shad eased up on his horse after looking back to see young Andy, pale and windblown, clinging precariously to her seat on the galloping dun. As soon as he slowed to a trot, Miss Libby recovered her breath and rediscovered her tongue.

"Put me down, Mr. Jones. I'd rather walk than have you manhandling me."

"Manhandling," he muttered. It was the second time the lady had accused him of that. "I'm not even touching you, Miss Libby." He raised the reins off the stallion's neck. "Look. Both hands accounted for."

It wasn't his hands that were bothering her. It was being pinned between those two rock-hard arms—one bracing her back and the other snug against her midriff. It was being cradled between two denim-clad, hard-muscled thighs. It was the warm tickle of his breath at her ear. And every time she tried to lean her upper body away, her lower portions lodged more firmly against him. She'd never been plastered against a man before. It was extremely unsettling. And not at all as distasteful as she was insisting.

She was being ungrateful, too, and it galled her that the minute she was near this big cowboy her manners went up in smoke. Libby angled her head, encountering the firm line of his jaw beneath the stubborn set of his mouth.

"Thank you for coming to our assistance," she said.

Those full lips slid sideways and the tension in his jawline eased. His arms relaxed where they touched her. For a second, Libby thought she saw warmth seep into his deep brown eyes. Or perhaps it was only relief, for he sighed roughly.

"Glad I was nearby," he drawled. "Like I said, Miss Libby, this isn't Saint Louis. Riding at Paradise isn't like being on one of your bridal paths back East. Things can...well...happen out here."

Bad things, he'd wanted to say. But he didn't. He thought maybe she was scared enough already, judging from the trembling he could feel everywhere he touched her slim body.

"You didn't happen to get a glimmer of the person who fired on you, did you?" he asked her. When she shook her head, he added quickly, "Well, I doubt if it was anything. Probably just a cowboy trying out a new rifle and having no idea you or your daughter were anywhere nearby. I'll check into it, Miss Libby."

What he'd be checking into, Shad thought grimly, was the whereabouts of Hoyt Backus and every hand at Hellfire. There was little doubt in his mind just who had fired those shots. There was even less doubt about the reason. With Amos gone, the ranch would pass to his daughters. If they got scared off—or maybe even killed off—Hoyt would be first in line to buy it, with tears in his eyes and a big fistful of cash.

The lady sat so quietly then that Shad wondered if she was reading his mind.

"Don't you worry," he said, trying to reassure her. "You just need to be a little more cautious out here, especially with your daughter. Next time you two want to go out riding, I'll see that somebody goes along to keep an eye out."

"She's not my daughter."

"Pardon?"

"I said Andy's not my daughter."

"But I thought…"

"You thought wrong, Mr. Jones."

She straightened her shoulders and stared off over the horse's head, ignoring him. Shad glanced back at little Andy once more. Well, he hadn't noticed any particular resemblance, but then he'd also thought the little girl was a damn little boy. Where Miss Libby was concerned, he realized, his instincts were no longer to be trusted.

He studied the dark-haired lady now—the soft curve of her cheek, the dark length of her eyelashes, the little tilt of her nose. Just as she was ignoring him, he tried to ignore the petal pink of her lips and tried not to think of the feel of them under his. He tried to banish the sudden desire to taste them again.

His entire impression of the lady's circumstances shifted once again, this time like a rug being pulled out from under him or the ground heaving beneath his boots. If she wasn't a mother...if she'd never...if Miss Libby was a maiden lady...

If that kiss he'd stolen from her was indeed as innocent and virginal as it had felt...

A tremor worked its way through him, bone deep. Old memories shuddered in his brain—spiderwebs shifting on a sudden, inexplicable draft in a long-locked room. He shook his head to clear it.

"Mr. Jones." She hissed his name.

"Ma'am?"

Rather than reply, the lady aimed a hot glare in the direction of his lax left arm, lying across her skirt. He jerked it up as if her black-skirted lap had grown hot as a cast-iron griddle, muttered something that was a cross between an oath and an apology, then stared straight ahead.

He'd be on another kind of griddle tonight, Shad thought morosely. His bunk was bound to become a bed of white-hot coals when the dream returned. And it would. He knew that as surely as he knew he had broken his vow once again, as surely as he knew the delicate sway and the surprising warmth of Miss Libby in his arms.

The sun had climbed high overhead. They were still a good mile from the house, threading their way across the flat land through stands of mesquite and clumps of prickly pear. Every once in a while a frilly-leafed branch of mesquite would tickle across Libby's cheek or a horsefly would persist in buzzing around her head. She found those irritations preferable to the constant feel of Shadrach Jones, hard against her back.

The harder she tried to ignore him—pretending the solid warmth of his chest was no more than the leather-backed seat of a coach, that his arms were merely the oaken arms of a chair—the more she was aware of him. And the more she was aware of him, it seemed, the more she babbled to Andy in an effort to distract herself.

She'd spent the past half hour pointing out places where she'd picnicked with her mother years ago, sounding like a schoolmarm as she identified trees and shrubs and wildflowers, as well as the various birds that their horses flushed from cover.

"See those flowers over there, Andy?" Libby pointed left to a carpet of delicate pink. "Those are primroses. We have those in Saint Louis, too."

The child, more comfortable in the saddle now, nodded. "What are those red ones?" she asked in a tone more polite than curious.

Libby frowned, chewing on her lower lip. For the life of her, she couldn't recall the name of that particular flower. She ought to know it, too. She used to pick armfuls of the crimson blooms. The name was on the tip of her tongue when the man behind her whispered softly, "Indian paintbrush."

A mere breath, as if the breeze had whispered in her ear. A warm breeze. Too warm.

"I knew that, Mr. Jones," she muttered, leaning

forward, away. "It's paintbrush, Andy. Indian paint-brush."

"It's pretty," the little girl replied, her attention drifting off in the opposite direction now. "Oh, look over there, Miss Libby," she called out. "Puppies!"

Libby swung her gaze toward the thin carpet of shade beneath a mesquite tree where she saw a lump, a lifeless pelt that resembled a cast-off fur coat. The lump appeared still, then suddenly there was a tiny, furry ripple of movement at its edge. Puppies!

An oath scorched her ear now as Shadrach Jones pulled back on the reins. His arms tightened around her for a moment, then he slid off the back of the horse.

Libby clung to the saddle horn.

"Stay here," he told her.

"What's the matter, Mr. Jones?"

If he heard her question, he ignored it as he turned and strode toward the low-branched mesquite. Andy, who had slithered down from her mount, was several cautious steps behind him. It was the closest the little girl had approached a male voluntarily, and Libby watched with growing interest as the big cowboy squatted down beside the prone animal and Andy drew even closer to him.

Shad swallowed an oath that felt more like a sob as he gazed down at the dead animal. It was Black Bess, no doubt about it—one of the best cowdogs they'd ever had at Paradise. She could flush the or-neriest bull from the thickest, thorniest cover, and when other dogs would hang back with their tails be-tween their legs, Black Bess would charge ahead, yapping almost as if she were singing.

Damn fool female. This was her first litter. She

should have had sense enough to crawl into the straw-lined box he'd readied for her behind the bunkhouse instead of running off like some wild thing. Or maybe he should have had sense enough to rope her in these past few days.

"Is she dead?"

The little girl's voice came from just behind him. He turned to find her staring down, her blue eyes glistening and her lips quivering. When he nodded, a tear broke loose and skittered down the child's cheek. He felt half like crying himself.

"She's gone, but she left a couple of pretty little pups," he said softly as he scooped up one of the wriggling balls of fur and held it out to Andy. "Here."

A light sparked in the child's eyes and she reached out, then drew back as if Shad were offering her a handful of hot coals.

"He's not going to bite you, sugar." He held the puppy closer to her.

Her wary gaze met his for a single, telling moment, then slanted away. It wasn't the tiny animal that worried her, that cautious look said. It was him. The big animal. Quite clearly, she didn't want to touch him, even if it meant not getting to hold her little heart's desire.

It rocked him for a moment. What the hell could happen to someone so young to cause a reaction like that?

"I won't bite, either," he added. "How 'bout if I put this little fluff ball down on the ground and you can pick him up when you're ready?"

Once the puppy was down, the little girl glanced at Shad once, as if suspecting a trick of some sort.

When he raised both hands in a gesture of surrender, Andy snatched up the little animal and cuddled it against her shirtfront.

He turned back to Black Bess. There wasn't an unusual amount of blood so he didn't think she had bled to death giving birth to her litter. Running his hands over her thick coat, he searched for whatever might have killed her. It wasn't long before he found it—a clotted red hole in her skull, just beneath one ear. The dog had been shot.

Shot! It didn't make any sense at all. Shooting at game and predators, Shad understood. Even drawing a bead on people had its own horrible logic. But not this.

"Can we keep them?" The child's tiny, wavering voice broke into his bleak thoughts.

He shifted on his haunches. "Think you can manage all three of these squirming little things and still stay on that horse?"

She nodded with confidence bordering on eagerness, but Shad wasn't quite as certain as she was. He removed his hat and lifted up the two pups still nestled against their lifeless mother, plopping them into the deep felt hollow.

"Put that little guy in there, too," he directed Andy as he began unbuttoning his shirt.

"What are you doing?" she asked, a newly fearful note in her voice.

"Making us a proper basket for toting pups," he said, grinning as he wrenched his arms out of his sleeves.

What in the name of heaven was the man doing? Still perched precariously atop Shadrach Jones's big stallion, Libby gripped the saddle horn more tightly to keep herself from sliding sideways to the ground. She'd been watching the boyish child and the virile cowboy with such interest that she'd almost forgotten about the unfortunate dog. Andy would move toward the man, as if drawn by some invisible bond, then she would skitter away only to move toward him once more.

She had been thinking how very odd it was that a child so frightened of the male sex should be drawn to such a perfect specimen.

And he was perfect, Libby thought, unable to tear her gaze away from the beautifully sculpted chest he'd just uncovered. She was entranced by the way the muscles curved then gave way to corded ridges at his belt line. She was nearly bewitched by the suggestion of the sheer power those muscles contained, and her mouth went dry at the sight of so much sunbaked, caramel-colored, luscious and glistening skin.

The impropriety of his undressing—out here in the middle of nowhere in front of two females—was slow to dawn on her, but dawn it did once her eyes had had their fill.

"Mr. Jones," she hissed as he approached her. "Is that really necessary?"

His dark eyes—insolent, amused, challenging—met hers. "Yes, ma'am. I figured the shirt would go a mite easier on you than the pants. But if you'd rather I did it different…"

His bronze fingers were already at his belt buckle when Libby called out, "The shirt will do, thank you very much."

Now his mouth curled with lazy insolence. "You're right welcome, Miss Libby."

The child had scrambled back up on the dun. Shad handed her the makeshift basket of puppies and was pleased that she took it from him so readily, without more than a slight tremor in her fingers.

"Hold 'em tight now, sugar. It's a long way down to the ground," he told her, though he doubted she'd let those little critters get more than an inch away from her. Her eyes were shining like Christmas morning as she cradled the shirt-wrapped hat on her lap. It was the first time he'd seen the kid even halfway happy, he thought.

"Let's go, ladies." He snatched up his horse's reins and pulled him in the direction of home.

"Aren't you riding, Mr. Jones?" Miss Libby's voice floated down over his shoulder while he kept his eyes on the terrain ahead.

"I'll walk awhile."

"It won't do your injured leg much good," she added after a moment. "I notice you're favoring it some."

Truth to tell, the snakebite was beginning to ache no end, and there was nothing he would have liked better than to swing up on Stormy for an easy lope back to the ranch. Considering Miss Libby's prissy reaction when he took off his shirt, though, he'd decided he'd best keep his half-naked distance.

"You need to get off that leg," she said now. "I suggest that you ride. More than suggest. I insist." There was a faint echo of Amos in her tone.

Shad stopped in his tracks, his fingers clenched around the reins. The stallion snorted, then gave his shoulder an impatient shove.

"It's too far for you to walk, Miss Libby," he told her slowly and distinctly.

"I was suggesting that we ride the way we did before, Mr. Jones. Double."

Double, he groaned inwardly. What the hell did she want from him anyway? One minute she was regarding his bare chest with squinty-eyed disdain; the next minute she was asking—no, she was demanding—that he plaster all that naked skin against her. The lady made him feel dizzy as a damn yo-yo.

Libby leaned forward, as far as possible, when he mounted and settled behind her. Once more those brawny arms pressed against her, only now they were uncovered—hard as oak, a blend of bunched muscle, taut sinew and strong, ropy veins. It was difficult to tear her gaze away. Even more difficult not to breathe in the purely male fragrance—all leather and sunshine and sweat—that suddenly surrounded her. And she could barely breathe as it was, because her heart seemed to be stuck somewhere in the vicinity of her throat. She swallowed hard to dislodge it.

"If it discomfits you all that much, Miss Libby, I'd just as soon slide off and walk."

"Nonsense," she said with a sniff.

"Suit yourself."

"I usually do."

"Uh-huh."

He gave the stallion a kick that sent the animal forward at the same time it pressed Libby back against all that bare skin. She rode in silence the rest of the way back to the ranch, for fear that if she spoke her voice would come out all wrong—ragged as her breath, erratic as the beat of her heart.

It wasn't Shadrach Jones at all, she told herself. It was just that she'd had so little experience—none really—with men that her body seemed to be behaving at such perverse odds with her mind. The one was whispering yes while the other was muttering no, leaving her in an unaccustomed and speechless dither.

Once more she found herself wishing she was more like Shula, who would be reveling now in the hard arms of this big, bronze cowboy, sopping up his heat and fragrance like a female sponge, glorying in his naked nearness. Just as Libby herself was doing right this minute.

Lord help me, she thought woefully. The last thing Libby wanted was to be like Shula. No. That wasn't quite true. The last thing she wanted was to be this close to Shadrach Jones ever again.

Shula peered from her bedroom door as Libby came down the hallway. From her tousled curls and loose wrapper, it was obvious that Shula had just awakened from a nap—or a beauty sleep as she preferred to call it.

She arched a finely shaped eyebrow in Libby's direction. "Couldn't you have gotten any closer to him, Libby?"

"I beg your pardon?"

Shula opened her door wider. "You heard me." Her bracelets jangled as she motioned Libby closer, then she planted a hand on each of her sister's shoulders and turned her full circle. "Good," she said. "No sweat stains."

"What?" Libby croaked.

"Perspiration," Shula said with the air of a schoolmarm instructing a particularly dull-witted pupil. "Men perspire, Libby. Well, actually, gentlemen perspire. Men like Shadrach Jones just sweat. Surely you noticed that while you were sitting smack in the middle of his lap."

Shula inspected the sleeve of the riding habit more closely now while she murmured, "Lucky for you that you're wearing black. The stains barely show."

Blinking and nearly speechless, all Libby could do was sputter. "I was not sitting in his lap."

"You were, too. I saw you." Shula rolled her eyes. "I don't know why you're getting so flustered. You're twenty-five years old, after all. If you want to sit in a man's lap, you're certainly entitled."

Although her mouth was moving, Libby simply couldn't get any words out. It was true—all of it. She *was* twenty-five, and she *was* flustered, and she *had* been sitting smack in the middle of Jones's lap. Worse, she had savored every single minute of their close contact, and Shula seemed to be all too aware of that fact.

"Good Lord, Libby. Stop looking as if you'd just been caught with your hand in the cookie jar." Shula smiled—her full lips hovering between a leer and an expression of genuine delight. Then she winked. "It's perfectly all right to dally with the help," she said, "as long as you don't get carried away. You wouldn't want to let something like that get too serious."

"Serious?" Libby echoed numbly. Her lips felt wooden all of a sudden and a feeling of disorientation gripped her, making her light-headed. She was the big sister, wasn't she? The one so accustomed to imparting quiet counsel and sage advice. But now it was Shula who seemed older, wiser and better versed in the ways of the world while Libby felt dizzy and confused.

"You know what I mean." Shula lowered her

voice as she tugged her sister's sleeve, drawing her conspiratorially close in order to whisper. "You might want to fall into *bed* with him, honey, but you certainly wouldn't want to fall in *love* with Shadrach Jones."

Chapter Eight

"**I**'d rather fall in a vat of boiling oil."

In the middle of the night, long after Shula's outrageous remark, Libby bolted upright in her bed, muttering through tightly clenched teeth. Her hands were fisted in the jumble of covers on her lap.

"Fall into bed with Shadrach Jones! I'd rather be strung up by my heels over a bed of hot coals. Or walk over a bed of nails. I'd rather..."

Her protests sputtered to a fuming silence as she stared bleakly into the darkness. Why was she going on like this? Why now? She should have informed her sister exactly where she could stow her unwanted and unsought advice, instead of just walking dumbly away, slamming her door and then hiding out in her room the rest of the afternoon and evening.

She had even taken her evening meal in her room, pretending to be too grief stricken and too distraught to be a fit companion. In short, she was behaving just like Shula—all heart and no head. All gush and no grit. It wasn't like her at all.

But then she hadn't been acting like herself ever since her arrival in Texas. No. That wasn't true. She'd been fine those first few hours in Corpus Christi. She'd been sane and solid up until her encounter with Jones. After that, she'd become a bellowing, screeching and—yes, dammit—quivering wreck.

And now here she was locking herself up in her room to escape the problems she ordinarily met head-on.

"Coward," Libby grumbled into the dark. Then she blinked as if a bright light had flashed through the room. What exactly were her problems? Or, she wondered dismally, who?

She'd be hard-pressed, she realized, to blame her current misery on her father, even though the man had caused her untold heartache in the past. For once, it wasn't Shula who was making Libby's life miserable. It certainly wasn't little Andy. If anything, the child had seemed to be deliriously happy with her hatful of puppies when they'd returned from their ride this afternoon.

Their ride. That sensual, skin-tingling, sweat-stained ride. No doubt about it. Her problem was Shadrach Jones. It wasn't so much what the man said or did—even though his high-handed ways made her see bloodred—but his mere presence that made her behave uncharacteristically, that had her flustered and flummoxed and just plain foolish.

She'd never been the least bit interested in the opposite sex. She still wasn't, only suddenly there was this man—this collection of muscle and bone and warm breath—who was wreaking havoc upon her. The man must have some chemical in his body that reacted instantly and explosively with some chemical lurking in hers. He must possess some mysterious magnetic force that pulled all her sane and sober tendencies sideways, that left her mind unbalanced and in a miserable dither. There was no other way to explain it.

And there was nothing in her experience that told her how to deal with these disconcerting feelings except to stay away from the man who provoked them—stay the *hell* away from him. Only how she'd manage that Libby didn't have a clue. She couldn't hide out in her bedroom indefinitely. Returning to Saint Louis was the obvious answer, but there was her father's funeral to consider and to leave so soon wouldn't just break young Andy's heart, it would also put the little girl back within her father's lecherous reach. They couldn't go back. Not yet.

Which left a single alternative. Shadrach Jones and all his chemicals and strange magnetics would just have to go. The sooner, the better.

Knowing the dream awaited him, Shad had drunk an extra cup of Eb's tar-black coffee. He would have sat up all night playing cards, but the atmosphere in the bunkhouse was glum, almost funereal, befitting the circumstances.

Amos was dead. Shad kept forgetting. Or not forgetting so much as not being able to comprehend the finality. It was like waiting for a second boot to hit the floor.

Reluctantly he had bid the men good-night and had headed for his private quarters at the far end of the bunkhouse. When he had finally fallen asleep, it was with a kind of belligerence—still dressed and with his arms crossed tightly over his chest. When the dream came, he aimed to dream it different.

But he couldn't.

Feathers and flames. They consumed him once more, each sight and sound and smell as real, as palpable and as painfully exquisite as they had been twenty years before.

Once more he could hear the hot droning of locusts in the elm whose branches clawed at the clapboard. Once more he was sleeping naked in that stifling room beneath the eaves of the parsonage, dead tired from clearing acre after acre of mesquite and scrub oak, bone tired at the age of fourteen just from growing. That summer his wrists had shot right past his sleeves. His shirt buttons popped off just from breathing, and his new stepmother was always sewing them on, sometimes before he could get out of the shirt. He'd stand, hardly daring to breathe, staring at her honey-colored hair and watching her tongue skim her lower lip then settle in the corner of her mouth as the backs of her cool fingers pressed against his hot skin and she wove the needle in and out, back and forth, interminably.

And now—now—she was climbing the narrow stairs. He heard her nightdress whisking at her legs. She whispered his name. He smelled the delicate scent of clover deepening as she came closer, turning heavy and ripe as roses.

Her touch—feathers at first—struck him dumb. He was stunned, speechless. His tongue was useless until she touched it with her own. His hands were cumbersome, cold and stiff as spades, until she lifted her gown and shaped them to her breasts.

"You want me, Shad. You know it."

He didn't know anything just then. He was nothing more than a tinderbox, and when she straddled him, he went up in flames, instinct taking over where awk-

*wardness and uncertainty left off, a summer's worth
of temptation ripping through him like a jagged bolt
of lightning.*

*Then it was done—over in moments, for he hadn't
known to do anything but explode inside her like stars
on a velvet heaven, like fireworks on a hot July sky.*

*The door downstairs clicked open. The dream sped
up. It became a blur of slick and scrambling bodies,
his father's implacable footsteps coming up the stairs,
her screams, and moonlight glinting on the gun.*

A rough hand jostled his shoulder and Shad
snapped upright on his bunk. Eb stood there in his
rat-gray long johns, shaking his head.

"You shouted out," the old man said. "I thought
maybe that snakebite was troubling you."

"No. I'm all right."

"You sure?"

"Sure I'm sure," Shad snarled. "Thanks," he
added gruffly, watching the old sailor shuffle back
toward his hammock, envying him the sweet sway of
his sleep.

They collided in the dark kitchen.

Libby, fortified by her decision to fire Shad and
much too wide-awake to sleep, had left the sanctuary
of her room and had padded barefoot down the staircase and across the vestibule. Shad, meanwhile, having decided that sleep was comparable to suffering
the tortures of the damned, had gone to the kitchen
to check on Black Bess's pups. He was leaving just
as Libby came in.

They walked right into each other. For Libby, it
was like hitting a six-foot two-inch brick wall.

"Ooph!" Her breath sailed forward and Libby

would have stumbled back except the wall had arms that clasped her—hard. She stood there then, through no effort of her own, in a solid and all-encompassing embrace. In Shadrach Jones's embrace. She would have known it anywhere, in darkness or by the light of day. It was strangely familiar. Secure and unsettling all in the same moment.

The wall swore. Softly though, like the sound of rough bricks shifting, sliding into place, seeking the perfect fit. It was followed by the coarse scrape of whiskers on her temple, and the slow spread of big, familiar hands on her back. Her breath was already gone, and now Libby's mind seemed to have fled, as well. No little voice whispered *Don't*. Nothing cautioned *Beware*. Her head was empty except for the sound of her own heartbeat. How the devil could it beat so hard and yet feel as if it were holding still?

When she shook her head in bewilderment, her lips brushed his cheek and she discovered another paradox. Prickly soft. A miracle of flesh and hair. Her tongue slid out to test it further.

A deep, breathy curse blew across her ear, sending ripples of heat all through her, and Libby shivered as if taken by a sudden chill. Another contradiction, as confusing as it was intriguing. She found herself lifting on tiptoe, like ivy inching up the shady side of an edifice, seeking light and warmth, seeking and finding the mouth that slanted over hers. The kiss unfurled like a new leaf, all tender and soft and moist as his tongue skimmed hers. Heat curled through her from the top of her head to the tips of her toes, prompting her arms to slide up and twine around his neck.

Shad's groan was lost in the depths of the kiss. He

felt like a sleepwalker whose dream had stalked him from his bunk to the big house, only to slam up against him now in the dark kitchen. Only he wasn't dreaming. Every inch of his body had snapped wide-awake at the feel of Miss Libby, all boneless and purring in his arms. A little she-cat. No. A lady cat. He had to struggle to remember that this particular breed could be all limp and lovey one minute, then hissing and spitting fire the next.

Still, he couldn't tear himself away. "Lady, lady, what are you doing to me?" he murmured against her lips. It wouldn't have surprised him in the least if she had replied throatily, "You want me, Shad. You know it." How the hell could he help it?

But what she said was "Stop," or more exactly moaned the command while making no attempt to obey it herself. If anything, she clung to him more and her mouth seemed to issue a sweeter, deeper invitation to which Shad immediately responded. His brain was barely functioning now, its rich supply of blood having surged elsewhere.

She moaned once more just before muttering, "I am not going to fall into bed with you."

"No, ma'am," he managed to rasp against her wet lips. He hadn't asked her, had he? Had he? Hell, he couldn't think anymore. How any man could kiss, converse and sweat bullets simultaneously defied his current powers of comprehension.

A moment later, though, when she had plucked her mouth from his and had balled her hands into hard little fists against his chest, Shad vaguely understood that the kiss was over.

She stepped back, out of his arms. "You need to

leave," she said at the end of a ragged breath, then repeated it more forcefully. "You need to leave."

Leave. Shad blinked in the darkness. It wasn't that he didn't recognize the word so much as it was his distinct impression that when Miss Libby said "leave" she meant more than just ambling back to the bunkhouse and packing it in for the night. She meant Paradise.

Until a moment ago there had been nothing Shad had wanted more than to put several counties—big Texas counties—between himself and Amos's daughter. But now...

He told himself his sudden reluctance to leave wasn't because of the kiss. Rather it just plain galled him that she wanted to boot him out. After all he'd done! After he'd spent a miserable few hours in that high-toned eatery with a noose around his neck and next to nothing on his plate. After he'd risked life and a particular limb to save the kid from a rattler. After all that, Miss Libby's gratitude left a lot to be desired.

"Mind telling me why?" he asked, surprised at the churlish, even childish note in his voice. That along with a certain huskiness left over from all the kissing.

A match scraped and flared across the room, bringing her big, glossy eyes into view for a second before the flame went out.

"Damn," she muttered with a certain huskiness of her own.

More matches then. Resisting his natural urge to help, Shad leaned against the door frame, cocked a leg and crossed his arms, while half a dozen matches scritched and scratched and snapped in two before one finally caught and held, bouncing Miss Libby's shapely little shadow from wall to wall. How any one woman could be so beautiful and so ornery all in the same breath was beyond him. But then Shad reminded himself that Miss Libby Kingsland wasn't a woman at all. She was a lady. That was a whole different breed.

The glass chimney trembled against the lamp as Libby reseated it. She turned up the wick while trying to maintain control of her shaking hands. Blast the man. Once she was within a foot of him she became an incompetent dolt. Kissing him made her stupid and senseless, yet he'd had the gall to ask what *she* was doing to *him*. Firing him, that's what. Sending him far away. Preferably downwind so those outrageous chemicals of his could no longer combine with hers to send her head spinning or turn her insides to warm, wet mush.

She pushed the lamp to the center of the table, yanked out a chair and sat, then folded her hands in what seemed like a very businesslike posture. He didn't have to know it was simply to quell the shakes.

"Now, Mr. Jones," she began, forcing her voice to stay level and her eyes to meet his, "if you've got wages coming or any back pay that's owed, I'll be happy to—"

"Just hold on, lady." He shouldered off the door frame, then crossed the kitchen's terra-cotta tiles in what seemed like a single stride. "If this is all because of one little kiss…"

"Little!" Libby's voice climbed to an altogether unpleasant register—a screech, really—and her hands flew up off the table. She restrained them by clasping them in her lap, then swallowed hard to subdue her vocal chords. "I'd hardly call that little, Mr. Jones."

Flipping a chair around, he straddled it as if it were

a snorting, bucking mustang. "How the hell would you know, Miss Kingsland?" he growled.

"Well, I..." Libby drew in her lower lip. The answer was painfully obvious. She didn't know. But if what she'd just experienced had been a little kiss, she didn't even want to think about the havoc a big one might wreak in her. The very notion made her stomach quiver. "We were discussing your dismissal, I believe."

"All right." He crossed his arms over his chest. "Go ahead."

"I want you to leave."

"You already said that."

Libby crossed her arms now. "Well?"

"Well what?"

"Go." She angled her head toward the door. Once he was gone, she thought, she'd be able to breathe normally. However did he manage to suck up all the air in a room, leaving only scraps for everybody else to breathe?

But he wasn't going. He seemed stuck to that backward chair as if he were glued to it by the seat of his pants. The pants—she couldn't help but notice—that were pulled so taut across his thighs. The thighs that had cradled her so solidly that afternoon. She could actually see the power in those hard curves, could almost feel... Her eyes snapped back to his face only to discover the most irritating grin she'd ever seen.

"You've got a lot to learn about firing, Miss Libby," he said.

"Perhaps you'd like to instruct me, Mr. Jones." She narrowed her gaze, and added, "I'm sure you've been through the process countless times."

He nodded, seemingly unperturbed by her scorching glare. "Yep, but never on the wrong end of it. I've fired some men over the years, and I watched your daddy send more than a few men packing. But there wasn't one of them that either one of us booted out unjustly or without giving him a good reason why."

"A reason? That's all you need and then you'll go?"

Again he nodded. "Yes, ma'am." Then his voice dipped disturbingly low, fairly rumbling in his chest. "If you've got one."

Libby sniffed. Surely she could think of something other than the embarrassing truth. Well, couldn't she?

Jones's eyebrows rose quizzically as he sat there, all patience now and paternal wisdom and apparent permanence. "Do you have a reason?" he asked.

"Of course I do," she snapped. Fool man. Just give me a minute to come up with one.

He continued to sit there, shifting once to drape his arms over the back of the chair. No doubt doing it just to rattle her concentration with those rolled-up sleeves that exposed wrists as thick as tree limbs and forearms the color and density of oak.

She needed a reason, dammit, and the only one her flummoxed brain could produce was the truth. "You unsettle me, Mr. Jones. When you're around, I find I can't think clearly. And..."

One of his dark eyebrows climbed higher.

"And my heart starts feeling like it's going to explode."

Squeezing her eyes closed, Libby let out what remained of her breath. There. She'd said it. She'd given him the silly reason. Let him laugh if he wanted. At least now he would get up off that damnable chair and go.

He wasn't laughing though. She couldn't hear anything, in fact. Not a suppressed chuckle. Not even a breath. When she worked up the courage to look at him, fully expecting to see that cockeyed grin, he wasn't even smiling. In truth, he looked quite grim.

"That's the reason," she said softly. "The only one I can offer you."

He shot up out of the chair as if the glue that had held him there had suddenly caught fire. "To tell you the truth, Miss Libby," he said abruptly, "I was planning to ride out right after Amos's funeral anyway."

"Oh." The word came out with more surprise than relief.

"Unless you want me gone sooner."

"No." Her gaze flew up to his, then fluttered down. "What I mean is, I'm sure my father would want you to stay for the services."

"All right."

Without another word, he shoved the chair back beneath the table, then strode out of the kitchen. Libby listened to his boot heels ringing on the marble floor in the vestibule. When she heard the front door close decisively, she let out a little sigh.

There. Her problem was solved. The man was leaving. Once her father's funeral was over, she wouldn't have to worry about her head spinning or her heart exploding anymore.

She drummed her fingers on the table. That was just what she wanted.

Chapter Nine

"And so, my fellow mourners, let us contemplate that other Paradise where Amos Kingsland now resides," the Reverend Hewlitt intoned from the portable pulpit beside the open grave. "For surely he has gone to the place of angels where he stands now looking in their shining faces."

As the minister droned on, at the back of the crowd Eb Talent leaned closer to Shad and whispered, "Shining faces! I'd venture where the Captain is right now he's more than likely looking up the undersides of their flowing robes." The old man spat a wad of tobacco. "Getting his eyebrows singed, too, what do you wanna bet?"

Shad stifled a laugh as he nodded. He and Eb and the rest of the boys had had their own memorial service for Amos the night before in the bunkhouse, all of them getting drunk as hog-nosed skunks while they traded stories of their late employer. Tall, Texas stories. But true ones. Not the pap this preacher was spreading on the crowd. Of all the things Amos Kingsland had been in his life, saint surely wasn't one of them. Wherever he was right now—heaven or hell—the old conniver was probably having himself a hearty laugh at these festivities.

Quite a turnout, actually. Shad's gaze drifted over the bowed heads of a senator, two congressmen and a score of local dignitaries before it came to rest on Miss Libby's prim little black hat. He'd made it a point to avoid her for the past two days, once even diving headlong into a pile of hay when she showed up in the barn. Not exactly the way for a man to behave. More like a mouse. Still, this was one mouse who had no intention of getting caught by a wily she-cat.

Miss Libby was as wily as they came. Shad was sure of that now. How else could he explain the way she made him feel like a damn yo-yo, up one minute and down the next, jerked this way and that? Hell, she'd kissed him senseless, all the while telling him to stop. Then she'd fired him and told him she wanted him, all in the same sweet breath.

He'd beat it out of the kitchen as fast as he'd been able to. He should have saddled up and ridden out that night, he told himself now, instead of hanging around to pay his last respects to Amos. The respect he'd given the man while he was alive was plenty. That ought to have been enough. But here he was, listening to some Methodist drivel while contemplating Miss Libby's black straw bonnet, the tilt of her head and the pale smoothness of her cheek.

Eb's bony shoulder nudged his arm. "You ain't still figuring on lighting out right after this, are you?"

Shad wrenched his gaze away from the lady in order to look down on the grizzled old sailor. He hadn't told Eb that Miss Libby had given him his walking papers. Apparently she hadn't told anyone, either.

"Nothing to keep me here now that Amos is gone," he muttered.

"Just Paradise." Eb shrugged. "Those girls are going to need a good man to hold this whole shebang together." He angled his head toward the burly man sitting on the fringe of the gathering of mourners. "Hoyt looks like he's sitting on a spring over there. Soon as the Captain's planted, he's going to be making Miss Libby and her sister an offer."

"Let him." Shad turned away. Let somebody else keep that old coyote away from the door. Let some other fool stay here and get shaken up then booted out.

Behind his back, Eb sighed wistfully. "I always figured the place meant something to you, Shad. Guess I had it wrong."

"I guess you did," Shad muttered.

Libby's graciousness was wearing dangerously thin as she stood beside the grave, accepting the interminable and florid condolences of Senator Vance Hull. Yes, her father had been a big man even by Texas standards. A stalwart pioneer. Most certainly a man of vision. Yes, indeed, Amos Kingsland could have been governor if he'd so chosen.

Too bad he cared for cattle more than he did for people. Too bad land meant more to him than family. What a shame...

Her own political leanings? She had none, and if she did she planned to do her leaning at home, in Missouri.

She was almost relieved when a large paw clasped her upper arm and a voice boomed, "'Scuse me a minute, Senator. I need to have a couple words with

Miss Libby.'' The next thing she knew, Libby was being ushered away from the sputtering politician while Hoyt Backus's bourbon-sotted breath wafted around her head.

"Damn buzzard," Hoyt growled. "We sent him to Washington just to get rid of him."

His hand clamped more tightly on her arm as he shouldered through the crowd, propelling her to its edge. It was, Libby decided, like being escorted by a determined, whiskey-swilling and cigar-smoking grizzly. Being manhandled was one thing; being bearhandled was infinitely worse.

"Mr. Backus, please."

"Call me Hoyt, honey." He drew up so abruptly then that Libby would have pitched forward if he hadn't still had a death grip on her arm.

Libby wrenched away from him, straightening the seam of her sleeve as she hissed, "Say whatever it is you have to say, Mr. Backus. I'm listening." She shot him a fierce glare then, and discovered not a gruff bear glowering down on her but a rather sheepish human being.

He swept off his hat and clasped it to his massive silver belt buckle. "I'm sorry about your daddy, Miss Libby."

"Thank you, Mr. Backus."

"Hoyt."

"Hoyt," she uttered through clenched teeth. "Thank you. But was it really necessary to drag me off to express a simple condolence?" She reached up now to repin the hat that had loosened during that dragging.

"Well, this is business, you might say, honey. Real private business. I didn't want half of Texas to get an earful of it.'' The man was crushing his hat now in his big hairy fists.

She'd been warned about this. Just about everyone at Paradise had told her that her father's former partner was eager to get back the property that he had once shared, that he would do or say just about anything to achieve his goal, that if he couldn't buy it legal and outright he might resort to more underhanded means. But this burly hat crusher didn't look particularly like a threat to Libby. If anything, he reminded her of a bashful boy. And, if her eyes weren't completely deceiving her, wasn't that a blush creeping up over the collar of his shirt?

''Now that Amos is gone and you're in charge, Miss Libby...well, what I mean is between you two Kingsland sisters, you strike me as the one who's all business.'' The crimson flush climbed higher on his neck. ''That's not saying you're not just as pretty as your little sister, mind you, it's just—''

''I don't know that I am in charge,'' she said, cutting him off before he worked his tongue into a knot trying to flatter her. ''I haven't any idea what my father's wishes were. His attorney only arrived from Corpus Christi this morning.''

''That'd be Bob Cleland?''

Libby nodded as she gazed around the mourners until she saw the elderly, white-haired lawyer whom she had met only briefly just prior to the funeral. There had been a twinkle in his pale blue eyes and an amused twitch to his mouth, both of which had struck her as wholly inappropriate for the occasion. Right now the man appeared to be having a glorious time, shaking hands and patting backs as he mingled among his cronies.

"Mr. Cleland plans to read my father's last will and testament this afternoon, Mr. Backus," she said, quickly adding "Hoyt" before he corrected her and called her "honey" again. "Any business about Paradise will have to wait until after that. Now if you'll excuse me."

She had only managed a single step away from him when Backus reached out and clamped his hand around her arm once again.

"It's not about Paradise, Miss Libby," he implored. "Just listen up a second, will you?"

"Let me go."

"Whoa now, honey..."

Libby tried to jerk out of his grasp, but he only held her more tightly.

"You've got the wrong idea, gal. It's personal business I'm aiming..."

A shadow knifed between them suddenly as a deep voice rumbled. "Let the lady go, Hoyt."

The viselike grip eased immediately. "Hell and damnation!" Backus growled. "Can't a man have one minute for a private conversation around here?"

"Didn't look to me like Miss Libby was enjoying her end of the conversation," Shad drawled. A little smile twitched at the corners of his mouth.

A lethal smile if ever Libby had seen one. For a second she almost felt sorry for Hoyt Backus, who was punching his hat back into shape now while he glared at the interloper.

Their little glaring contest offered Libby an opportunity to observe the man she'd been avoiding for the past two days. He was wearing a black suit coat— snug across the shoulders, she noticed, and a bit short in the sleeves—over a pair of pressed denims. His white shirt fairly glowed in contrast with his deep tan skin and his boots were polished. No dust today. No sweat. In fact, the clean, sweet fragrance of soap that wafted toward her seemed suddenly as threatening as the impending brawl. She stepped between the two potential combatants, deliberately facing Backus.

"Perhaps we'll be able to continue our conversation later, Hoyt," she said.

The big man grunted, gave his hulking shoulders a shrug, then shot one last look at Jones before lumbering off. She stood there a moment, her arms clasped and her back stiff, willing herself to turn around and face the man she had fired.

"Goodbye, Miss Libby."

As softly as he spoke it, the word still managed to thunk in her stomach like a rock. *Good-bye.*

"Hoyt'll try to throw his weight around, just like today." She heard him shift his own weight onto one leg. "Keep an eye on him. Your daddy always did."

She turned, shading her eyes to look up into his face, finding it handsomer than ever and reminding herself that she was doing the right thing. The best thing. The only thing. "Where will you go, Mr. Jones?"

"Corpus, more than likely. For a while anyway." *What the hell do you care, lady?*

She tilted her head and her damn hat with its black feathers and bows shifted on its perch of glossy hair. "Do you have family there?" she asked him.

"No, ma'am." *A little late to be hauling out your social graces, ma'am, if you don't mind my saying.* Shad was starting to feel like that damn yo-yo again so he didn't mind one bit when Bob Cleland walked

up behind Miss Libby and laid a soft, lawyerly hand
on her shoulder.

"We're getting ready for the reading of the will,
Miss Kingsland."

Libby blinked. She had forgotten herself—again—
as those chemicals worked their confounded magic on
her. She didn't need magic. She needed a dose of
sanity, which she was certain her father's will would
soon provide. "I'll get my sister," she responded.

"Oh, no need." The attorney smiled at her and
once again Libby detected that odd, almost efferves-
cent twinkle in his eyes. They seemed to bubble like
champagne. "Your sister is already up at the house
awaiting us."

On pins and needles no doubt, Libby added sourly
to herself. "I'll be right along, Mr. Cleland."

"Very well." The man's entire countenance was
practically fizzing now as he added, "You, too,
Shad."

"Pardon?" The big cowboy looked as stupefied as
Libby felt. More, if that was possible.

"Come along, both of you," the white-haired attorney directed, clasping them each by an elbow.
"This shouldn't take long."

"After you, ma'am."

With a crisp nod, Libby whisked past Shad's outstretched arm into her father's office where Shula was
already ensconced in a chair on one side of the massive desk.

As soon as Libby sat beside her, Shula leaned over
and hissed, "What's he doing in here?"

"Don't ask me, Shula," Libby snapped. "It's not
my last will and testament, you know."

"I know that." With her lips crimped then, Shula settled back, rearranging her skirt over her knees while her gaze kept slithering sideways to the man who had planted himself on one side of the horsehair sofa. After a long moment she sighed and said in a voice like lemonade laced with honey, "Well, I certainly don't begrudge him a legacy. Although judging from those clothes, the man hasn't the foggiest notion of how to spend money. It's a shame really, don't you think? Oh, and I meant to tell you when you first came in, Libby, your hat's not sitting right. It's kind of sliding off the side of your head." Shula smiled fetchingly. "Want me to fix it for you, honey?"

Libby unclenched her teeth just enough to utter curtly, "No, thank you. I'll do it myself." But instead of making repairs, she plucked the pins out, snatched the hat off and plopped it in her lap. "Where's Mr. Cleland?" she said irritably. "I thought he was right behind us."

"And so I was, my dear, with the exception of a small detour," the lawyer said as he came through the door and proceeded to the big oak and leather chair behind the desk.

The elderly man seemed quite fragile when he lowered himself into Amos Kingsland's huge chair. The springs barely complained beneath him. Suddenly Libby found herself wishing she had seen her father sitting there, grumbling as he made entries in account books, swearing when the figures failed to add up right, smiling when they did. The desktop was no doubt scarred from his big boots. She decided she'd take a look once the will had been disposed of. After all, the desk would be half hers then.

If Shula approved, she might even have the huge

piece of furniture shipped back to Saint Louis where it would always remind her of how hard her father had worked turning a desolate stretch of land into Paradise. Of course, she thought sadly, it would also be a constant reminder that his efforts had come at the expense of and by the exclusion of his family. Maybe the desk wasn't such a good idea.

The attorney sat there now, methodically removing papers from a worn leather satchel. Having been in such a hurry to convene this meeting, he seemed to be almost dawdling now. Shula cleared her throat impatiently. Over on the sofa, Shadrach Jones recrossed his long legs.

Libby was glad her father had remembered his foreman in his will. She hoped it would take some of the sting out of his abrupt dismissal. Although, she thought, the man hadn't looked particularly stung when he'd come to bid her goodbye. If anything, he'd seemed anxious to be on his way.

She found herself wondering now what or who awaited him in Corpus Christi. She wondered, too, when she passed through the city on her return to Saint Louis, if she would see him. Not that she wanted to, of course, but...

Shula's arm pressed against hers as she leaned close. "Is this old geezer practicing for a paper-shuffling contest or preparing to read a will?" she whispered. "Do something, Libby."

After a sigh, Libby edged forward in her chair then ventured, "I believe we're all ready, Mr. Cleland, if you'd care to proceed."

There was a knock on the office door then. Not a tentative tapping, but several big-knuckled blows that had both Libby and Shula pressing their hands over

their hearts. But before anyone could say a word, the
door swung open and Hoyt Backus lumbered in. The
dark scowl on his face disappeared as soon as his eyes
lit on Shula.

Libby whispered to Shula, "What's he doing
here?" But Shula only plucked at the fabric of her
bodice, much too taken aback herself to reply.

"Have a seat, Hoyt," the attorney directed, giving
his assemblage of papers a decisive tap on the desktop. "We're all here now, Miss Kingsland. I suggest
we begin."

Hoyt Backus lowered his bulk onto the sofa, and
out of the corner of her eye, Libby could see Shad
shift to his left, putting a bit more distance between
himself and the newcomer. Then it was quiet in the
office. So quiet Libby could almost hear Shula's
nerve ends twitching. Or were they her own?

"I suspect," Cleland began, "we've all heard
enough testimonials to Amos's character and fortitude
to last us a good while. I would, however, like to add
a personal note of my own. I knew your father, Miss
Kingsland—" he paused to look at Libby, then
shifted his pale eyes to Shula "—and Miss Kingsland,
for three decades. Although he was in considerable
pain during the final weeks of his life, there was no
question that his mind was as sound as it had ever
been during our long acquaintance."

He paused then, suspiciously, letting his gaze fall
on each one of them in turn, and finally allowing it
to come to rest on Paradise's foreman. "You'd agree
with that, wouldn't you, Shad?"

Shad nodded, then he crossed his arms over his
chest. "What I hear you saying, Cleland, is that any-

body'd be a fool to dispute whatever's in his will, right?''

"Exactly. Thank you for putting it so succinctly."

"My pleasure."

"We attorneys tend to—"

"Oh, for heaven's sake, Mr. Cleland," Shula snapped. "Nobody's going to have any complaints. Let's just get on with it."

By now Libby wasn't so certain as she watched that peculiar glint return to the attorney's eyes. The man obviously knew something they didn't. Something that amused him no end.

"I can't speak to the soundness of my father's mind toward the end, Mr. Cleland, but I can assure you that my sister and I are prepared to honor his last wishes."

"I'm happy to hear that, Miss Kingsland."

Tickled pink was more like it, Libby noted as the man continued.

"Amos had a will of long standing, but he sent for me two weeks ago in order to make some revisions." He laughed softly now, contemplating the papers in his hands. "They were—how shall I put it?—rather unorthodox."

A little groan burbled in Shula's throat and she slumped perceptibly lower in her chair. Libby unconsciously began chewing on a fingernail.

"Unorthodox," Cleland repeated, "but legal all the same."

From the sofa a deep voice drawled, "I wouldn't want to rush this or anything, Cleland, but you want to just put a rope around it and get it branded?"

"Very well then." The lawyer glanced at the papers once more. "There are a few minor bequests, none of which is really worth mentioning at this point, so let me proceed to the matter which concerned Amos above all else. The disposition of Paradise.''

Shula leaned forward ever so slightly. Her foot, which had been jiggling impatiently, held still.

''It was Amos's profound wish to leave Paradise, its acreage in the amount of eight hundred thousand acres, its livestock, its residence including all contents and outbuildings...''

The man paused now to move the top page to the bottom of the pile, aligning all four corners with agonizing precision.

Shula had sucked in a breath just moments before, and as far as Libby could tell, her sister was still holding that anticipatory air. The only person in the room who appeared completely unconcerned with the proceedings, perhaps even oblivious of them, was Jones. Even Hoyt Backus at his end of the sofa seemed to be suspended an inch or two above the horsehair upholstery, awaiting the lawyer's next words.

Bob Cleland resumed now, not by forging ahead but by repeating. ''Its residence including all contents and outbuildings to whichever of his daughters, Elizabeth or Shulamith, within ten months of his demise, marries his longtime and trusted employee, Shadrach Jones.''

Shula screeched as she shot up out of her chair. ''He gets it all? That big dirty cowboy gets it all? That's ridiculous.'' She pointed an accusing finger toward the sofa now and her voice rose even higher. ''Well, just look at him, Your Honor...I mean...Mr. Cleland. The man obviously doesn't know the first thing about money. He…he doesn't even have a decent suit.''

As shocked by her sister's outburst as she was by the contents of the will, Libby grabbed a handful of Shula's skirt and yanked her back into the chair. ''Sit down and close your mouth, Shulamith Kingsland,'' she warned. ''Right now.''

''There's more,'' the lawyer said calmly. ''Shall I continue?''

''More?'' Shula snapped. ''More of what? There's nothing left.''

Libby cast her a scathing glance before she nodded to the man behind the desk. ''Please,'' she urged him. ''Continue.''

''Amos's will directs that, in the event such a marriage fails to take place within the allotted time, then Paradise, its acreage, the livestock, et cetera, et cetera, are forthwith bequeathed to Hoyt Backus.''

''Oh, my God,'' Shula moaned pitifully just as a big hat sailed across the room and the owner of Hellfire boomed joyfully, ''Hot damn.''

Chapter Ten

Then all hell, or at least a goodly portion of it, broke loose in that little office at Paradise. Shad sat on the sofa as a numb witness while Shula threw a fit the likes of which he'd never seen before. When she up-ended Bob Cleland's leather satchel and scattered papers all over the carpet then began to batter the old man with his own briefcase, Miss Libby had given her sister a flat-handed slap and had led her weeping from the room.

Hoyt, meanwhile, had sat at his end of the sofa, enjoying Shula Kingsland's dramatics as if they were the finest Italian opera. "Ain't she something to behold," he had murmured more than once. He had left shortly after the women did, but not before eyeing his old foe's office as if it would soon be his own.

Shad couldn't think of a single reason why it wouldn't be. He continued to sit there, wallowing in glum silence while the lawyer scooped up his snow-fall of documents. He'd never expected to inherit a penny from Amos, never given it a passing thought. But then when Bob Cleland had invited him to the reading of the will, it had occurred to Shad that maybe Amos had left him a little something after all. Not only had he been touched being remembered that way, he'd also been sitting there earlier, smiling to himself while imagining the speed with which he could divest himself of his inheritance that very night if he got on the road to Corpus fairly soon.

Shaking his head now, he muttered a soft little curse.

"It couldn't have come as a complete surprise, Jones," the lawyer said as he angled papers back into his satchel. "You know better than anybody how Amos felt about this place."

Shad's mouth hardened. "Yeah. He loved it more than his wife or his daughters. Still does, even in his grave."

"Probably," the elderly lawyer agreed, resuming his seat at the desk. "There's no question that Paradise was his first and foremost concern when he changed his will. He held you in high regard, you know. Like a son."

"Well, now, that makes sense—setting out to ruin his *son's* life the same way he ruined his daughters'."

Bob Cleland placed his elbows on the desk and steepled his fingers. A tiny smile played at the edges of his lips. "I take it then you're not particularly interested in marriage…"

Shad snorted.

"Even if it's only a marriage of convenience that would make you the largest landholder in the state."

Another snort gave way to an oath. "Amos knew damn well I never had ambitions like that. Hell, if I'd had, I wouldn't have worked for somebody else all these years." He glared at the lawyer. "I never wanted the responsibility. Still don't. And I can tell you for damn sure I don't want a wife.''

"From what Amos told me, you were largely responsible for Paradise's success these past years."

"Yeah, well," Shad grunted, "I worked hard. It's what he paid me for. But..."

Cleland arched a white eyebrow. "But what?"

Shad was quiet a moment, staring down at the pattern of the carpet before finally raising his gaze to the attorney's. "But I always knew I could leave anytime the notion struck me. Just saddle up and ride away. Somehow that made the staying easier."

"Yet you stayed," the attorney observed. "How many years? Fifteen? Sixteen?"

"About that."

"And you're still here now." Cleland latched his briefcase and pushed it aside. He stared at the man on the sofa thoughtfully, then said, "You could have gotten up and stormed out of here the minute the reading concluded."

"I should have," Shad said through clenched teeth.

"Perhaps." The elderly man leaned back in the large chair. "Or perhaps Amos knew you better than you know yourself. He was, you know, quite confident that you'd stay, that you'd continue to oversee Paradise and that he was leaving his life's work in competent hands."

"Confident, was he?" A harsh laugh broke from Shad's throat. "And what about his daughters, Cleland?"

"What about them?"

"Was the damned old fox so confident of their greed that he supposed they'd be willing to go along with this...this marrying nonsense?"

"Quite frankly, Jones, yes. Yes, he was." One white eyebrow arched upward on the lawyer's forehead. "Aren't you?"

Shula had lain prostrate on her bed for nearly an hour, weeping, saying nothing after announcing that she would be far better off lying in a dark little grave alongside their father. Her hands were clasped with wan grace across her stomach. All she required, Libby had decided, was a single, funereal white lily.

Despite the fact that Shula didn't respond, Libby kept apologizing for the slap she'd inflicted on her downstairs. Intending merely to bring the raving redhead to her senses, Libby had packed some of her own distraught emotions into the blow and had nearly knocked her sister's pretty head off her shoulders. She felt terrible about it now, especially with Shula lying there so damnably quiet.

"It isn't the end of the world, Shula," she said with a helpless little sigh.

Shula opened one eye, then the other. "A lot you know, Libby." She was up and off the bed then, stalking toward the dresser to inspect the pink welt on her cheek. "If you ever hit me again," she warned, glaring at Libby in the mirror, "I'd appreciate it to no end if you'd do it somewhere other than my face."

Ashamed again of losing control, Libby's gaze fluttered to her lap. "I'm sorry, Shula. I truly am."

"Oh, that's all right." Shula's voice was almost breezy now. "It's nothing a little powder can't disguise. And it did get my head back to working order. Now, let's stop lying around feeling sorry for ourselves, Libby, while opportunity's just slipping like so much sand through our fingers. Are you going to do it or am I?''

Libby, who hadn't been lying around nor feeling sorry for herself, looked confused. "Do what?''

Shula was dabbing a pink powder puff to her cheek now, but she didn't miss a beat and didn't even blink when she responded, "Why, marry that big, dirty cowboy, of course. What else would I be talking about?''

Several hours after the reading of Amos's will— several hours and half a bottle of Pilar Delgado's best rye whiskey—Shad slumped lower in his chair. His long legs angled out from beneath the opposite side of the table, threatening to trip anybody who walked past, but no one, it seemed, had any intention of getting anywhere near the glowering man except Pilar herself.

The whore gave Shad's boots a solid kick before planting herself in the chair across from his. Her brown eyes were still muddy from the tears that had pooled in them when Shad had given her the envelope containing Amos's five-hundred-dollar bequest. "No need to bother the ladies about this,'' Bob Cleland had whispered conspiratorially when he'd asked Shad to deliver it.

"Business is no good tonight,'' Pilar complained now. "Everybody's sad.''

"Hell, what're you sad about, Pilar? You're a goddamn heiress.'' He drained his glass, then filled it to the brim once more.

She lifted one hand to the bosom of her loosely gathered blouse, touching the envelope safely tucked inside. "And you? Are you a rich man now, Shad? What did Señor Kingsland leave you?"

"Everything," Shad muttered. "Nothing. A kick in the teeth."

"You're not sure?"

He shook his head, staring glumly at his whiskey glass, wishing he were either dead drunk or stone-cold sober rather than on this soggy middle ground where he couldn't forget his problems or reckon with them, either one.

"Maybe you need to come to bed," Pilar said, angling her head toward the back room.

Maybe he did, Shad thought, but not with Pilar. In the eight or nine years since Amos had set the woman up a chaste but convenient distance from the ranch, just about every man at Paradise had been in that back room and buried himself in her voluptuous brown body. Eb Talent. Even Amos a time or two. Everyone but Shad. He wasn't sure why, but it had something to do with sharing. And that didn't make a whole hell of a lot of sense when the women he visited in Corpus were whores no different from Pilar. But somehow they managed to maintain the illusion that they were there for him alone.

Of course, that hadn't stopped the sloe-eyed, full-hipped Pilar from pursuing Paradise's only holdout. The woman considered him a challenge. Or a gelding. Shad wasn't always sure which.

He was more than a little grateful, then, when Bowley Arneson ambled over from the bar, tapped Pilar on her bare shoulder and whispered something in her ear. Pilar nodded. Giving Shad a long, rather wistful look, the woman rose and headed for the back room.

"Hope I ain't interrupting anything, boss," the bow-legged cowboy said, grinning down at Shad.

Shad shrugged. "We were just talking."

"That's what I figured." He gestured toward the men still slouched against Pilar's makeshift sawhorse and pine-plank bar, all the while fingering the silver dollar intended for Pilar. "Me and the boys figured we best get our business done early if you're still planning on cutting out those calves on the south range tomorrow."

Was he? Shad blinked up at Arneson. With Amos's funeral and his own abrupt dismissal, he hadn't given much thought to work schedules at Paradise. He'd been planning on cutting himself out, actually, rather than the calf crop.

"Boss? There's a story buzzing around about you leaving. Somebody said that dark-haired daughter of the Captain had given you the boot." The cowboy shifted his weight onto a single bent leg. There was a glint of worry in his eyes and a note of panic in his voice when he asked, "She ain't in charge now, is she? 'Cause if she is..."

"No." The denial came out so forcefully it took Shad completely by surprise, as if someone else had spoken it. "I'm in charge, Bowley."

"Phew. Well, that's a mighty big relief. The boys'll all be glad to hear it, Shad. Right glad. It wasn't so much that we didn't want to be working for a couple of women, mind you. We just didn't want to stand around and watch Paradise go all to hell with the Captain gone." He reached out to grab Shad's hand, shaking it vigorously. "Sure is good news. I believe I'll just go back to the bar right now and let the other boys know so's their time with Pilar won't be spoiled none.''

"You tell them to go ahead with the cutting like we planned, will you, Bowley?" Shad said. "I'll ride down there as soon as I can tomorrow and give you some help with the branding.''

"Will do." The cowboy's head bobbed up and down, then he fairly danced a jig on his bowed legs as he returned to his companions at the bar.

A moment later a small cheer resounded in the smoky room as the men all raised their glasses in Shad's direction.

"Good news, boss," one of them called.

He lifted his own glass in return while a grin pulled at the corners of his mouth. "Wouldn't want to ruin any man's evening with Pilar," he drawled. "Don't you boys stay out so late you're not worth beans tomorrow.''

Despite the fact that they all nodded their heads in vehement agreement, Shad was pretty sure he'd be dealing with a half-dozen red-eyed, wrung-out cowboys tomorrow.

It wasn't until he had ridden halfway back to the ranch that it actually dawned on Shad that he'd decided to stay. The sudden realization sobered him up like a pail of ice water right in his face, and he pulled back on Stormy's reins so hard and unexpectedly that the big stallion nearly stumbled.

"Sorry, fella," he murmured as he dismounted. The horse snorted, then with his reins trailing on the ground, he followed a few feet behind his master.

The moon was just shy of full, and it cast a shimmering blue light on the grass-beaten trail between Paradise and Pilar's place. Shadows seemed to drift like blue silk scarves from one mesquite bush to another, and somewhere deep in the iridescent darkness, a javelina snuffled softly as it poked through the brush.

"Amos, Amos, Amos." Shad shook his head as he walked along, his thumbs hooked in his back pockets and his eyes on the ground ahead. "What the hell were you thinking when you made that confounded will?"

Shad's mind wandered back to the day he met the man who was wreaking havoc on his life right now. He smiled crookedly in the moonlight, thinking how he'd wreaked his own brand of havoc on Amos way back then.

After that bloody night in the parsonage, he'd been on the run for almost five years, living by his wits and a gun and not much else. Desperado, they had called him. Dangerous. Hell, he supposed he had been; or looked dangerous, if nothing else, wearing his buckskin breeches and moccasins, his hair parted and plaited, his already-dark skin burnished from sun and wind. But Amos hadn't been afraid. In fact, Amos Kingsland was the only man who ever got the drop on him.

Shad had carved out a nice little career for himself as a cattle raider, working his way south through Texas, picking off mavericks, branding them with his own *Double D,* then selling them to outfits trailing north to the railhead. He'd stolen at least two hundred head from Paradise until the day Amos had sneaked up behind him and poked the cold barrel of a .45 in his ribs.

He'd thought he was a goner for sure, but the big man with the bristly beard had laughed and said, "If

Play TIC-TAC-TOE and get FREE GIFTS!

HOW TO PLAY:

1. Play the tic-tac-toe scratch-off game at the right for your FREE BOOKS and FREE GIFT!

2. Send back this card and you'll receive TWO brand-new Harlequin Historical™ novels. These books have a cover price of $4.99 each, but they are yours to keep absolutely free.

3. There's no catch. You're under no obligation to buy anything. We charge nothing — ZERO — for your first shipment. And you don't have to make any minimum number of purchases — not even one!

4. The fact is, thousands of readers enjoy receiving books by mail from the Harlequin Reader Service® months before they're available in stores. They like the convenience of home delivery, and they love our discount prices!

5. We hope that after receiving your free books you'll want to remain a subscriber. But the choice is yours — to continue or cancel, any time at all! So why not take us up on our invitation, with no risk of any kind. You'll be glad you did!

YOURS **FREE**

A FABULOUS **MYSTERY GIFT!**

We can't tell you what it is...
but we're sure you'll like it!

A FREE GIFT –
just for playing
TIC-TAC-TOE!

DETACH AND MAIL CARD TODAY!

First, scratch the gold boxes on the tic-tac-toe board. Then remove the "X" sticker from the front and affix it so that you get three X's in a row. This means you can get TWO FREE Harlequin Historical™ novels and a **FREE MYSTERY GIFT!**

PLAY **TIC-TAC-TOE**

YES! Please send me all the gifts for which I qualify. I understand that I am under no obligation to purchase any books, as explained on the back of this card.

(U-H-H-08/98)   **246 HDL CH56**

Name
_____
(PLEASE PRINT CLEARLY)

Address _____ Apt.# _____

City _____ State _____ Zip _____

The Harlequin Reader Service® — Here's how it works:

Accepting free books places you under no obligation to buy anything. You may keep the books and gift and return the shipping statement marked "cancel." If you do not cancel, about a month later we'll send you 6 additional novels and bill you just $3.94 each, plus 25¢ delivery per book and applicable sales tax, if any.* That's the complete price — and compared to cover prices of $4.99 each — quite a bargain! You may cancel at any time, but if you choose to continue, every month we'll send you 6 more books, which you may either purchase at the discount price...or return to us and cancel your subscription.

*Terms and prices subject to change without notice. Sales tax applicable in N.Y.

If offer card is missing write to: Harlequin Reader Service, 3010 Walden Ave., P.O. Box 1867, Buffalo NY 14240-1867

BUSINESS REPLY MAIL
FIRST-CLASS MAIL   PERMIT NO. 717   BUFFALO, NY

POSTAGE WILL BE PAID BY ADDRESSEE

HARLEQUIN READER SERVICE
3010 WALDEN AVE
PO BOX 1867
BUFFALO NY 14240-9952

NO POSTAGE
NECESSARY
IF MAILED
IN THE
UNITED STATES

you put half the effort into raising beef as you do stealing it, boy, you might just make a halfway decent cattleman.''

How many nineteen-year-old kids, Shad wondered now, had been offered jobs while their prospective employer held a Colt aimed at their hearts? How many of them remained dry palmed and surly, sneering down a long, nickel-plated barrel as he had done that day?

"Jobs don't work out for me."

"Why's that?"

"I got a past," he'd answered bluntly, ready for the man to tell him to move on or else to put a bullet in him.

But Amos had only laughed again, pinning Shad with those steely blue eyes of his. "Better get yourself a future then, son."

Even now, sixteen years later, Shad could still hear that rough laughter and those gruff words. *Better get yourself a future then, son.*

Well, he hadn't gotten himself a future exactly; it was more like a solid present, a day-to-day existence that suited him perfectly. He'd stayed at Paradise knowing he could pick up and leave anytime he wanted. Or run, if he had to.

Run. It occurred to him that after twenty years there was probably nobody even looking for him anymore. Or maybe there never had been. But you never knew. Given the choice between pinning a murder on a half-breed or a preacher, Shad was pretty certain which one the law had picked.

Run. A man could stay on the run from his past, but how could he run from his future? Shad angled his head up at the moon-drenched sky now. "That's what you did, isn't it, Amos, you old buzzard? You gave me a future without once asking me if I wanted it or not.''

He didn't—goddammit! Much as he loved Paradise, it wasn't worth being shackled to a wife. What had the lawyer called it? A marriage of convenience? Well, it wasn't convenient for him.

During his ruminations, Shad had veered off the trail a ways. About a quarter mile from the big house now, he could see a few lights burning upstairs. He was wondering if Amos's daughters were still awake, sitting cross-legged on a bed and cackling like witches while they greedily plotted their own futures, as well as his. Then his boot crunched down on something peculiar.

Squatting, he discovered a pair of broken field glasses. One of the lenses had popped out and shattered under his weight. He squinted through the remaining lens, aiming it toward the house. Damn thing looked close enough to touch.

Miss Libby wove in and out of his view as she paced back and forth in her room upstairs. Her white cotton gown looked prim and starched, but the wealth of dark wavy hair that spilled over her shoulders was anything but prim. It looked wanton and wild, just begging a man to run his fingers through it. Shad found his own fingers were itching to do just that as he yanked the field glasses from his face.

Heat flared across his cheeks, as well as in his groin. Shame pricked at his conscience suddenly, making him feel like an errant schoolboy. He wasn't the spying type. He'd never gotten any kind of thrill from just watching. His thrills were much more direct than leering at a woman from a quarter mile away.

Somebody had been, though. Somebody had been hunkered down out here in the dark, training his sights on the big house. When? His gaze encompassed the surrounding area now, and rested on the remnants of a fire. He tested a charred branch with a callused fingertip and found it still warm to the touch.

Who the hell…? His grip tightened on the binoculars. Maybe he was going off half-cocked over nothing, Shad told himself. They'd had more than a few problems with trespassers at Paradise. Eastern bird-watchers mostly. Odd, pasty-faced people who didn't seem to have anything better to do but travel halfway across a continent to gawk at whooping cranes and scissor-tailed flycatchers.

"Run 'em off," Amos had always said. "I don't want some bird-loving fool nailing my hide to the wall because he got chased by one of my bulls or ruined a pair of fancy shoes by stepping in a cow pie."

Hopefully it was just some "bird-loving fool" who'd dropped his binoculars and beat it when he heard somebody coming. Still, Shad wouldn't put it past Hoyt Backus to send a man over, under cover of dark, to keep an eye on the Misses Kingsland, especially now that Paradise was almost within his hairy grasp.

"Almost," he muttered as he lofted onto Stormy's back. "Almost ain't worth squat, and you know it, don't you, you old spying coyote? That and a nickel will get you a cup of coffee. Almost ain't having, Hoyt. Not Paradise anyway."

The lights were all out in the big house when he rode in, but the bunkhouse was lit up like a tree on

Christmas Eve. After he'd bedded Stormy down, Shad pushed through the bunkhouse door and was immediately greeted by half a dozen grins, the biggest of which was tobacco stained and belonged to Eb Talent.

"What's going on?" Shad asked, not sure he really wanted to know.

The grins merely widened without offering any replies. Whatever was underfoot, no one was volunteering to tell him. Or maybe nothing was going on; maybe since the Captain's death he was so used to glum faces that normal smiles caught him unawares.

Shad sighed. "I'm going to hit my bunk. Don't you boys sit up grinning all night. There's lots of work to get done tomorrow."

When he walked into his dark quarters at the far end of the bunkhouse, Shad didn't bother with a lamp. He pitched his hat onto the table to his left, and when he heard it hit the floor, he blamed his faulty aim on Pilar's whiskey.

Lord, he was tired, he thought as he draped his gun belt over the peg on the wall. He felt as if he could sleep right through to the following week. No bad dreams tonight, he told himself as he dropped wearily onto his bunk, then found himself flailing in empty space before sprawling on the floor.

He lay there a moment, too stunned to make a sound, wondering how he could have missed something as big as a bed in a room no bigger than a jail cell. It was only when Eb Talent walked in carrying a lantern shoulder high that Shad realized there'd been no bed to miss. The room had been stripped bare.

''What the hell's going on here?'' he grumbled, hauling himself to his feet.

Eb still wore that stained grin, the edges of which nearly touched his ears. ''I figured you knew, Shad. Miss Kingsland ordered all your gear moved out.''

''No, I didn't know.'' Shad slapped the dust from where his bed used to be, off his shirt and pants. So she'd gone and fired him anyway, he thought. So much for your daughter's greed, Amos. So much for that future. He scowled at Eb. ''Mind pointing out where Miss Libby pitched my clothes?''

''Didn't pitch 'em,'' Eb said. ''Had everything moved up to the house. Every stick and stitch. And it wasn't Miss Libby, Shad.'' The old sailor closed one eye in a slow, sly wink. ''It was the other one. That pretty-as-a-picture little Miss Shula.''

The little girl's head snapped up when Shad came through the kitchen door and, clutching a puppy to her chest, she scuttled deeper into the corner.

Shad swore softly. In all the commotion of Amos's funeral, he had completely forgotten about Black Bess's pups. ''Looks like you're taking real good care of those little ones,'' he whispered to the child.

Andy bit her lip, refusing to look at him for a moment. Then her eyes fluttered up to Shad's face. ''There's something wrong,'' she whispered as she held up a glass eyedropper in a trembling hand. ''They won't take any of this milk.''

''Did you warm it?''

She shook her head, sending a sheaf of raggedy hair across her forehead. Her eyes flooded with tears. ''I forgot.''

Much as he longed to lay his tired, whiskey-sodden

bones down in a bed, Shad went to the cast-iron stove and got a fire going. "We'll just heat up a little pan of milk," he told the child, "and those balky critters will be fat and happy and sound asleep in no time."

After he'd tested the inch of warm liquid with a fingertip, Shad carried the pan to Andy's corner of the kitchen. He sat down beside her as close as he dared, praying that the little girl wouldn't start yelling bloody murder and wake everybody upstairs.

"Hand me that dropper, sugar." He held out his hand palm up and was relieved when she did as he'd asked. "Now pass me that pup and we'll get down to business." She did that, too, and sat watching quietly while Shad coaxed the warm white fluid into each of the tiny black balls of fur. It wasn't long before the pan was empty and the puppies were full.

"You're doing a fine job with them, Andy. Good as their mama," he said, placing the last sleepy animal back into its flannel-lined basket.

The little girl blinked sleepily and lifted a hand to cover a yawn.

"Tired?" Shad knew the answer, but wondered if this stubborn, wounded little creature would admit that any more than she admitted the fact that she was a girl.

"Sorta," she said, then retracted it with a shake of her head and a quick "Not really."

"Tell you what. Since I'm an old night owl, how 'bout if I take over these midnight feedings?" He grinned. "We'll be a team. You be the day mama and I'll be the night mama."

Her eyes darkened and narrowed. "A man can't be a mama."

"Well, honey," he said with a ragged sigh, "if I

wasn't just playing mama to those pups, I don't know what else you'd call it." He leaned his shoulders back against the wall then and let his eyes drift closed a second, wondering what in all creation he was doing sitting on a kitchen floor playing mama to three puppies and a girl when he ought to be slung out on a mattress someplace. Anyplace. Right now he didn't care much.

"You look tired." Her voice was soft and tentative as a breeze.

Shad opened one eye to find her looking at him curiously. Like he was—well—human. Not a big step, he thought, but at least it was in the right direction. "I'm so tired I could sleep sitting up right here." He bit down on a yawn before he added, "Might have to, too, seeing as how Miss Shula stole my bed."

"She and Miss Libby argued something awful," Andy said.

"Yeah? Who won?"

The little girl's brow furrowed beneath her ragged hair and her lips pressed together as she gave the question serious consideration. Finally she asked almost shyly, "Does the winner get to marry you?"

Shad merely raised one cautious eyebrow, which the child seemed to take for an affirmation because she grinned suddenly and responded with gleeful certainty, "Well, then it was Miss Shula because I heard her say that's what she was going to do."

"The hell..." Shad clenched his teeth on the oath and lowered his aching head. When he looked up a moment later, Andy was standing at the door, staring at him.

"Your bed's upstairs in the room right next to Miss Shula's," she said quietly. "I heard her say that, too.

I'll show you the way if you want.'' While she stood there on one foot like a dainty little waterbird, awaiting his reply, her gaze flitted to the window. Her face froze for a second, and then it cracked open in a scream.

Chapter Eleven

Andy! The screams wrenched Libby from her fitful dreams. Without a second thought—without her wrapper or her slippers, either—she fumbled along the dark hallway and half stumbled down the staircase. By the time she reached the bottom, the blood-chilling cries had stopped, but the walls still seemed to reverberate with them, and Libby was certain they had come from the kitchen.

She pushed through the door into the little lamp-lit room. "Let her go, you filthy beast!" The words tore from her throat the moment she saw Andy in the grip of Shadrach Jones.

"Now wait a minute, Miss Libby."

"Get away from her," she screeched, advancing across the kitchen toward him.

He eased his hands from the child's shoulders, then held them up defensively as he muttered, "Kid, help me out here, will you? Miss Libby's under a real wrong impression of what was going on when she came in."

Andy responded by reaching out for a handful of white gown and yanking on it like a bellpull. "Please,

Miss Libby," she cried. "Stop. Please stop. He wasn't hurting me. He wasn't. Shad was helping me."

"Helping you?" Libby pulled the child protectively toward her. "I don't understand. Why did you scream, Andy? What happened?"

"I saw him."

"Saw who, honey?"

"My father." Andy pointed to the window. "Out there."

"Oh," Libby said softly. She drew the trembling child closer to her hip, one hand on her fragile shoulder, the other stroking her rumpled hair. "Oh, dear." She had thought that Andy was improving, getting stronger not only physically but mentally. But if the girl continued to see her father in every strange male and imagined him lurking in every shadow, then there was still a great deal of healing to be done. Not to mention a great deal of apologizing.

Her gaze flickered to the tall cowboy now, expecting—after her false accusations—to be skewered by his dark, merciless eyes. But the light that greeted her was warm with sympathy and the curve of his mouth was gentle, almost tender. Surprisingly so.

He shook his head, indicating the window. "Must've been the wind or the moonlight," he said. "I checked."

"There, Andy. You see? It wasn't anything at all. I suspect your eyes are just tired from being up so late." She tipped the little girl's chin up, studying one eye and then the other while nodding her head with mock solemnity. "That's what it is, all right. Pure and unadulterated fatigue. It's no wonder you're seeing things."

"I'm not that tired." Andy stiffened with anger. "And I didn't see *things*. I told you I saw *him*."

"All right," Libby murmured in an effort to soothe her. "What do you say we talk it all over in the morning after we've both had a good night's rest?" Libby feigned a yawn, which immediately coaxed one from the child. "See, sleepy girl. Come on. I'll take you back upstairs and tuck you in all safe and tight."

Andy shrugged away. "I can go by myself," she muttered as she stomped toward the door. "I don't care if you believe me or not, Miss Libby. Or him." She aimed a hot, hurt glare in Shad's direction before running from the room. Her footsteps thudded on the stairs then sounded overhead more like a gang of rowdy boys than one angry little girl.

Cocking an ear toward the ceiling, Libby sighed with frustration and murmured to herself, "She gets so mad when nobody believes her."

"Yep."

Her back stiffened. She had nearly forgotten the man was standing behind her. Now she became aware of the heat his big body generated as he stood there waiting, no doubt, for her apology. She imagined the insolent grin on his lips and his lazy, slant-hipped stance. "I'm sorry, Mr. Jones, for jumping to that awful conclusion."

"That's all right, Miss Libby. I guess I would have gone off half-cocked, too." The deep voice behind her paused for a moment. "Best not be roaming around the house in your nightdress from now on, though. There *was* somebody snooping around outside."

"What?" Libby whirled around. "But you said..."

Shad angled a hip onto the table and crossed his

arms. "I said it for the benefit of a little girl who'd just had her socks scared off her." His gaze lowered briefly to the bare toes that were peeking from beneath Libby's gown, then moved slowly back up to her face. "Looks like you did, too." He chuckled softly. "And then some."

It was only then, under that warm-eyed scrutiny, that Libby realized she was, for all practical purposes, naked, even though her skin was suddenly as hot and flushed as if she were wearing a fur coat. Her hands knotted into fists and she fought to keep her arms at her sides, not wanting to give him the satisfaction of witnessing her distress as she made a foolish attempt to cover herself.

"Well, I'm not a little girl, Mr. Jones," she snapped, "so please don't think you have to lie to ease my mind. I insist that you tell me the truth."

The truth? Shad groaned inwardly. About the only truth he knew right then was a curve of hip the lamplight revealed through her thin cotton gown, a hint of dark warmth between her legs and the shape of her unbound breasts, their centers hard and pink as rosebuds under a veil of white frost. Just aching to be plucked.

He gritted his teeth as he shrugged out of the dark suit coat he'd been wearing all day. "Here," he said gruffly, shaking it out before he draped it around her shoulders, then drawing his hands away before they did some damn thing he'd be sorry for. "Hope it doesn't smell like horse."

She sagged for a second under the sudden weight. Then she surprised him by lifting one shoulder to nuzzle her cheek against the dark lapel. She whispered,

"It smells like you," and a jolt of desire ripped through him, nearly bringing him to his knees.

"Truth is, Miss Libby," he said, forcing his brain back on a safe and proper course, "there were fresh footprints outside the window. I'd have followed them, but I didn't want to leave the girl alone."

"Could it have been one of the hands? Perhaps someone just couldn't sleep and..."

"I doubt it. Not one of Paradise's hands anyway." He narrowed his eyes. "Any chance she really did see her daddy?"

Libby shook her head. "John Rowan's in Saint Louis. In jail, I hope, where he belongs. But that doesn't explain who was spying on us, does it? Or for that matter why anybody would want to."

"Hoyt would," he said bluntly. "It's him or one of his men. I'd be willing to bet on it."

"But why?"

"He wants Paradise, Miss Libby. Wants it bad enough to do whatever he has to do to get it."

She frowned, her dark eyebrows drawing tight, and she tugged his jacket more closely about her as if she'd taken a chill. "Paradise." The word left her lips like a curse, then she raised her eyes slowly, leveling them on his like a loaded side-by-side. "What about you, Mr. Jones?" she asked. "Do you want Paradise bad enough to do whatever you have to do to get it?"

Lord, the lady could be direct when she wasn't all tied up in knots. It was just like talking to Amos sometimes. A softer version, though, with sweet curves and dark hair half caught in his coat collar, half drifting over her shoulders. He grinned. "Is that a proposal, Miss Libby?"

"Certainly not," she snapped. "Why, it's preposterous that my father would have suggested such a foolish arrangement. Surely you're not considering it." She blinked then. "Are you?"

"I didn't say I was planning to marry anybody, did I?" he drawled. "Maybe I just like the idea of being a burr under ol' Hoyt's saddle for a couple of months." His grin widened. "And maybe, Miss Libby, I'll stick around awhile on account of you."

She clutched the big coat closer, further concealing herself, as her chin ratcheted up to a stubborn angle. "Merely to torment me, I suppose."

He hadn't known he was going to admit what had just come out of his mouth, hadn't even known he was thinking it until the words "on account of you" had slipped out. And now Shad wasn't sure why he took a step closer to her, or why he reached out to trail a finger along her soft cheek. It must have been the devil at his back, prodding him forward against his better judgment.

"Torment or tempt you," he said huskily, "the way you tempt me."

Her cheek flared beneath his touch and her blue eyes fluttered up to his. "It's...it's not intentional."

"Doesn't matter," he breathed. "It's happening all the same." Leaning forward, he brushed his lips over hers, feeling them quiver slightly and whisper apart, feeling the sweet, shy warmth of her invitation, and needing it. God! Suddenly needing nothing else.

When his arms slid under the jacket, surrounding her with solid heat, Libby thought she had caught on fire. The kiss had already blazed along every nerve in her body, and now his touch was burning her flesh, turning her brain to ashes. She couldn't think. Worse, she didn't want to.

Wanting to run, inexplicably she found herself moving closer, twining her arms around Jones's muscular neck, threading her fingers through his thick hair, drinking his wet, whiskeyed kisses like a craven dipsomaniac or a woman dying of thirst. A little moan caught in her throat, throbbing there like the purr of a kitten.

Shad lifted his head a fraction at the sound, drew back just enough to read the desire in her unfocused gaze.

"Don't stop," she whispered, standing on tiptoe, straining to bring her mouth back to his.

She might as well have been talking to a locomotive with bad brakes, Shad thought grimly as he gave her his mouth again. Stop. He hardly recognized the word. The fact was, since his very first experience, he had never had occasion to stop. For him there had never been hand-holding, hugs or any other boyish gestures meant to warm up and win over a girl. And pleasurable as it was, kissing wasn't some parlor game.

Kissing was preamble. Overture. It was the slow, sweet, breathless climb up the near side of a hill. And Shad was already dangerously close to the top and the subsequent headlong tumble down the far side. Kissing wasn't, as Miss Libby seemed to think, for its own sweet sake.

He needed more. Lord, even if it earned him a curse and a slap. Sliding his hand under her nightdress, he took the weight of one full, warm breast in his palm. As his thumb grazed its rigid peak, Shad could feel the shock wave running through every inch of her body, and the hot, hard currents pulsing in his own. No one had ever touched her this way before.

He knew that instinctively, and knew he'd pay a heavy price for being the first to breach Miss Libby's prim defenses.

Instead of cursing him, though, as he had anticipated, she made a whimpering sound against his mouth. Instead of hauling back and hitting him, her slim arms rode up higher on his shoulders while her fingers twisted tighter in his hair and her hips pressed into his. Lord Almighty! The lady may not have known quite what she wanted, but she definitely wanted more.

Lady! The word flared in his brain like a match. Or maybe she knew exactly what she wanted and precisely how to get it, the way another lady had so many years ago. He gathered a fistful of her long hair, then dragged her head back.

Just inches from his now, her mouth was wet and glistening, swollen from his kiss. Her dazed eyes opened slowly.

"What do you want from me, lady?" His voice was rough and strained. He wound her hair tighter, further exposing the sleek white column of her neck. "What are you doing to me?"

At his back then Shad heard the polite but insistent clearing of a throat. "I'd say the answer to both those questions is pretty obvious, wouldn't you, Mr. Jones?"

Shula clucked her tongue. Her heels clicked on the tile floor and her gown rustled as she came into the kitchen. "And, Libby, for heaven's sake. If you wanted him for yourself, why didn't you just say so?"

The sun had come up through strands of pink and lilac clouds the next morning even though Libby had prayed fervently that it wouldn't. Her other prayer—that everyone else in the house would miraculously disappear, or if not that, at least sleep until well past noon—had also been ignored.

Shula, perversely and probably on purpose, had arisen at the crack of dawn. She sat across the breakfast table now, shining like the sun itself above clouds of lilac ruffles while offering sweet, sisterly advice between bites of toast.

"It's nothing to be ashamed of, Libby. Gracious! You're sitting there looking like a fallen woman when all you did was lose your balance for a minute." Shula bit off a corner of toast, chewed thoughtfully for a second, then asked, "That was all you lost, wasn't it, honey?"

Libby unclenched her teeth just enough to respond, "No, Shula. I lost most of my dignity and all of my self-respect."

Shula waved a dismissive hand. "They weren't getting you anywhere as far as I could see. What I meant was..."

"I know what you meant," Libby snapped.

"Well, you went tearing out of the kitchen so fast last night, I really couldn't tell." She giggled then. "Of course, from what I could see of Shadrach Jones, I'm guessing you never got that far. The poor man was, well, fairly hot and bothered." She arched a knowing brow. "Lathered as a stallion, actually."

"Oh, please." Libby's face flamed, sparking her temper. She banged a fist on the tabletop. "Not one more word, Shula. Do you hear me? Not one more word. It's bad enough to wake up wanting to die without having to endure all of your foolish drivel."

"I was only trying to help," Shula whined.

"Don't help. Don't advise or counsel. Don't keep giving me those knowing little looks." Libby lofted an eyebrow now in imitation of her sister, then lowered it menacingly. "And most of all, Shula, don't sit there telling me everything is simply fine and dandy when it isn't and never will be again. Ever."

Ever, Libby repeated to herself, ignoring Shula's wounded expression and turning her gaze toward the window where the flat, sunstruck plains of Paradise stretched out as far as she could see. Nothing would ever be fine and dandy again.

It wasn't simply that she'd made an utter fool of herself the night before. Behaving foolishly in the presence of Shadrach Jones was something she'd almost grown accustomed to. The fact that she had kissed him again didn't surprise her one bit. The shocking revelation had been the feelings that kiss had released in her—hunger and thirst and a wanting so hot it had threatened to consume her very soul— and the knowledge that she would have done anything to abate that hunger, to quench that thirst, to satisfy that flaming desire.

If it hadn't been for Shula's timely entrance, Libby knew she would have lain down on the cool tiles of the kitchen floor and allowed the man—even begged him—to have his way with her. And to her complete and everlasting shame, Libby knew she would have continued even after he had left no doubt that he was, like her father, a violent and brutal man.

What do you want from me, lady?

Everything, she would have said. Or said nothing, but given everything all the same.

"Thank you, Shula," she said now, turning back

to her sister. *For saving me from myself* went unexpressed.

Shula continued to stare at the slice of toast she was buttering so diligently. Her lower lip was still puffed out in a pout. "You're welcome, Libby, I'm sure. I do have some experience in affairs of the heart, you know. I'm more than happy to step aside. It doesn't really make that much difference to me which one of us marries the man." She set her knife down with deliberation. "As long as one of us does."

"Well, then you do it, Shula. With my blessings." Libby pushed back her chair from the table and stood up. "I'm going home."

"But you can't," Shula gasped.

"Can't I? You just watch."

Libby strode from the room leaving Shula to contend with the toast that had flopped, butter-side down, onto her ruffled lap.

There were two things she needed to do before she left, and Libby wasted no time in heading for the little grove of live oaks behind the house where she stood, her head bowed, beside her father's grave.

Fresh earth was mounded over the site and strewn with flowers from dozens of funeral bouquets. There was no headstone yet. Her father's will had directed that he be buried here at Paradise, but had failed to specify a memorial—a surprise, Libby thought, in that he had specified everything else.

She tried to imagine words chiseled deep in stone. "Here lies Amos Kingsland," she whispered. "Captain. Cattleman. Lover of Paradise. Alone."

Having come merely to say a cool and dutiful

goodbye, Libby suddenly found her eyes filling with hot tears and her legs giving way.

"Damn you," she sobbed, sinking to her knees beside the grave. "All I ever wanted was to come back. I loved it, too. I loved Paradise. All those years. Now I'm here and it's too late."

Libby cried then as she hadn't cried since that day fifteen years before when her mother had prodded her into a carriage and taken her away. Her heart heaved, felt older than the earth itself as it sundered along a buried fault line, breaking all over again.

Finally, exhausted and unable to cry anymore, she gathered her skirts and struggled to her feet. Scrubbing the brine from her cheeks, Libby cast a last mournful glance at her father's final resting place. "Captain," she said quietly in a voice now firmly under her control, "I would have made you proud if you'd given me half a chance."

The second thing she needed to do was take a final ride to bid a last goodbye to Paradise. Only now Eb Talent stood in her way.

"I'm sorry, Miss Libby," he said, staring down at his boots as he wrenched his felt hat through his gnarled fingers, "but I got orders. You ladies aren't to go riding out unaccompanied."

"Whose orders?" Libby demanded.

"Why, Shad, ma'am." The old man cocked his head and squinted at her as if to say "Who else?"

Who else, indeed! Well, she didn't have time to waste arguing with Eb. Anyway, there would be enough arguing later—hours of it probably, long, nattering hours—when Shula realized just how serious Libby's intentions were.

She gave a small sigh of surrender. "All right, Eb. Then I'll be needing someone to accompany me."

The man scratched his head. "Nobody's around. Only..."

"You're around, Eb," Libby observed with as much sweetness as she could spare for the old sailor.

"I don't ride. Not no more. Not with my bum legs. See, all the boys are down south, and the only one who's here...besides me, I mean..." His voice trailed off.

"There's someone else?" she asked. "Can he ride?"

"Oh, he surely can, ma'am. Better 'n most. But, you see...well, he's catching a few winks."

"At this hour of the day?" Libby drew herself up imperially now. "I want you to go wake the laggard immediately, Eb."

He shifted his weight from one bum leg to the other. "Oh, Miss Libby, I don't—"

"Either you wake him to accompany me on my ride," she warned, "or I'm going by myself. Is that clear?"

Eb nodded. He plopped his hat back on his head, then sauntered toward the barn door, muttering, "He ain't gonna like this one little bit. He's gonna blow up like a thunder squall off the Yucatan. Nail my hide to the mast, Miss Libby, and yours, too, I expect."

For the life of him, Eb couldn't understand why a fellow whose bed was up in the big house would choose to stretch out on his bedroll here on the bunkhouse floor. Still, after a decade and a half, he couldn't pretend he knew Shadrach Jones much better than the first day he came to work for the Captain.

"If he steals anything," Amos had said, *"shoot him."*

Eb shook his head now as he stood in the doorway watching the big man sleep. They hadn't had to shoot him after all. And Shad didn't have to steal, because he'd earned the Captain's confidence and trust through years of hard work.

The man's qualities were obvious—his strength and honesty, his savvy and ability to lead men. But knowing what a man was didn't always tell you who he was, Eb thought now.

At Paradise, as in the rest of the West, you didn't ask questions, but took a fellow for what he was. A hard worker was just that, and his past was no more important than the clothes he'd worn last week. With Jones, though, there was always the suspicion that those cast-off garments might be stained with blood.

The notion never made it any easier to wake him. No, sir. Nor the fact that he was sleeping with his hands locked in fists, the cords of his neck distended, and his closed lids twitching like theater curtains behind which a deadly drama was taking place.

"You go wake him, Eb," the boys would always say, putting on grins to hide the fear that their foreman might not wake quite right, that he could strangle a man or snap his neck, believing him to be one of the devils in his dream.

"You go wake him, Eb," the old man muttered now, just loud enough to get the job done.

He could see the nightmare end when those bronze lids stilled. Then Shad woke the way he always did, jackknifing up, alert for trouble. "What's wrong?"

"Nothing much. Well, something." Eb battened down for the storm. "Miss Libby wants to go riding."

Chapter Twelve

Out behind the bunkhouse, Shad yanked on the shower rope to bring a bucketful of water down on his head. His low-muttered, ground-out oaths turned to a single, sharp expletive when the cool water cascaded over his soapy head and shoulders, then he knuckled the moisture from his eyes and slicked back his hair.

He'd had about six hours of sleep during the past few days and only a fraction of that had been restful. His eyes felt like two holes drilled in his skull. He probably looked like the devil's breakfast, which was fine with him. Maybe Miss Libby would keep her distance.

Lord knows he'd tried to put some distance between himself and the lady last night. After he'd left Miss Shula grinning like a cream-fed cat in the kitchen, he'd tossed a saddle on Stormy and run the poor horse flat out for five miles toward Corpus with the wind blowing at his back like the very breath of Satan and his body still burning from the lady's kisses.

Coward, he'd cursed himself when he'd finally

pulled back on the reins. Running to put out the fire when any sane man knew you stood your ground or dropped to it or you went up in flames. He was high-tailing it like a boy with his pants on fire. But he wasn't a boy anymore, no matter what his nightmares kept telling him. He was thirty-four, not fourteen. Not some dizzy-headed, fumble-fingered kid who didn't know the first thing about women. And no matter how real and how bloody those dreams seemed when he was having them, they weren't real. They were dreams. Mere figments. Nothing more than dark clouds storming in his brain. Dreams, goddammit. A man didn't run away from those.

A man didn't run away, period, he berated himself. Certainly not on account of a female who got his blood so hot his brain kept boiling over. He wasn't a kid running from home and trouble now, but a man hotfooting it away from obligations. There were dozens of cowboys depending on his direction. There were cattle and fences; wells to be dug; Amos's new Brahma bull to be bred to the best stock. There were Amos's daughters, who didn't know a thing about their father's plans for Paradise, and Hoyt, who didn't give a damn about those plans but wanted to put his own dirty thumbprint on the place.

And there was that sad, bedraggled little girl. Not that she was his responsibility, but he wondered what in the world a person could do to erase a child's miserable past. Nothing maybe. God knows his own past was still haunting him twenty long years down the road. But something maybe. Something to keep little Andy from drowning in bad dreams. To set her on a solid course toward the womanhood that awaited her.

He had angled his head up toward the night sky

then and imagined Amos looking down at him from beyond the stars with a grin cutting across his craggy features.

"All right, Amos," he had muttered as he touched his heels to his horse, turned him back to the heart of Paradise. "You've got a rope on me good and tight. I'll grant you that. But I'm not holding still for the branding, old man. We'll just have to figure out some other way to work this all out."

Some other way, Shad thought now as he ran a towel briskly over his body. "Marriage," he growled. Amos hadn't been any good at it. What in blazes had given the Captain the notion that Shad would be any better? Or hadn't that mattered to the old man as long as his Paradise was safe and secure? Hadn't anything else mattered? Or anyone?

Libby had run inside the house to don her riding habit after Eb had gone to wake her companion. She was coming out the front door now, so absorbed in securing the chin ties of her black silk hat that she wasn't aware of the man who stood between two saddled horses until he yelled at her.

"You're not wearing that municipal park getup today. Not if you're riding with me."

"I beg your pardon?" Libby knotted the bow firmly at her chin as she crossed the yard toward Jones, almost glad the first words out of the warm mouth she'd kissed the night before were crude and curt. Otherwise she might be tempted to feel something besides the anger that was surging through her now.

"This is called a riding habit, Mr. Jones. *Riding,* as in *horses. Habit,*" she snapped, "as in *custom-*

ary.'' Her eyes narrowed. ''Aren't you supposed to be working today?''

''I am working. Believe me. Now go change,'' he growled.

''Go to blazes.''

He went to the bunkhouse instead, leaving Libby fuming and slapping her riding crop across her palm. By the time he stalked back, she wouldn't have been surprised if smoke had streamed from her nostrils and flames shot out of her mouth when she said, ''You certainly don't expect me to wear those?'' She pointed the riding crop at the folded pants and shirt he carried, one garment per fist.

''You will if you want to ride with me.''

He thrust the clothes at her chest, and Libby promptly let them fall to the ground. ''I don't want to ride with you, Mr. Jones. I'm quite happy to go alone.''

''Fine. Be my guest, Miss Libby.'' He gestured toward the little dun nearby. ''Go ahead.''

Libby glared at the western saddle on the dun's back even as she felt the tight gathers of her skirt tightening all the more. Even if she managed to raise her left foot high enough to fit it through the stirrup— a doubtful prospect to begin with—there was no way she would ever be able to get her right foot over the horse's back to the other side. Not without ripping her skirt all the way up to her waist.

''Where's my mother's saddle?'' she asked.

''In the tack room.'' His mouth hooked in a grin. ''Hanging on the wall. A good two feet out of your reach.''

Crossing her arms now, Libby gritted her teeth and stared at the clothes on the ground. She didn't know why she was being so willful when the thought of the freedom those clothes would afford her was beguiling. And she did so long to fully enjoy this final ride before she went home.

She avoided Jones's eyes as she bent to pick up the faded denims and the white cotton shirt. "These aren't yours, I trust," she said, shaking them out for further inspection.

"No, ma'am. They belong to a seventeen-year-old hand who sprouted out of them over the winter. They're clean, Miss Libby, if that's what you're worried about. I expect they'll do. Hips might be a bit snug, though. And the shirt."

His gaze settled on her bodice momentarily before returning to her face. Libby's face colored as much from the man's appreciative scrutiny as from the memory of his touch. The touch that had been so gentle and bewitching before the cowboy's true nature and his innate violence had surfaced. Her heartbeat faltered. No need to worry about that, she reminded herself. She was leaving, and taking her fluttering heart with her.

Without a word to concede defeat, Libby carried the clothes into the house.

Shad stretched out in the shade of the bunkhouse, intending to catch a few much needed winks during the hour or so he figured it'd take Miss Libby to change. He'd barely gotten comfortable before she was coming back out the front door.

Lord Almighty! If young Ethan Ditch had ever filled out his denims and work shirt the way that lady did, every man at Paradise would have questioned his own manly inclinations. The dark fabric was molded to her hips like icing on a cake. As for the shirtfront...well, the buttons were working hard to keep both halves in place.

She had taken off the stupid hat and brushed her hair back into a glossy, ribboned hank—a switch as pretty as a curried mare's. As she strode toward him now—legs long and lovely as a Thoroughbred's—Shad regretted ever imagining she'd be easier to ignore in men's garb.

"I'm ready," she said so stiffly her mouth almost cracked getting the words out.

"Yeah. I can see that." Shad levered to his feet, settled his hat on his head and walked past her to where he'd left the horses. He swung up on the roan mare, then rested both arms on the horn while he cocked his head toward Miss Libby. "Need help?" he drawled, baiting her on purpose now, blaming her for once again heating up his blood.

"No, thank you." The stirrup was a stretch for her leg and it took her a bounce or two before she had enough heft to mount. She squirmed a bit, settling her backside in the saddle, causing Shad to sit up straighter and resettle himself in his.

"*Señorita!* Wait!" Antonia waddled across the side yard, skirts caught up in one hand and a burlap sack in the other. "I prepared a lunch for you. *Aqui esta.*" She handed the sack up to Libby.

"That was very thoughtful of you, Antonia."

"Oh, not me, *señorita*. It was—"

"Got enough in there for me?" Shad asked, cutting off the woman before she deflected the thanks toward him, preferring Miss Libby's scowls to any show of gratitude.

Antonia nodded.

"Will you keep an eye on Andy for me, Antonia?"

Libby asked. "I asked her to come along, but she didn't want to leave those puppies of hers."

Again the woman nodded. "Señor Shad already told me. When he asked me to prepare the food for you, he told me I must keep the child inside the house. But that will not be so difficult. With *los perritos* in my kitchen, so is *la niña*." Antonia winked, then turned back toward the house. "Enjoy your ride, *señorita*."

"Thank you, Antonia." After securing the burlap sack to her saddle, Libby arched an eyebrow toward her riding companion. She ought to thank him, too, she realized but the words stuck in her throat. Silence was safer even if it was rude, she decided.

"Shall we go?" she asked him. Then, without waiting for his reply, Libby jammed her heels into the dun's sides and took off at a gallop.

Any man who had spent a good portion of his life trailing cattle north knew how to sleep in the saddle as well as how to wake—fast as a shot—the way Shad just had.

Miss Libby sat angled back, one hand on the reins, the other braced on the dun's rump. From the set of her mouth and the strained patience in her eyes, it was obvious she had just asked him a question.

Fancy that. After treating him like an invisible tailwind for over two hours, the lady deigned to speak. And he hadn't heard a word of it.

"Pardon?"

"The fences, Mr. Jones. They weren't here fifteen years ago. I thought my father was committed to open range."

Shad glanced at a span of board running between

two cypress posts, noting a loose top rail. "He was," he said, peeling himself from the saddle and stretching once his boots touched the ground. "Until he started his breeding program five years ago. Then the fences became sort of a necessary evil." He reached into his saddlebag now for the hammer and penny nails he always carried there.

At the fence now, his knee jammed against the two-by-four and, his mouth bristling with nails, Shad hammered the loose board back into place. He might have managed to miss his thumb if he hadn't been aware of a pair of blue eyes burning into his back. He might have cursed a blue streak, too, if not for those delicate ears.

"Tell me about the breeding program," she called.

He turned. She was climbing down from the dun and walking toward him. The intensity of her gaze was more than a little reminiscent of Amos when he wanted an answer to a question—now. Shad pulled his banged thumb from his mouth.

"It's complicated," he said gruffly. It was also not a subject he was inclined to discuss with a female. This one in particular.

She tipped her chin up. "So then I assume you don't understand it all that well yourself?"

It was the devilish light that danced in her eyes which goaded him to respond. "Oh, I understand the breeding program all right, Miss Libby. Every in and out of it, you might say. I just don't think it a fit subject for a lady such as yourself."

Her cheeks reddened, but she stood her ground, even angled her chin more aggressively. "Don't think of me as a lady, Mr. Jones. Think of me as the potential owner of Paradise."

His big hand splayed across his heart while a smirk played across his lips. "Why, Miss Libby! Is this another proposal of marriage?"

"I should have known I couldn't have a serious discussion with such...such an oaf," she snapped, turning her back on him and returning to her horse. Thanks to her anger, she mounted the animal without hesitation or undue clumsiness, and promptly left the leering cowboy in her dust.

This ride—this final farewell to Paradise—wasn't turning out the way Libby had planned. For the past two hours, instead of regarding everything as if it were the last time, she'd been looking at the place— truly seeing it—for the very first time. It occurred to her that the Paradise she'd carried for so long in her heart wasn't the real ranch at all. Only the memories of a ten-year-old child. The bellowing voice of her father and her mother's wails. Ghosts. Good ones and bad, but ghosts all the same.

This morning the land stretched out before her in all its glorious, rugged reality, leaving no room for memories. She wasn't ten years old anymore. Her mother and her father were dead. And Paradise—from one horizon to the other, as far as her eyes could see—was here and now.

What Libby saw now wasn't a place reserved for a child's frolicking picnics. It was a working ranch. An enterprise. A vast one. The more she looked, the more her curiosity grew. Questions kept popping into her head. She didn't remember fences. Why had her father enclosed so much acreage? Why was the land more brushy now? And what, for goodness' sake, was this confounded breeding program all about?

It wasn't such a surprise, she had to admit, that

Paradise's foreman found her curiosity rather foolish and her questions merely idle chatter. After all, it was a bit late to be saying anything but goodbye.

Goodbye!

The phrase sank to the pit of her stomach where it settled like a rock. What choice did she have? She had to go home. The alternative…was riding toward her now. The only way he could have outdistanced her, Libby decided, would have been by jumping the fence twice and racing like the wind. The superior grin on his face implied that he had done just that. Dammit. He was easier to endure when he was fast asleep, lagging behind her.

She lifted a hand to shade her eyes, calling, "You look tired, Mr. Jones. Perhaps this would be a good time to stop for our lunch."

"But why a board fence?" Libby asked. Her legs were crossed Indian-fashion and her arms were propped on her knees. "Why not barbwire? Wouldn't that be cheaper and easier to maintain?" She took a quick bite of one of the rolled tortillas Antonia had packed.

Shad's food stuck in his throat, making speech a near impossibility, as he watched Miss Libby's lips make contact with the tortilla. How she turned the mundane act of eating lunch into brazen images of making love he wasn't sure. How her cool indifference had turned to hot curiosity was a mystery, too. The lady plain boggled him.

"They use barb over at Hellfire," he said, "and the cattle have the scars to prove it."

She nodded as if she understood, then continued to do sensual things with her lunch. Shad uncapped his canteen and took a long swig, hoping to cool his rising temperature.

"I don't recall that there was so much brush when I was a child," she said now, gesturing to the pasture across the fence line. "Or am I just remembering wrong?"

"A lot of cattle did a lot of grazing in those fifteen years, Miss Libby. When the good grasses are gone, old Mr. Mesquite moves in."

She smiled a little private smile. "It's not all that different from Saint Louis, actually. The rich folk move west to bigger, better residences, leaving the common folk to take over their old neighborhoods."

"You miss it?" He handed her the canteen, praying she'd drink a little less erotically than she ate. "Saint Louis, I mean? The city?"

"Not today."

Now her lips glistened and a bead of water trickled down her chin. All he could think about was catching it with his tongue, Lord help him.

"I don't miss it a bit," she continued. "In fact, right this minute Paradise strikes me as...well...paradise."

It struck Shad that way, too, but for wholly different reasons, he was sure. And when Miss Libby made another inquiry about the ranch's breeding program, he wondered if she wasn't somehow reading his mind.

"Better than tell you, why don't I show you." He levered up from the ground, offering her a hand that, surprisingly enough, she grasped. Then, rather than just stand there battling his need to kiss her, Shad walked to his horse. "Well, come on if you're coming," he called back to her gruffly, in hopes he could ignite the ill temper she'd displayed earlier. She was a whole lot safer when she was bristling with anger.

He took off, racing along the fence line. Libby followed as best she could, trying to avoid the sharp thorns of mesquite and to guide the dun around big patches of prickly pear. She lost sight of the roan and its rider for a few minutes, then when she saw them again, Jones had dismounted and was standing with one boot hooked on a fence rail and both arms braced over the top.

Across the fence, only a few yards away, was the most magnificent animal Libby had ever seen. Well, the second most, perhaps. But given the competition—the big cowboy and the enormous gray bull—she wasn't going to get close enough to pin a ribbon on either one of them.

"He's magnificent," she breathed, moving to stand beside the man at the fence, unable to take her eyes from the great animal, who must have stood a good six feet at the rippling hump on his neck and weighed a solid ton. His great black eyes took her in and seemed to find her harmless enough. The bull stomped one big hoof and flicked both large, flopped-over ears as it lowered its muzzle to a clump of grass.

The magnificent specimen at her side, she realized, had cocked his head and was giving her a look of mild surprise, as if he couldn't quite comprehend that a mere woman would appreciate good stock.

"That Brahman," he said, "can go miles between watering holes and survive a whole summer of hot sun and sparse grass." He aimed a finger at the grazing beast. "See that loose hide. It helps keep him cool. He doesn't seem to take sick the way other cattle do. So you're looking at the breeding program, Miss

Libby. Your daddy was hoping to start a whole new breed from this...er..."

"Gentleman cow?" Libby offered, amused at the sudden hint of crimson in Jones's bronze cheeks.

"Yes, ma'am."

"Bull, Mr. Jones. It's quite all right to say it. I'm not one of those fussy ladies who swoon in the face of reality. Tell me more."

She listened intently then as he told her of her father's plans for the future, of the Captain's hopes and dreams for the ranch. There was better cattle to be bred, smarter and quicker horses, hardy grasses to be cultivated, brush cleared, wells dug, more. So much more. There was still a lifetime of work left to be done. The question now was—whose lifetime?

The cowboy's tone was even and measured, yet that lazy drawl managed to convey a deep, almost fierce pride. It was obvious that the man had had a hand in all those plans, that they were his dreams, too. And it was clearer than ever to Libby why her father had entrusted his life's work to his foreman. The marriage Amos had dictated in his will didn't seem quite so insane anymore, but sensible and ever wise. Though it was still a decision of the head rather than the heart, Libby was beginning to realize it took a lot more than just loving Paradise to run the place.

When he concluded with a sigh and said softly, "Well, that's about the sum of it," Libby said, "You love it, too, don't you?"

"Paradise?" He thumbed back his hat as he stared over the fence at the massive hindquarters of the Brahman. "I don't know about love, Miss Libby. I respect it. I appreciate its potential. I know it like my own skin.'' He laughed softly. ''Hell, I hardly know anything else.''

''If it's any consolation to you, I believe my father made the right decision in leaving Paradise in your care.''

He looked down at her now, his dark eyes narrowing and his mouth pulling tight. ''He didn't leave it to me, Miss Libby. The fact is, all Amos intended with that confounded will of his was to make me a permanent employee.''

Libby blinked beneath his searing gaze. The man was direct, to the point of rudeness, but she appreciated his honesty. ''You don't think much of marriage, do you, Mr. Jones?''

''No, ma'am, I don't.'' The heat in his eyes increased. ''Do you?''

''But...but the alternative,'' Libby stuttered. ''What's going to happen if Hoyt Backus gets his hands on all this?''

''He'll do just what he's done with his place. Move in too many cattle and overgraze it all for the love of the almighty dollar.''

''How many cattle are too many?'' she asked, thinking no place had more than Paradise.

''Ten acres per head is a good rule, but Hoyt likes to squeeze in all the beef he can. Sometimes five or six acres per head.'' He jerked his thumb west. ''Hellfire's so twisted with mesquite now you can hardly ride half a mile in a straight line. Which is one of the reasons he wants Paradise so bad. He'll do okay when the weather's mild, and he'll raise three or four times the beef he does now, but he'll have enormous losses when it's too hot or freezing cold and his underfed

and underwatered stock isn't healthy enough to with-
stand the extremes.''

"What about all my father's plans?" Libby asked.

"Well, for starters—" he pointed once more at the
big slate gray bull "—our magnificent friend here
will be bred to each and every old cow who can throw
down a calf. And then those calves will be bred every
which way until all of that old gentleman's fine qualities are dissipated like so much smoke in the wind.
A good breeding program is a long-term proposition,
not a fast-turned buck. In short, Miss Libby, Hoyt'll
bring the whole damn place to ruination.''

That had been her suspicion—indeed, her worst
fear—but to hear the fate of Paradise described so
vividly made Libby's stomach churn. "I'd hate to see
that happen," she murmured.

"Yeah. So would I." His voice was low, nearly as
plangent as her own.

She raised her eyes to his. "Which brings us back
to my father's will and the subject of marriage. I have
to tell you, I don't believe in marriage, Mr. Jones.''

He met her gaze with a calm directness. "Neither
do I, Miss Libby." Then once more his hand—
bronzed by wind and parentage, callused from long
years of work, capable and strong and full of grace—
swept over the landscape, encompassing thousands of
acres in a single, smooth motion. "But I do believe
in this.''

"Yes," she whispered. "So do I. More now than
ever before.''

Chapter Thirteen

They rode silently back to the house, neither one of them, it seemed, having any desire to pursue their earlier conversation about the disposition of her father's will in general, marriage in particular. While the notion itself no longer struck Libby as quite so preposterous, the very idea of her marrying anyone, let alone a man as violent as Shadrach Jones, remained out of the question. She recalled the way he'd manhandled her in Corpus Christi, the way he'd bruised her with his kiss. If she'd never even been interested in a lapdog, she thought, why in the world would she consider taking up with a wolf?

Of course, a marriage of convenience, simply for the sake of Paradise, was something entirely different. It would certainly accomplish what they both wanted, which was to preserve the ranch and see it prosper.

Could they do it? she wondered now, letting the dun follow in the big roan's tracks, lagging back in order to study the object of her improbable thoughts.

In the shade of his hat, dark hair went spilling over his collar. Below that, wide shoulders and a broad back seemed about to split the seams of his shirt. And farther down, where all that muscle narrowed to a trim waist, the bullets on his gun belt glinted every once in a while when the sunlight caught them just right. Or just wrong, she corrected herself. Once again, she thought that if the idea of marrying was outlandish, it was even more outlandish to consider marrying a gun-toting, bullet-belted, half-Indian, hot-tempered man.

She'd seen enough violence—the rough grabbing and the hard backhanded slaps her mother had endured first with one husband, then with the next—to last her a lifetime. Let Shula contend with it. Shula, who didn't remember their father's bullying ways and who seemed unaffected by their stepfather's harsh treatment of their mother.

Let Shula do it. Let her stand—or cower, as the case might be—beside Shadrach Jones and oversee this empire. Let her become an empress here. For all of Libby's love for Paradise, it wasn't worth the price she'd have to pay.

They were nearing the house now, where an unfamiliar carriage was parked near the front door and men and horses loitered in the nearby shade. As if to confirm what she'd just been thinking, she saw Jones's hand move to his hip and settle on the butt of his gun.

"Who is it?" she asked, urging the dun forward.

"Hoyt."

"What do you suppose he wants?"

He let out a harsh little laugh. "Other than Paradise, Miss Libby? Just trouble, I guess."

"Well, don't give him any." Her voice was level despite the fact that Libby's stomach had just worked itself into a tight knot. She could see Hoyt Backus's men more clearly now. All but two of them wore guns, and the two who didn't stood with rifles cradled in their arms. "Don't aggravate them," she told the man at her side.

He gave her a look of wounded innocence that seemed to say "Who, me?" Then he dismounted and walked casually toward the group of men. Libby was left to scramble off the back of the dun and hurry in his wake.

Don't aggravate them! Hell, Shad thought, he knew how to handle these boys, the majority of whom were hot-blooded, hardheaded Mexicans who liked to flex their muscles now and then. You stood up to them. You joshed them. And you never pressed their prickly spines to the wall.

"Menendez," he said, eyeing the stocky man who had stepped forward from the group. "You're a long way from Hellfire, aren't you?"

"Closer than you might think, Jones." The man slanted his head toward the house. "The boss is inside talking to the Kingsland woman." His mouth curved upward now against the droop of his black mustache. "He's making plans, I reckon, for taking over here."

"In a pig's eye!" Libby shot forward, her hands fisted at her sides, her chin poking up into the Mexican's face. He seemed to find her fury downright funny. So did his compadres. A little wave of laughter ran through their ranks.

So much for not aggravating them, Shad thought wearily as he looked down at the lady who had just stuck her hand in a nest of wasps and was daring them to sting. He was calculating the odds—seven wasps against one sleepy, beleaguered cowboy and one hot honeybee—when the front door slammed and Hoyt's voice boomed out.

"Hold on, boys. Didn't I say this was a social call and I wanted everybody to be Saturday clean and Sunday quiet?"

The Hellfire hands murmured and stepped back as their boss strode into their midst. "Go on. Saddle up," he told them, and they complied with only a small amount of teeth-gnashing and muted cursing.

Relieved as he was to have the confrontation over, Shad wasn't any too glad to be gazing down into Hoyt Backus's beefy and now beaming face.

"Hoyt," he drawled, "you look like the cat who just lapped up the cream."

The man slapped a brawny hand on Shad's back. "Maybe I did, Jones. Maybe I did. I've just passed a very pleasant time with the prettiest little redhead the good Lord ever put on this earth."

"My sister doesn't speak for me, Mr. Backus." Libby inserted herself between the two men. "Whatever deal the two of you might have agreed on—"

"Call me Hoyt, honey," he said, cutting off her words as well as her breath when he clasped an arm around her shoulders and pulled her against his side. "The only deal we talked about was whether or not it would be seemly to throw you girls a party so soon after your daddy's demise."

Libby didn't have to search her brain very hard to come up with Shula's response. "Let me guess, Hoyt. Shula said it wouldn't be seemly at all." She batted her eyelashes now and made her voice fairly drip with honey. "But she does so love parties and she's sure our daddy wouldn't want us sitting around wringing our pale hands and eating out our little hearts with grief."

The man looked surprised but still enormously pleased. "That's about the gist of it, Miss Libby." He clasped her more closely before letting her go. "I best get back to Hellfire now and see to this shindig." He started toward his carriage, then stopped. "You're invited, too, Shad. Hell, bring everybody. Tell 'em to wear their dancing shoes. We'll have us a high old time."

The carriage canted precariously as the big man climbed in. Libby and Shad watched while Hoyt and his surly entourage rolled out of the yard.

"He doesn't strike me as a man bent on making trouble," Libby said almost to herself.

Shad's gaze was still fastened on the roiling dust the men left in their wake. "Strikes me more as a man bent on making love."

"Love!" Libby exclaimed. "To whom?"

His eyes locked in her direction now and he grinned. "Why, to the prettiest little redhead the good Lord ever put on this earth, that's who."

"That's absurd," she snapped.

"Don't tell me, ma'am. Tell Hoyt."

"He says I remind him of Mama." Shula stood in front of the pier glass, clutching yards of yellow organza to her bosom. "What do you think, Libby? The yellow or the pink? Personally, I think the yellow makes me look as if I've only just recovered from the grippe. The pink, on the other hand..."

"The man has ulterior motives, Shula. I wish you'd use your head for thinking instead of for coordinating clothes."

Her sister whirled around to face her now. "Well, you're a fine one to talk, Libby Kingsland, sitting there in that outrageous getup. When I first saw you, I thought you were Andy. With hips! You don't catch a man by trying to look like one, for heaven's sake."

Libby's gaze surged heavenward. "I'm not trying to catch a man."

"Well, you better. Lord knows I'm no circus performer. I can't be juggling both of them."

"Then don't."

Now Shula rolled her eyes. "What? And find myself, two months from now, with a third-class steamboat ticket in my hands and nothing else? No, thank you."

She'd been sitting on the edge of the bed, and now Libby sank down wearily on her back. "Oh, Shula, is it worth all that to you? Why can't we just go back home and pretend none of this ever happened? Pretend Paradise never existed? We were happy, weren't we?"

"Happy? Living in squalor?"

Libby took in a long breath and let it out slowly. "It was hardly squalor."

"Compared to this, it was." Shula's wrists jangled as she gestured around the room. "Anyway, we can't go home."

Something in Shula's tone had Libby sitting up again, narrowing her gaze on the woman who was now absorbed in tracing the origin of a loose yellow thread. "What do you mean we can't go home?"

"I never noticed before what shoddy work that Pine Street dressmaker put out," Shula murmured, ignoring her sister. "There's enough loose thread here to make a whole new gown."

"I asked you a question, Shula. Why can't we go home?"

"You're such a pest, Libby." Shula yanked on the string and pulled it loose.

"Then just answer my question and I'll leave you alone. Why can't we go home to Saint Louis?"

Shula sagged into a chair, the dress crumpled in her lap. She chewed her lower lip a moment, avoiding Libby's eyes. "We just can't, that's all." Her lashes fluttered toward her sister now. "Anyway, Andy's much better off out here. You said so yourself."

"Don't tell me you've suddenly taken to worrying about Andy and what's waiting for her back there," Libby said with a sniff. "Besides, I have a feeling that, even with his daughter gone, John Rowan's probably gotten himself into enough trouble to warrant half a lifetime in jail. We'll just keep our eye on Andy awhile. We'll keep her in the house with the front door locked twenty-four hours a day. For however long it takes."

Libby frowned, picturing the house on Newstead Avenue and remembering how Rowan had battered and bruised their door. "Maybe I should have an extra bolt installed," she mused. "And the back door could be reinforced, I suppose, with—"

"It's gone, Libby."

"The back door?" Libby blinked. She tried to envision their kitchen with a gaping hole where the door was, just to the right of the dry sink. There was a loose screw on the bottom of the escutcheon that she'd been meaning to tighten and then forgot in all the fuss and flurry of their Texas trip.

"No," Shula said wanly. "The house."

Now the sorry vision of a vacant lot formed in

Libby's thoughts. Rubble and weeds and broken glass. She blinked again, realizing she was looking at tears trickling down Shula's cheeks. She could barely gather breath enough to ask, "What do you mean, it's gone?"

"It wasn't my fault, Libby," Shula sobbed. "It was all those grubby, grabby bill collectors. Nasty little men with nasty little mustaches and dirty finger-nails." An indignant flame burned through her wet eyes. "Cheap customers in cheap suits with the pants too short and the sleeves way down to their hairy knuckles. Awful—"

"You lost our house, Shula? To bill collectors? You lost our entire inheritance from Mama?"

Shula nodded, then shook her head, then nodded again as her tears increased.

"You lost everything?" Libby's voice was so hollow it sounded as if her heart had just been ripped from her chest. "Everything?"

"Everything," Shula whispered. "Except for..."

"For what?" Libby pressed, her cold insides warmed by a sudden ray of hope.

Shula sniffed back her tears. "My clothes. That's about all we've got left. And just look at them," she murmured dismally, once more picking at yellow threads. "I don't know how that Pine Street woman dared charge what she did for such shoddy workman-ship. She called herself a *couturier,* too, Libby. Why, she's nothing but a seamstress. And a poor one at that."

Two days later Libby found herself absorbed in those same pale threads, only it was she who was wearing the yellow organza dress now and riding in the back seat of a carriage bound for Hellfire.

Andy, in denims and her ungainly homespun shirt, was slumped in the seat beside her. Libby glanced her way, for a moment envying the child her comfort. Unlike Andy, who had won her own battle of "What to Wear to the Party," Libby had surrendered—grim lipped and without grace—to Shula's nattering insistence that she had to wear "something other than mouse gray or squirrel brown." And now she was chasing the ends of threads and trying to breathe in one of Shula's doll-size corsets that was pushing her less-than-doll-size bosom up to her chin.

In the front seat Shula was hardly visible beneath a pink parasol. But their driver was all too visible with his wide shoulders and dark hair curling over the white collar of his shirt. Another of Shula's victims, Shad was wearing one of Amos's suits—a let-out black coat and a pair of taken-in and let-down pants and a silk cravat that seemed to be choking him.

Libby hadn't seen him for two days, not since Shula's news that their mother's bequest now belonged to dressmakers, milliners, shoemakers and "nasty bankers." After that stunning revelation, Libby had virtually secluded herself in her room, partly out of the fear that she might awake from her daze to discover her fingers locked around Shula's pale throat, but mostly in the hope that she would be able to conjure up a solution to their problem.

She had considered going to Corpus Christi and telegraphing the bank in Saint Louis to confirm Shula's story, but then had decided her sister wouldn't lie—about being rich, perhaps, but never about being broke. Briefly then, she had deliberated contacting the bank about a second chance, thinking perhaps if she and Shula both took on jobs that they could scrape together enough cash to get the house back. But a vision of Shula playing kitchen maid had put a quick end to that. So, aside from printing money or marrying Shadrach Jones, Libby hadn't been able to think of any way out of their current poverty.

They would simply have to accept their reduced circumstances, she had decided. When she'd informed Shula of that fact, her sister had laughed—guffawed, actually.

"You do all the accepting of reduced circumstances that you want, Libby," she had said. "Personally, I'm planning to accept a proposal of marriage."

From Jones? Libby wondered now as she focused on the two passengers in the front seat and watched their shoulders touch every now and then when the carriage swayed. Neither one of them, she noticed, drew back as if the contact had been distasteful. As a matter of fact, over the course of the journey, they seemed to be sitting distinctly closer than they had been originally.

"Are you feeling all right, Miss Libby?"

She turned to the child at her side. "Yes, of course, Andy. Why?"

The little girl shrugged. "I don't know. Your hands are all twisted up and your mouth looks like you've been sucking on a lemon."

"Nonsense." Libby unfisted her hands and unfurled her tense lips in a smile. "I'm fine." Try as she might, she couldn't disguise the irritation in her tone. "Why wouldn't I be fine?"

Andy shrank back farther into her corner of the seat. "I was just asking, that's all."

Libby patted her knee. "I appreciate your concern, honey. And I'm sorry I snapped at you. I'm fine. Truly."

Why wouldn't she be fine? Libby thought sourly as her fingers plucked again at stray threads. She was destitute. She was wearing a dress that pulled her in painfully and pushed her out shamefully. She was planted in the back seat of a bumpy carriage, forced to watch all that shoulder touching going on up front, not to mention Shula's eyelash batting and Shad's responsive grins. And, last but hardly least, she was on her way to a party she didn't want to attend at a place appropriately named Hellfire. Why, in the name of heaven and all the saints above, wouldn't she be fine? Dandy. Absolutely peachy.

Shad passed the carriage's reins to his right hand in order to ease a finger beneath his tight collar and cravat. About the only saving grace, he thought, was that the collar wasn't attached to a leash. Not yet, anyway. Maybe never.

The oath he might have sworn, if he hadn't been strangling, broke deep in his throat. Seemed that's about all he'd been capable of uttering these past few days.

"There you go again," Eb had said to him just yesterday when they'd been taking inventory in the tack room. "What in tarnation are you swearing about, Shad? If you ask me, a fella in your position oughta be celebrating instead of skulking around here swearing all the time."

"My position?" Shad had snarled.

"You stand to inherit the biggest spread in Texas

just for choosing between two females, one prettier than the other. Your plate's full, Shad. Leastways as far as I can see.'' The old sailor winked then, broadly and knowingly. ''Guess you're just complaining 'cause it's hard making up your mind between the oatmeal cookie and the raspberry tart, huh?''

In spite of himself, Shad had laughed. ''Well, that's one way of putting it, Eb.''

He wasn't so sure about the varieties of sweets Eb had described, though, Shad thought now. At least he'd never reacted to an oatmeal cookie the way he reacted to Libby Kingsland. As for her redheaded sister...well, Eb might not have been too far off that mark.

Unlike Miss Libby, who didn't seem to know what she wanted from one minute to the next, Miss Shula had made her desires most eloquently known beginning with this remade suit of Amos's he was wearing. He'd adamantly refused, not only to attend the shindig at Hellfire, but also to stand like some cigar-store Indian while Antonia cut and pinned the pants and coat. But Miss Shula had worn him down, and finally doing just what the lady wanted seemed easier somehow than having to stand in the breeze of her batting eyelashes or to listen to her flap her gums.

Which was how Shad found himself in his current position, holding the horses to a trot on his way to Hellfire, watching the raspberry tart jiggle beside him and feeling the oatmeal cookie do the same directly behind his back. He let out a silent sigh of relief when Hoyt's big two-story, white-painted house came into view and the burly man rushed out to greet them. Not that he was so happy to see Hoyt, but he was starting to get a headache from listening to Miss Shula's bracelets clanking every time she spoke, which was constantly. Between the jiggling and the clanking and Miss Libby's stony silence, Shad couldn't hear himself think.

The carriage rocked to a halt amid a throng of other vehicles. From what Shad could see, it looked as if half the population of South Texas had turned up in dark frock coats and pale dresses. Fiddle music was in the air and, even though this was Hellfire, the smoke that drifted from several deep pits carried the enticing aroma of roasting beef rather than brimstone.

Hoyt bounded down from the wide front porch, agile and eager as a boy. Though he offered a hearty welcome to the other occupants of the carriage, his eyes dwelt on Miss Shula. The man was smitten, purely dumbstruck, as far as Shad could tell.

"Just look at you, honey," he said as she melted out of the carriage into his brawny arms. "You're prettier than any sunset I ever saw." While Miss Shula appeared to be trying to conjure up a modest blush, Hoyt linked her arm through his and led her away.

Shad sighed and slanted an arm over the seat back. His two remaining passengers looked about as happy as he was to be there.

Chapter Fourteen

The night was warm. Nearly sweltering. Libby had watched the darkness come rolling across the Hellfire sky like a blue wool blanket with scores of tiny moth holes for the stars to twinkle through. She'd spent most of the evening contemplating the sky from her vantage point near the punch bowl.

Now the familiar sound of an armful of bracelets broke through the waltz the fiddlers were playing.

"Libby, for heaven's sake," Shula hissed at her. "You haven't budged from this table all evening. People are going to start taking you for a servant. Or a drunk." Shula eyed her suspiciously as she refilled her own cut-glass cup. "Good Lord, you *are* drunk!"

"I most certainly am not." The indignance in Libby's tone was undercut somewhat by a faint slur. She deliberately slowed her speech to counter it. "I am desh...destitute, Shula. I am poor. Penniless. But I am *not* drunk."

Shula jerked a lace hankie from the depths of her bodice and began dabbing at her face. "I don't know what I did to deserve this. Showing up at a lovely party with a ragamuffin who'd rather die than dress properly and a man who acts like he's wearing a snake around his neck instead of a starched collar." She flapped the scrap of lace directly under Libby's nose. "And now this! My sister's pickled as a herring. What will people think?"

"They'll think we're awful," Libby giggled. "They'll think we're common as weeds." She crooked a finger to motion Shula closer and then lowered her voice to a conspiratorial whisper. "And then do you know what will happen?"

"What?"

Libby smiled a little sloppily. "They'll think about Paradise. They'll consider all that land and all those cattle and all that lovely money, and they'll keep being ever so nice to us."

Shula's pouty lips barely softened. "Well, you're probably right about that. But we haven't got Paradise yet, have we? And I don't see you doing one single thing to make sure that we will. All you're doing is making a fool of yourself," she snapped, "while I'm doing all the work."

"All the juggling," Libby corrected, wagging a finger at her sister.

"One of us has to." Shula drained her cup and thumped it down on the table. "One of us has to marry one of them, or we can kiss Paradise goodbye."

"You can marry them both, Shula. Lord knows you've been batting your eyes at both of them all night."

Shula plucked at a flounce on her bodice. "Well, at least now I know the reason you've been over here sulking and pouring half the punch bowl down your throat. You're jealous."

"I am not."

"You are, too, Libby. You've been standing over here all night glaring daggers at me while I was dancing and flirting my fanny off with that big cowboy of yours. And I can't for the life of me understand why it's so hard for you to admit you have feelings for the man."

While she spoke, Shula was flapping her lace hankie in Libby's face, which, from Libby's perspective, was more like a red flag in the face of a bull. "I don't," she insisted, adding a snort and a stamp of her foot for emphasis.

"You do, too."

"Do not."

My God, Libby thought, they were arguing like a pair of six-year-olds, and the worst part of it was that Shula was right. Libby had been nearly sick with envy watching her sister in the arms of Shadrach Jones. The fact that he didn't seem particularly to enjoy the dance hadn't made a bit of difference while his dark hand splayed out on Shula's back and his chin rested against her red curls.

The reason she had dived headlong into the punch bowl had been to put out the fire that sight had ignited in her. But she had put it out. And meant to keep it out.

"This is pure silliness," she announced to her sister. "You can think whatever you want, Shula. You usually do, so I'm not going to waste my breath arguing with you."

Shula shaped her lips in a victorious smile, then she aimed a warning glance at the punch bowl. "If I were you, Libby, I wouldn't be wasting any of that breath around lit matches, either. You're liable to go right up in flames, honey.''

It wasn't to avoid lit matches that Libby was making her way to Hellfire's barn now, but rather to peek in on Andy. Earlier in the evening, the child had announced her intention of escaping from the grown-up festivities in order to play with a new litter of kittens in the big building behind the house. Libby had had some reservations about letting Andy out of her sight, and now she felt more than a little guilty because, during her stint at the punch bowl, she hadn't spared the child a thought.

Fiddle music followed her along the dark path behind the house. The barn loomed up, gray against a black sky, but its door was open and a warm, golden light spilled in her direction, beckoning her.

Libby drew up just outside the door. Inside, light from a single lantern warmed the hay bales to a rich amber hue while it cast two shadows across the dusty, hay-littered floor. Two shadows, tall and small, with hands outstretched and linked. Two shadows moving together in three-quarter time. Shad was teaching Andy how to waltz! Libby moved a little closer now, still out of the light, and leaned against the door frame, watching in wonderment.

The big cowboy, so agile on horseback, moved with an equal grace on the makeshift dance floor. Andy's tiny hands nearly disappeared in his, but the smile on her face was enormous. Then she stepped forward when she should have stepped back.

"Oops," she giggled. "Sorry."

"You're doing fine, honey."

"But I stepped on your foot."

"Didn't feel a thing," Shad said as he continued to lead her along the edges of an imaginary square. "I was just thinking about what you asked me earlier. About dresses."

Andy's face tilted up. "You mean when I asked you what was so good about them?"

"Yup." He smiled down at her. A smile that, although it was directed at Andy, caused Libby's stomach to quiver perilously. "One good thing about dresses is they hide a lady's feet when she's dancing."

"So she can make mistakes and nobody will know?"

"Uh-huh."

Andy lowered her eyes now to measure her steps again. "If that's all, then I guess dresses aren't so great," she muttered.

"Well, now, I said it was one good thing. I didn't say it was everything."

"What else?" the child challenged. "I bet you can't think of anything else."

"Sure I can." He closed his eyes a moment. "Take Miss Libby, for instance."

"What about her?" Andy asked.

What, indeed? Libby wondered, leaning forward just a bit and just in time to see the grin that slashed across Shad's formerly serious face.

"Miss Libby sure looked pretty in that yellow dress," he drawled.

Did she? Libby's gaze fluttered down the length of pale organza, then back to Shad's dreamy expression.

"How a person looks isn't important," Andy said petulantly. "Miss Libby says so herself. What's important is how a person acts."

"That's true, but..."

"That's what Miss Libby says." The child's chin snapped up and she lost track of her feet. "Oops. Sorry."

Oh, hush, Andy, Libby was thinking. Let the man go on, for heaven's sake. Nobody had ever called her pretty before. It was always Shula who garnered those compliments. Suddenly Libby thought she knew just why her sister enjoyed them so. Shad's words were bubbling in her head like champagne.

"Dresses are dumb," Andy proclaimed.

"Okay."

"You agree?"

"No." Shad laughed softly. "I'm just being agreeable. There's a difference."

"You're supposed to argue, Shad," the child insisted. "That's what grown-ups do. But I guess you're right about Miss Libby. She does look pretty tonight."

He nodded in agreement, then chuckled. "Even if she is five feet higher than a kite."

"I most certainly am not." Libby pushed off the door frame and stepped—well, stumbled—into the light. She glared at the offending hem of her dress and then glared harder at Shad. "How dare you say that, Mr. Jones, especially to a child?"

"Miss Libby!" Andy exclaimed. "Come see. Shad's been teaching me how to waltz."

Libby felt her indignation—righteous as it was—crumbling in the face of the little girl's joy. "I did see, Andy. You were very graceful. As if you'd been dancing for years. Go on. I didn't mean to interrupt you."

"No. I guess I'm tired. Dancing's harder work than

I ever knew.'' Her glance swept around the interior of the barn. ''Maybe I'll try to find where that mama cat carried her kittens off to. Why don't you take my place and dance with Shad for a while? He's not tired at all, and he's ever so good, Miss Libby.''

Having issued that invitation, Andy skipped away in search of kittens, leaving Libby and Shad standing there with music playing and only golden lantern light between them.

Libby stared at the floor. Her cheeks grew hot with embarrassment. If she thought she could have managed it without falling on her face, she would have whirled around and run out the door. If she could have found her voice, she would have reassured Shad that she didn't expect him to dance with her on the silly and misguided expectations of a child. If she could have bored a hole through the hay-littered floor that moment, she would gladly have dropped through it and disappeared—forever.

His deep voice broke the silence. ''How 'bout it, Miss Libby?''

A bronzed hand stretched toward her, drawing hers with the force of a magnet. She was in his arms then, moving to the music, the way she'd longed to be all evening. Libby closed her eyes. Her yellow dress was swishing against Jones's solid legs. His warm breath was riffling against her ear. She was pretty. She was waltzing. She was perfectly pickled, and she didn't care one little bit. Her feet were hardly touching the ground—until one of them came down hard on the toe of a boot—and then her head came down from the clouds.

''Sorry,'' she sputtered into the lapel of his jacket. ''Perhaps we shouldn't...I'm not very good at this.''

Stiffening now, she tried to pull away, but the hand at her back was unyielding, drawing her more firmly against him.

"Shh. I'm good enough for the both of us," he whispered at her ear. "Relax, Libby. Dancing's just like making love, only all dressed up and vertical."

Shad had meant it as a joke for the most part, but when those blue eyes snapped up to his, he wished he'd bitten off his tongue before letting the lady know the direction of his thoughts. There was shock in her expression, along with the required indignation, but underneath all that prim effrontery, there was curiosity and punch-drunk desire.

That's why he'd come out to the barn in the first place, to get away from Libby's smoldering gaze that had driven him half-crazy while he was dancing with her sister. And now here he was dancing with her when he should have been running away, holding her close when he should have been putting miles of moonlight between them. Here he was, wanting her. Again. Always.

"I...I wouldn't know." Her lips stammered while her eyes darkened with a woozy indication that she'd like to know, like to sample that other, older, horizontal dance. Like to be kissed, if nothing else.

There was nothing in the world right then Shad wanted to do more. He slowed the waltz to a mere sway now and bent his head to taste a corner of that beguiling mouth. Soft. Sweet with sugar. Whiskey warm. His tongue sampled the seam of her lips. "Libby," he whispered, unsealing them, drawing forth a wet little moan from deep in her throat.

The music diminished. The barn itself seemed to vanish as all of Libby's senses honed in on this moment, this man, this stunning kiss. What had begun as a tentative touch had deepened to a fierce possession—a clash of tongues and teeth that sent sparks shimmering through her and shot flames along every nerve. Her arms rose as if buoyed by heat alone, and her fingers found the strong cords of Shad's neck and the hard line of his jaw before they wove through the wealth of his long, warm hair.

She was dizzy with him—with the warm play of his tongue on hers, with the heat of his hands as they moved over her and the wild beat of his heart against hers. Dizzy with the taste of him and with the mingled fragrances of leather and soap and man.

Then he suddenly gentled the kiss to a mere brush of his lips over hers. "We've got company," he murmured.

"What? Who?" Libby forced her glazed eyes to focus. Andy stood staring up at her with a face as pale and blank as the moon.

"He's here, Miss Libby," she said dully.

This time Libby didn't have to ask who. Nor did she have to ask Shad to let her go. He had already done that, and was on bent knee now, eye level with the child.

"Your daddy, Andy?" he asked. "Where did you see him, honey? Tell me."

Her gaze flickered toward the door. "One of the kittens got out. I went after it." Her breath snagged and her lips trembled. "He's out there."

No sooner had she spoken than Shad was up and out the door. Libby knelt down to take his place, clasping the little girl's shoulders, intently searching her face.

"There are dozens of men here tonight," she said.

"Guests and ranch hands and others. Maybe you only saw someone who reminded you..."

Andy shook her head. "It was him." Her tone was listless, without its usual rancor or insistence. "I know it was him. I heard him."

A frown creased Libby's brow. Seeing phantoms struck her as somehow less disturbing than hearing them. "He spoke to you?"

"Nobody sounds like him. My mama always said he must have eaten gravel as a boy. He sounds...I don't know...scary."

"What did he say?"

Now Andy's lusterless eyes brimmed with tears. "He said he saw me dancing. He said I'd burn in hell if I ever did it again. And..."

"And what, honey?" Libby urged.

"He said he was going to kill Shad for touching me. That only he could do that because he's my father and he loves me and I belong to him." Tears exploded from her eyes as her voice broke with racking sobs. "I don't want him to love me like that, Miss Libby. He hurts me."

"Oh, sweetheart." Libby's voice broke, too, and she pulled the trembling child into her arms, crooning to her and stroking her ragged hair. "He won't hurt you, Andy. Never again. I promise you."

Libby rocked her then, lifting her eyes to see Shad come back into the barn, shaking his head.

"Nobody out there," he said quietly.

"She claims she heard him," Libby whispered over Andy's head. "She said he told her terrible things. And he threatened to kill you."

"Come on." In a single motion he had brought

both of them to their feet and was propelling them toward the door. "We're leaving."

Libby halted. "Surely you're not taking this seriously?" Her gaze canted meaningfully toward the child at her side as she added quietly, "I don't think I have to remind you that there's a rather vivid imagination at work here."

"No, ma'am." His jawline hardened and his grip on her arm tightened. "And I don't think I have to remind you that there's only one person who stands to benefit from my being six feet under Paradise instead of standing on it."

A chill raced along Libby's spine. It seemed so obvious now, and the threat she had consigned to Andy's imagination was suddenly very real. But it wasn't little Andy who was in danger. It was Shadrach Jones. If he were dead, there would be no question that Paradise would find its way into other hands. Into huge, hairy paws. "Hoyt," she whispered as Shad pressed her to the door.

"Let's get your sister and go home, Miss Libby. Now."

"Now?" Shula's tongue clucked, a metallic "tsk" that echoed the noise of her bracelets. "You must be crazy, Libby. I'm not leaving now. Why, the party's only just begun."

Clamping her sister's elbow in a viselike grip, Libby growled, "We're going. I'll explain it all later."

"You can do your explaining to somebody else, Libby Kingsland." Shula jerked her arm away. "I'm having fun for the first time in weeks—in months!— and I'm not leaving."

"Of course you're not leaving, honey." Hoyt lumbered up behind Shula and draped a beefy arm around her shoulders. "Now what's all this fuss? What's your hurry, Libby, honey?" His mouth slid sideways in an oily grin. "Where's the fire?"

Right under her temper, Libby thought, and the heat was increasing. She was about to accuse the hairy brute of attempted murder when a low voice sounded at her back.

"No fire, Hoyt. We're just taking a scared little girl back to Paradise where she belongs." Shad brushed past Libby to stand within inches of Backus. He stabbed a finger into the man's huge chest. "Don't you ever use that little girl to get to me. You hear me, Hoyt? If it's me you want, you come straight for me. Me, not her."

Shula gave a little snort. "I knew it! What's that little snip up to now? And shame on you, Libby. You ought to know better than to believe another one of those cockeyed stories Andy's always making up. That little girl's sense of what's what is about as jumbled as her hair, if you ask me."

"Which nobody did," Libby promptly and hotly reminded her. What had begun as a confrontation between two sisters had expanded into a very loud foursome. The fiddlers were still fiddling, but she noticed now that numerous guests had turned their attention toward the increasingly heated discussion. Then, quite suddenly, a half-dozen armed Hellfire cowboys—the same rough-looking crew that had visited Paradise earlier—took up a menacing stance behind their employer, their hard eyes all leveled on a single man. Shadrach Jones.

The threat of violence snapped like lightning in the air. Libby could feel her knees turning to liquid.

"Please." Her voice was little more than a squeak. "Let's go." She nudged Shad's sleeve, feeling the whiplike tension there. If he heard her, he was ignoring her as his hot glare raked from man to man. Anger seemed to have blinded him to the odds before him. Or stupidity, considering that his life had just been threatened by this ugly bunch.

"You can tell your men the same goes for them," he warned Hoyt. "If I so much as catch one of them even looking at that little girl, he'll spend the next twenty years wishing he hadn't."

The man Libby recognized as Menendez surged forward, but Hoyt planted a restraining hand on his arm. "All right now, boys. No call to get rough. Shad and I are just exchanging a few opinions here. We're about done." His gaze slid to Paradise's foreman. "Isn't that right?"

"I've had my say," Shad snarled in reply. "Let's go, Miss Libby. Miss Shula."

Breathing a deep sigh of relief, Libby was about to turn toward the carriage where Andy was waiting when Shula planted her hands on her hips and howled indignantly for all of Hellfire and half of Texas to hear, "Who died and made you king, Shadrach Jones?"

For a second—for one horrible, heart-stopping, mind-numbing instant—a moment when the Hellfire roughnecks were snickering and Amos Kingsland's voice roared in her head like thunder—Libby stared at Shad's huge hands as they doubled into fists. She bit her lip, wincing in anticipation of the brutal crack across her mother's—no, her sister's—cheek. "Daddy, don't," she wanted to scream.

Then those big hands flared open, relaxed for the blink of an eye before they snatched up Shula and draped her like a pink shawl over his broad shoulders.

"Your daddy, Miss Shula," he growled as he strode toward the carriage. "Your daddy died and made me king."

Chapter Fifteen

Shadrach Jones was an absent monarch for the next few days, leaving Libby to bear the brunt of Shula's fury, which she was currently doing at the dinner table. With incredible patience, she thought, even though she was only half listening. By now she knew all of her sister's complaints by heart.

"And how dare he toss me over his shoulder like a sack of flour?" Shula spat for the thousandth time between bites of tender Paradise beef. "Just who does he think he is?"

"You said it yourself, Shula. King." Libby bit down on a grin. In this particular case, she had had to admit that she approved of Shad's rather high-handed behavior the other night. Had Libby herself possessed his strength, she would have picked up the defiant Shula like a sack of flour, too, and tossed her in the carriage.

Since that event, however, there had been no convincing Shula that Hoyt Backus meant anybody harm. And, in truth, the big hairy ape probably didn't intend to hurt Shula. The last thing he'd shouted as their carriage had pulled away had been, "Don't shoot, boys. I don't want one little hair harmed on that pretty red head.''

Shula was quiet a minute, slashing at a slice of beef on her plate as if she wished it were Shad's hide. Then she pointed her knife across the table at Libby and aimed an even sharper glare. ''Well, the king better get himself a queen, or else. We haven't even seen him in days. How do we know he hasn't just taken off?''

''He did take off, Shula. To round up cattle from the salt marshes on the coast. Somebody's got to work around here, for heaven's sake. You act as if Paradise is a place where money just grows on trees.''

Shula shoved her shoulders back against her chair and glowered the length of the table. ''There aren't any trees here, Libby. There's just heat and dust and big, stupid cows to keep it stirred up all the time.'' Slapping her napkin at the tabletop now, she launched a flock of dust motes to dance in a shaft of late-afternoon sun. ''See?''

Actually, Libby thought they were rather beautiful. Her gaze followed them to the source of light at the window and then her heart sailed into her throat when she saw something truly beautiful. Someone. Six feet of dusty cowboy slinging a long leg over the back of a horse, coming to ground with lean grace and weary gratitude. Shad. She hadn't realized how much she'd missed the mere sight of him until that moment. She hadn't realized quite how happy that sight could make her feel.

''He's back.'' The joyous little cry leaped from her throat as she pushed away from the table and raced for the door.

Shad gave his hat a slap against his thigh, squinting to keep the rising dust out of his eyes. For the past few days he'd been doing little else but eating dust and grit, he thought morosely. Well, when he wasn't chasing cattle or swatting at the gulf mosquitoes that swarmed like bees and bit just about as viciously. When he wasn't looking over his shoulder for the glint of a Hellfire rifle. When he wasn't thinking about one lady—Libby—by day and then dreaming of another, long-ago lady by night, all the while damning Amos again and again for getting him into this mess and damning himself for not knowing how to get out of it.

All he wanted right now was a hot bath followed by a cool and dreamless sleep. Mostly the latter. He could go the rest of his days covered from hat to boots with trail dust, he figured, but his tortured, sweat-drenched nights were beginning to wear him down by day.

He was hauling his saddle off of Stormy's back when the front door flew open and Miss Libby came flying out of the house like a little gray dove flushed from cover. A grin tugged at the edges of his mouth, but vanished when he caught sight of Miss Shula, all beady eyed and sharp clawed as a red-tailed hawk, right behind her sister.

Bracing the saddle on his hip, he touched the brim of his hat and drawled what was just about his least favorite word. "Ladies."

Libby drew up a foot or so away from him, her hand pressed to her heart, her blue eyes big and welcoming. "You're back," she said on a rush of breath.

"Yes, ma'am." And glad, Shad thought. Gladder

than he'd expected to be. The little quickstep his heart did purely astonished him.

There was hardly time to wonder at it, though, before the red-tailed hawk was elbowing the little gray dove aside and sinking her sharp little beak into him but good.

"You've got your nerve, being gone so long when everything here is at sixes and sevens." She cuffed him smartly on the arm, then jabbed her chin up into his face. "What I want to know, Mr. Jones, is what you plan to do about it. I demand to know your intentions. Now."

He sighed and shifted the saddle onto his other hip, then thumbed back his hat. "Well, Miss Shula, I'll tell you. Right now I intend to take a hot bath. After that..."

"I'm talking about our inheritance, you hulking idiot." She gave her foot a stamp and then jangled her bracelets under his nose. "I'm talking about marriage. I want to know what you've decided. And, if you haven't reached a decision yet, then I demand that you do it now. Right this minute." She tossed her red curls smartly. "After all, how difficult can it possibly be? You have to marry one of us. Either Libby or me."

It was a bit like watching two pots on a stove, Libby thought. One of them was bubbling up a storm, spilling over, its contents sizzling and popping on the hot stove top. The other—the dark, hard, cast-iron one—was simmering silently, but just as hot. Maybe hotter. Certainly more dangerous beneath that deceptive surface.

He hoisted the big saddle onto his shoulder now and held it with a single hand. "Tough choice," he drawled while his other hand scrubbed across his bristly chin and his gaze drifted from Shula to Libby and back.

Shula crossed her arms and tapped a foot. "We're waiting, Jones." Her gaze flicked sideways. "Aren't we, Libby?"

A swallow—dry as dust and horribly loud—was the best, in fact the only reply that Libby could manage as she stood there, holding her breath, envisioning the holocaust when the cast-iron pot had had it with simmering and finally decided to explode.

But he didn't. It was as if an invisible hand had just whisked him off the stove and plunged him in cool water. He smiled the most dazzling smile Libby had ever seen. It blazed across his dirt-streaked face.

"Well, I'll tell you, Miss Shula," he said, "your sister's already made it pretty clear that she doesn't think much of matrimony, holy or otherwise. Isn't that right, Miss Libby?"

Libby nodded dumbly. Half-blinded by his smile and still anticipating a bomb going off right in front of her, she could barely get her brain to function. Did she think much of matrimony? Well, no, she hadn't. Not until...

"So, the way I see it," he continued in a voice that was lazy, almost lulling, "that just leaves one lady up for grabs, you might say. And that would be you, Miss Shula." He widened that brilliant grin. "You correct me now if I've got this wrong."

Undaunted and apparently unaffected by his smile or his smooth, snake-charming tone, Shula lifted her chin and gave a little snort. "That's quite true. My sister has never expressed much interest in marriage.

Quite the opposite as a matter of fact. So I suppose that does leave just me."

"Uh-huh. That's what I figured." He shoved his hat back another notch as he gazed down at Shula contemplatively, almost speculatively. The way a horse trader might eyeball a chestnut mare.

Libby swallowed again, mortifyingly loud, and noticed that even Shula was forced to blink under that dark-eyed, disturbingly male scrutiny.

Her distress was short-lived, however, for once again her hands fluttered and her jewelry clinked and glittered in the sunlight. "Then I take it you've reached a decision, Mr. Jones?"

"Yes, ma'am. I have." He shifted his weight beneath the saddle, and then just stood there. Tall. Dusty. And utterly silent. He might have turned to stone then for all Libby could tell.

If a moment ever seemed endless, it was this one. Libby wasn't even breathing anymore and she could hear her own heart beating, slowly ticking off time like a ponderous grandfather clock. Or was it only Shula's foot, which had resumed its impatient tapping?

"Well?" Shula snapped.

"Let me put it this way." Shad cleared his throat. "And no offense intended, Miss Shula, but I'd rather be staked out and burned alive by my Comanche relatives than spend one minute married to you."

"What's wrong with Miss Shula?" Andy stood in the middle of the staircase, both hands wrapped around the banister as if she were hanging on for her life. "She came running up these stairs so fast she nearly knocked me down."

"She's upset," Libby said as she mounted the steps in her sister's wake. "It wasn't anything you did, Andy."

The child shook her head in bewilderment. "Something's sure wrong with her. She went right by me and didn't even say anything mean."

Little wonder, Libby thought. Her sister was probably fresh out of venom after sinking her fangs into Shad the way she just had. And although the grinning cowboy had prefaced his rejection with "no offense intended," Shula had taken great offense. Hot, hissing offense. She had told him—among other things—not only how she'd like to see him staked out by his savage relatives, but also exactly how many burning sticks she recommended they use in their fire…and elsewhere.

Shad had just kept grinning in the face of Shula's ire. And, oddly enough, Libby had stood there grinning, as well. Which hadn't made any sense to her at all under the circumstances. If Shad was turning her sister down, and if there wasn't going to be a marriage to satisfy the terms of her father's will, they could all just kiss Paradise goodbye when Hoyt Backus took over.

If there was anything left to take over. Judging from the sounds coming from Shula's room right now, the Princess was well on her way to tearing the palace apart.

"It might be a good idea to keep out of Miss Shula's way, at least for a little while, Andy." Libby gave the child's head a reassuring pat. "Just to be on the safe side."

"Yeah. Maybe I'll go out to the barn. Shad's back, isn't he, Miss Libby?"

With a vengeance, Libby thought, before replying, "Yes, he is, honey. Why?"

Andy shrugged. "Oh, I guess I just feel safer when he's around."

"You're not dwelling on your father again, are you, Andy?" Libby cupped the little girl's chin and turned her face up for a keen inspection. "Remember we talked about that. It isn't your father who's been scaring you, honey. It's somebody who's mad at Shad and trying to hurt him by playing some nasty tricks on you."

Her gaze slanting sideways, Andy murmured, "Yes'm, I know, but..."

"No buts about it, young lady." Libby gripped her chin more firmly, redirecting Andy's gaze so it met her own. "And no more thinking about him. You turn that imagination of yours on something else. Something that will make you feel good, like coming up with names for those puppies of yours. All right?"

The child nodded without enthusiasm, but then her eyes gleamed with curiosity. "Who's mad at Shad?"

As if on cue, the foot-stomping and drawer-slamming coming from Shula's room intensified, and the redhead hurled a curse out into the hallway that took the name of the Lord in vain as well as that of Shadrach Jones.

Libby rolled her eyes toward the ceiling and gritted her teeth as she muttered, "Does that answer your question?"

"Why's Miss Shula always mad at everybody?"

Because she's a spoiled brat, Libby was tempted to say. *Because she can't stand not getting what she wants. Or who she wants.* She bit her tongue out of ancient, habitual loyalty to her younger sister before actually replying, "She's just high-strung, I suppose."

Down the hallway now something hard hit the door. Another hail of curses quickly followed, causing the little girl to shiver.

"I think I'll go outside now before one of those high strings busts loose and comes down on me," Andy announced, then turned to trot down the stairs.

"That's probably a good idea," Libby agreed. If she had any sense, she thought, she would have gone outside with Andy. But instead she gripped the banister and headed up in the direction of all those snapping strings.

She entered the room with one hand raised, prepared to deflect a flying shoe or hairbrush, but she was completely unprepared for the sight that greeted her. There were dresses everywhere. The room looked like a tornado had gone through the ladies' department at an emporium, had tried on every garment and then had flung each one aside—on the bed, on the chair, on the carpet. Libby had witnessed scores of Shula's royal snits over the years, but never one of such grand proportions.

She made her way cautiously and on tiptoe around a discarded bustle and over a crumpled petticoat. "What in the world are you doing, Shula?"

From the center of the multicolored storm, her sister threw her a black look. "I'm organizing my clothes, Libby," Shula snapped. "What does it look like I'm doing?"

Actually it looked more like disorganizing, but Libby refrained from pointing that out. Instead she stood quietly, watching her sister yank yard after yard of lace and silken ruffles from the wardrobe and toss them in the general direction of an open trunk. "Why?" she finally asked.

Shula tossed a handful of stockings onto the bed. "For packing," she said briskly, as if any fool could see purpose in the chaos that surrounded her. "Do you suppose there are extra trunks around here someplace? Would you mind just taking a look around, Libby? I could use…"

"Packing!" Feeling light-headed suddenly, Libby shoved a dress aside and sat down on the bed. "Packing!"

"You heard me," her sister snapped as she jerked another garment from the wardrobe and inspected it for stains and tears.

Libby had heard her. She was thinking how a week or so ago those words would have thrilled her no end. She'd wanted nothing more than for Shula to agree to pack up and go home with her. Back to Saint Louis. Back where they belonged. But now everything was different. Libby was different.

There was a stitch of panic in her voice when she said, "We can't go back to Saint Louis. I…I won't go."

"Well, who said anything about you going anywhere, Libby? And who said anything about Saint Louis? Good grief, I wouldn't go back there if every banker in the city came crawling on his knees." Shula snorted and tossed her curls. "Which they'll no doubt be doing pretty soon, I imagine."

Libby sat there feeling like someone who had been seated too late in the theater and couldn't quite get the hang of the play. The harder she tried, the more confused she became. To make matters worse, the redheaded actress was regarding her now with the disdainful sympathy she ordinarily reserved for dull-witted fools.

As much as it galled her, Libby finally sighed and said, "I just don't understand, Shula. If you're not going back to Saint Louis, then where...?"

Shula's bracelets clacked and clattered furiously while she gave the dress in her hands a thorough shake before she lobbed it across the room. Then she beamed victoriously when the garment landed and its ruffles collapsed into an open trunk. "Hellfire, honey. Where else?"

"Hellfire."

It was a curse, not a name, when it ripped through Libby's clenched teeth as she walked toward the barn, kicking the hem of her skirt with each angry stride. "Hellfire and damnation."

She'd been cursing—under her breath and over it, too—ever since she'd left Shula to her packing. Cursing herself mostly for being so caught up in the present that she hadn't foreseen the future. She should have seen this coming. She should have known. From the minute her father's letter had come after all those years, she ought to have suspected. From the second his will was read, she should have had sense enough to realize how it all would turn out. Badly.

Right now she might almost have sworn her father had intended it that way. One last slap. One final, death-defying act of cold indifference to let his first-born daughter know—again—forever—that Amos Kingsland didn't give a damn. Not about her anyway.

And now it looked as if he hadn't given a damn about Paradise either, by allowing it to slip through her fingers and fall into the careless hands of Hoyt

Backus. Hoyt and Shula! Between the two of them, Paradise would come to ruin in the blink of an eye. Unless...

Libby shook her head. Shad had said it himself. She didn't think much of matrimony, holy or otherwise. And, quite clearly, neither did he if he found being burned alive preferable.

It was nearly dark now, and Libby reminded herself that the fate of Paradise wasn't her only worry at the moment. She hadn't seen Andy since the little girl had gone outside to escape Shula's wrath. For that matter, she hadn't seen Shad since he'd lit the fire beneath that wrath.

She lifted her hands now and cupped them to her mouth to call for Andy. Once. Twice.

"In a minute, Miss Libby," came the reply from somewhere behind the barn.

Libby's breath caught and a faint smile sketched her lips as she remembered all the nights in Saint Louis she herself had lingered outside long after dark, ignoring her mother's calls, unwilling to leave the stars that were shining high over Paradise to go back inside a cheerless, loveless house. Looking up now, she saw those same stars, the ones she'd wished upon for so many years. It struck her suddenly that those wishes had come true. She was here. She was where she had longed to be. And she wanted desperately, so desperately, to stay.

She rounded the corner of the barn.

"Oh, look out, Miss Libby," Andy cried. "Don't step on Abednego."

A little ball of fur went skittering along the hem of her skirt. Libby bent down to pick it up. "Abednego!

Where in the world did you come up with a name like that?''

"You said I oughta put my imagination to good use." Andy scooped up a second pup. "This one's Meshach. And there's..." Her little face darkened as she glanced around her. "Oh, dear. Shadrach's run away."

"He tried," a deep voice rumbled as Shad stepped around the other corner of the barn with the missing puppy wriggling and squealing in his grasp. He passed it to Andy before his dark gaze cut to Libby. "Didn't get far, though."

Her heart seemed to quit beating for a moment, then it made up for the lost beats by pounding furiously. She had the distinct feeling that Shad wasn't talking about the namesake pup, but rather about himself.

"Andy," she said quietly, "it's time for you to go in and get ready for bed."

When the child opened her mouth to protest, Shad cut her off. "You heard the lady, squirt. Maybe if you don't complain any, Miss Libby will let you keep these critters in your room tonight." He slanted a quizzical look at Libby.

"May I?" Andy cried. "Oh, please, Miss Libby, say yes."

"Well..." As Libby demurred, she was debating whether or not she wanted to be left alone, here, in the gathering dark, with Shad. Her head was telling her she didn't, but she could hardly hear the warning for the drumbeat of her heart. "Just this once," she finally said.

Andy yelped with joy, then scrambled after the puppies.

"Keep an eye on this little renegade," Shad said, squatting down to keep Shadrach from scuttling away.

Libby picked up Abednego and plopped him into Andy's arms. "You keep your bedroom door closed tight, Andy. Miss Shula will have a fit if one of these animals gets in her room."

Duly warned, the child nodded somberly. She stood there a moment, her arms filled with puppies, staring at the ground and mumbling something Libby couldn't understand.

"What, honey?" she asked.

"I said I was using my imagination again. Can an imagination make wishes, Miss Libby?"

"I suppose an imagination can do just about anything, Andy," Libby replied, reaching out to touch the little girl's cheek, remembering her own wishes aimed at stars overhead. "What is it you're wishing for?"

Andy's lashes fluttered up, revealing the shine of tears in her eyes. "I wish you were my mama." Her gaze slid shyly toward Shad then. "And I wish you were my papa. Instead of...instead of *him*."

"Oh, Andy..." Libby reached out for her, but Andy turned on her heel and, hugging her bundle of puppies, ran toward the house.

Libby rucked up her skirt, intending to follow, but a warm hand restrained her.

"Let her go," Shad said.

"But..."

"She's just wishing, Libby. It's harmless."

"Is it?" Libby sighed as she let go of the folds of her skirt. "I'm not so sure. She'll be disappointed, so terribly hurt when her wishes don't come true."

"Then she'll make new ones. Better ones," he said quietly. "That's called growing up."

Staring up at the starlit sky, Libby wondered if that was something she herself had failed to do. She couldn't even fathom new wishes. There were no better ones. Just this. Just Paradise.

She was vaguely aware that Shad had moved closer behind her. The heat from his body felt oddly reassuring, and when she tipped her head back, there was the surprising comfort of his shoulder. Libby let her breath out in a sigh. "My sister's upstairs packing. She's going to Hellfire."

He chuckled deep in his throat. "Heaven wouldn't have her, that's for damn sure."

"No. I meant…"

"I know what you meant, Libby," he said softly. "With me out of the picture, your sister's hell-bent on marrying Hoyt, I expect."

Libby nodded. *Hell-bent* was the perfect description of Shula's determination not to let the riches of Paradise slip through her fingers while her own determination seemed to have withered and died.

"You going to let her get away with it?" Shad asked her now, his voice a deep vibration at her back and a warm rush of air at her ear.

She shivered. "I don't have much choice. As you said, she's hell-bent. There's nothing I can do to stop her."

"Probably not. At least, not stop her from rushing off to Hellfire and Hoyt," he murmured as his cheek settled against her temple and the rest of him shifted even closer. "But you could sure put a crimp in her ambitions."

The warmth of his body was seeping into her de-

spite the layers of clothes between them, and the
soothing tone of his voice was making it difficult for
Libby to think—about Shula, about Paradise, about
anything but him. Libby sighed as much from frustration as from the pure pleasure of absorbing his
heat.

Shula, with all her ambitions in tow, was headed
for Hellfire. Paradise would soon be going to hell in
a handbasket. And she seemed incapable of doing
anything but standing here, mindlessly sopping up
Shadrach Jones the way a hot biscuit sops up butter.
"I'm afraid I don't know how, Shad."

"Easy, Miss Libby. Just marry me."

Chapter Sixteen

It wasn't the proposal he'd intended. Hell, he hadn't intended to propose at all, but merely suggest a way to keep the ranch intact, not to mention his own hide. And he'd spent the past few days convincing himself that this marriage of convenience business was just that—business.

Then Libby had come rushing out of the house looking for all the world like she was happy to see him, sending his heart tripping and stumbling for a minute in his chest. It had barely begun to recover when the raspberry tart had descended on him, reminding him once again that ladies were to be avoided like the plague.

Only here he was standing close as clothes to one of them, contemplating the pale curve of her neck, breathing in the sweet, flowery scent of her hair and—drunk on that alone, perhaps—asking her to marry him. God Almighty!

"In a manner of speaking," he added now before she got the wrong idea or concluded that he meant anything but business.

When she just stood there staring off into the dark, Shad wondered if she'd even heard him.

He tamped down hard on the nagging wish to have her turn—blue eyes as bright as day, a smile as warm as summer on her face—to have her throw her arms around his neck and to tell him yes, yes, oh yes. That wasn't what this was about, he told himself. It was about Paradise. Nothing else. And if it happened at all, this marriage, it would be a handshake deal and not a kissing one.

She did turn toward him then, blue eyes gray with worry and any hint of a smile being bitten from her lower lip. Delicate as a dove and twice as skittish. "I never intended to marry," she said somberly.

It wasn't a yes, but then it wasn't exactly a no. Shad felt a kind of loosening in his chest, as if his heartstrings had been tied in knots and now were unraveling. He couldn't help but laugh a little. "Well, neither did I, Miss Libby. I guess you could call us the victims of circumstances."

At that, her eyes flashed up. "My father's circumstances, you mean. I will not be a victim of any sort, Mr. Jones. I want to make that crystal clear."

"I understand," he said, even though he didn't have the least notion what she meant other than maybe feeling railroaded into something. Which she was. He damned Amos again. The Captain's daughter deserved better than being a pawn in the old man's scheme. So did he, he thought glumly. But then Paradise deserved better than being used like a strip mine for quick, easy cash.

"It's up to you, Miss Libby. I guess it just depends on how bad you want to save Paradise. And I guess I've decided I'm willing to try." He took a step back, the better to study her expression, before adding, "You've made it plain you don't hold much faith in matrimony, but we're not talking about a real marriage here, you know."

"No, of course not," Libby was quick to acknowledge. But a *real* marriage was exactly what she had been thinking of ever since Shad had broached the subject. Thinking of and—heaven help her—leaning toward. In spite of her misgivings, in spite of her fears, in spite of herself, she'd been picturing a true union between the two of them. Or three, counting Andy. Or four, counting Paradise.

Whatever disappointment she felt, she tried to banish it from her voice when she said, "I accept. I'll marry you, Mr. Jones."

"Well, then…" His hands twitched as if impelled to reach out for her, but he anchored them by hooking his thumbs through his belt. His habitual grin flattened to a stoic line. "That's that, I reckon."

His words hung like spent fireworks in the night air, and a strange awkwardness settled between them. Each took a step back, increasing the distance between them. They cleared their throats in unison. They were behaving, Libby thought, like youngsters left alone by the grown-ups—alone and at a loss for words. Hardly like a man and woman who had just agreed to marry, for whatever reasons.

And certainly not like a man and woman who had already shared some degree of intimacy. Was that never to be again? Suddenly the prospect of no more blazing kisses left her feeling unaccountably bereft. Cheated somehow. Her eyes lifted to Jones's face.

It was as if he read the yearning in her expression when he asked softly, in a voice that had the same effect as a caress, "What? What are you wishing, Libby?"

She opened her mouth to reply, but no words were there. Only an inarticulate longing. And then, before Libby could fashion even a bumbling answer, Eb Talent came stomping around a corner of the barn.

"Fine thing when the fella who's s'posed to be at the helm takes to hiding back here," the old man grumbled, "when there's a storm blowing up out front. And a redheaded storm, at that. Ain't none worse."

Shad gave Libby a final, lingering look before he sighed and said, "What's Miss Shula want now?"

"She wants to go to Hellfire," Eb said, planting his hands on his hips.

"Let her. Tell one of the boys to help you hitch up the carriage."

"She wants to go in the Captain's big coach. In style, she says." He lofted a glance heavenward. "Lord knows she's got enough luggage to fill it. So I spent a fair amount of wind pointing out that there ain't any fit roads twixt here and Hellfire. Told her real polite and every way I know how that the coach is liable to break a wheel or crack an axle before we ever get there." Eb shook his head now and fingered his whiskery jaw, then added plaintively, "She don't listen, that sister of yours, Miss Libby. Pardon my asking, but has she got some kind of hearing problem?"

Libby put a comforting hand on the old sailor's shoulder. "My sister's problem, Eb, is that she only hears what she wants to."

"Well, the only word she's hearing or saying right

now is *coach*," he muttered. "And that coach ain't going to Hellfire till there's a decent road."

"I'll go speak to her," Libby said. She glanced over her shoulder at Shad and raised one quizzical eyebrow. "Unless you'd like to have the privilege of setting the Princess straight."

A slow grin shaped his lips while he stood his ground. "I'd rather be burned alive, Miss Libby."

"I can't say I blame you." She returned a wearier version of the grin. "Sometimes talking with my sister is a frighteningly similar experience."

In order to get Shula to quit insisting on the heavy coach, Libby had to paint a picture of dire peril wherein the shattered vehicle's passenger was forced to trudge the many dark remaining miles to Hellfire. In the rain. Without an umbrella. Or her luggage.

Shula had pouted a moment, and then had proclaimed, "Well, I don't want to arrive on Hoyt's doorstep looking like some lost, bedraggled alley cat. Libby, have them take my bags out of the coach and put them in the carriage, will you?"

Two trunks wouldn't fit, no matter how much Shula had ranted and raved. Libby had promised to send them the following day. She had made one futile attempt to tell her sister about the stunning proposal of marriage she'd just received.

"Would you still go to Hellfire, Shula, if I said I was going to marry Mr. Jones?"

With a flip of her red curls and a resounding snort, Shula had replied, "That's the least marryingest man I've ever seen. Forget about him, honey. If he turned *me* down flat, you haven't got a snowball's chance in hell." She patted Libby's hand. "But that's all right.

You'll always have a home here at Paradise with me and Hoyt.''

Libby lay in bed now two hours after Shula's departure, considering her sister's final words. Even a snowball, she thought, was entitled to some measure of happiness and good fortune. She ought to be content to have received a proposal from "the least marryingest man" even if their union wasn't to be real. She ought to be thrilled having snatched Paradise from the grasp of Hoyt Backus and having insured that the ranch would prosper in the coming years.

She ought to be turning handsprings now that all of her youthful dreams were coming true. But what was it Shad had said about wishes? About new wishes being a part of growing up? Libby wondered now if she hadn't done some growing up since coming to Texas and if she hadn't acquired at least one new wish in the bargain.

From her bed, she could see a swatch of starlit Paradise sky, and wondered if there was a star up there she'd been unaware of or perhaps even ignored all these years. Which star was for wishing somebody loved her? Which one—out of a myriad of distant twinkling lights—was meant for Shadrach Jones?

"Clear night," Eb said. "All them stars and nary a cloud. It's gonna be a hot one tomorrow."

"Hot one tonight." Shad continued to rock in Amos's big chair, contributing little to the conversation while wishing the old sailor would either keep quiet for five minutes or amble off to his hammock in the bunkhouse. Shad needed to think, although he wasn't quite sure what it was that required mental stewing. He'd asked Miss Libby to marry him, and she'd said yes. Old Amos, wherever he was, ought to be smiling to beat the band now. Paradise was going to prosper. The new Brahman would sire a whole new breed. New wells would bring in welcome water. The whole damn place would thrive. That should have been that.

Only it wasn't. Shad kept wrestling with the notion that something wasn't right. Even now, despite the warmth of the night, a shiver skimmed down his backbone and raised the hairs on the backs of his arms.

Eb launched a stream of tobacco into the hedge of prickly pear that skirted the porch. "That big chair of the Captain's suits you, Shad. I'm betting Amos is real pleased with the way things have sorted themselves out, what with you marrying his daughter and all."

"I wasn't put on this earth to please Amos Kingsland," Shad snarled, "or to make his afterlife enjoyable."

"Didn't say you were, did I? God Almighty, boy. You're acting like a fella who's just lost his last nickel instead of one who's about to gain half-a-million acres and a pretty little bride."

Shad grimaced and continued to stare out at the dark sweep of starlit sky.

"You oughta be happy," Eb said, "right here, sitting in the Captain's seat, taking over at the helm. He built this place on a hill, you know, so's he could see the Mexes coming up from the south and the redskins sneaking down from the north. Course, things have settled down since the old days. There's hardly anybody left now to watch out for." Eb's gaze drifted west toward Hellfire. "'Cept Hoyt."

"Hoyt's enough." But even as he acknowledged a known enemy, Shad kept thinking about an unknown one. Glad as he ought to be with Paradise secure, he had the distinct feeling he'd been duped. Plucked naked and bump-skinned as a chicken. Picked clean as a greenhorn at a back table in a Corpus poker mill. Stripped down and used up by one of the ladies he'd sworn to avoid. And now he was betrothed to one.

Except it was sad little Libby, and that seemed to make all the difference in the world. She seemed to possess only the finer qualities of a lady. She said what she meant. She was gentle and loyal and kind. Unlike her sister, the raspberry tart, who said whatever was necessary to get her way and whose loyalty was to herself alone. They were like faces on opposite sides of a coin.

Or so he thought as he pictured the way she'd come running out of the house earlier today, making him feel…well…special somehow. As if he'd just come home. He'd never seen Miss Libby's side of a coin before, and he wasn't prepared to bet on it yet, thinking it was just her inexperience that accounted for her disposition. She simply lacked the skills her sister had.

Or did she? Hell, the lady'd made him want her from the minute he'd laid eyes on her. And now he'd asked her to marry him. How did he know that hadn't been her angle right from the start? How could he know—with a lady?

"Well, I reckon I'll turn in." Eb planted his hands on the arms of his chair and levered up on his bum legs. "Don't s'pose Hoyt'll be a problem once he gets word of the coming nuptials, Shad. I wouldn't sit out here stewing all night if I were you."

Shad wasn't quite done stewing, but he nodded to Eb anyway. "Don't roll out of that hammock of yours, old man."

He watched the old sailor make the trek to the bunkhouse, his legs wobbling and wide spread as if he were still on the pitching deck of a ship. But suddenly Eb drew up short, pointing toward the far end of the bunkhouse where an orange glow was just beginning to show above the roofline. "We got us a fire," he shouted.

Shad, who had seen it at the same moment, sent Amos's chair toppling backward as he shot to his feet. "You go roust the boys out of their bunks. Have them bring blankets and buckets. And plenty of 'em. Move those old legs of yours, Eb. Fast."

Shad's long stride had taken him around the corner of the building almost before Eb could react. Flames were already moving up the west wall, licking the paint off in long curls. It was obvious at first glance that this wasn't an accident—not a tossed smoke or an errant spark from a stove. The source of the flames was a pile of brush and paper trash that hadn't yet been consumed. The devil's own handiwork. A flaming gift from Hellfire if ever Shad had seen one.

He kicked at the brush pile to move it away from the building, then stomped on the scattered twigs and smoking wads of newspaper. By the time he'd done that, he was joined by a dozen wide-awake, union-suited cowboys.

They all knew what to do. In a land where a spark could ignite a thousand-acre conflagration in the blink of an eye, the men of Paradise exchanged shouts and oaths for only a moment before settling in to the grim task of beating and drowning the orange monster that was threatening to consume their quarters. Half of them smacked blankets against the side of the building while the other half strung themselves out at regular intervals to pass buckets of water from the pump.

From his vantage point on the roof, Shad directed the men below at the same time that he was swatting and stamping out the sparks that were coming down in brilliant showers and threatening to eat through the dry lumber to get to the banquet of bunks below.

For a minute, with his eyes burning from smoke and rising soot, while his sleeves kept going up in flames and his hair started smelling like somebody had just put a brand to him, all Shad wanted was to fill his lungs with cool, fresh air. He was tempted to climb down the far side of the building and keep walking. Let it burn. Let the wind rise and fling red embers over the whole half-million acres. Let the greedy flames of Hellfire take it all. No Paradise—no problems. He'd be a free man. The urge to get away was powerful, insistent.

And then he looked down at the line of weary men still passing buckets hand over hand, standing in mud now where the water had spilled to the ground. In the midst of that soot-streaked, sorry-looking, mud-swamped bunch stood an angel. A vision in a wet, white gown, her dark, damp hair tumbling over her shoulders and her slim arms straining under the weight of water-filled pails.

Lady. Libby. The face on the sweet side of the coin. Shad's breath caught fire in his chest, a blaze that had nothing to do with the actual flames around him. Then, as if she sensed she was being watched, she raised her gaze roofward, capturing his eyes through the haze of smoke. There was such courage and determination in those blue eyes that for an instant he thought he was staring down at Amos. But he saw something else in those eyes that Amos—for all his possessions—had never possessed. Warmth. Love. Shad didn't know what to call it, but it shone brighter than any flame. It lit up the night far beyond the reaches of the fire, and damned if it didn't light up his heart, as well.

"That'll do it, boys. Looks like we got it licked." After jumping down from the roof, Shad took the final bucket from the last man in line and pitched its contents against the charred wall of the bunkhouse. The last embers gave up with a wisp of white smoke as the weary ranch hands cheered.

"Let's hear it for Miss Libby, fellas," Eb shouted. "She worked as hard as any man here. Harder, maybe, considering her size. I'd say she did her daddy and all of us proud."

Another cheer was raised, and the men shook hands with Libby, one by one, shyly and somberly as they drifted back to their bunks. Shad stood back, letting her receive the well-deserved gratitude. He couldn't help but notice how the boys all respectfully averted their eyes from her wet, clinging gown. That was more than he could say for himself, though, and he thought if any of Paradise's hands gave her even half a leer, he'd fire the man on the spot. After he had pounded his sorry carcass into the mud.

With her cheeks smudged with soot and her hair all damp and matted, Libby Kingsland looked more beautiful right then than any woman Shad had ever seen. And she looked about done in by the time he crossed the muddy ground and cupped his hand beneath her elbow.

"Come on," he said softly. "You're about to fall over."

Libby sagged a little as if only then realizing just how wrung out she was. And then, having given up the first inch to her exhaustion, her legs buckled and she surrendered the final mile.

It felt so good being scooped up by a strong and ready pair of arms. What might have struck her as "manhandling" a week or two ago now seemed more a warm gesture of protection than an arrogant, brutish act. She felt safe. So safe. She lifted her tired, trembling arms to circle Shad's warm neck and pressed her cheek to his solid chest.

Although her body was exhausted, her brain kept moving at full tilt, trying to put words to the emotions she was currently feeling. Was it happiness? she wondered. Why would she be happy when a part of Paradise had nearly burned to the ground? But it hadn't. They'd conquered the fire. She had conquered it. *I'd say she did her daddy and all of us right proud,* Eb had proclaimed. She had saved a small piece of Paradise, thereby staking her very own claim on it. The place was more hers now than it had ever been.

Hers. And his.

She nestled more closely against Shad now, her body absorbing the warmth of his and the shock of each of his long strides as he crossed the yard to the house. There had been a moment earlier when Shad had been on the roof and Libby had been passing buckets below—a moment as bright as the fire itself—when their gazes had met and held. Without speaking, they seemed to have acknowledged a togetherness in the face of disaster. Without even touching, they had formed a bond. She felt it still.

He eased his grip and lowered her to her feet when they reached the front porch. Eb came hobbling up behind them.

"You okay, missy?" he asked.

"I'm fine, Eb. Just a little tired."

The old man sighed and swiped his hat off, revealing a stripe of white, soot-free forehead. "Damn," he muttered, "I hate fires. Hate 'em worse on ships, though they're bad enough on land. That wasn't no accident, was it, Shad?"

"Nope." Shad was scraping a muddy boot on the edge of a step. "I'd say it was about as deliberate as a pile of dry trash and a well-placed match can be."

Libby blinked. "Someone set the fire?"

"Someone." The word came hissing from Shad's lips. The meaning was clear.

"Hoyt," Libby whispered.

"One of the boys just told me he saw somebody skulking around earlier," Eb said. "Didn't recognize him. Didn't say anything at the time 'cause he figured it mighta been somebody new Miss Libby hired."

Shad scowled down at his boot. "No use beating the bushes for him tonight. That man and his matches are back at Hellfire now, I'd bet. You go on to that hammock of yours, Eb, and get some sleep. We'll figure out what we're going to do about this tomorrow."

With a shrug and a grumbled "good-night," Eb turned toward the bunkhouse.

"What *are* we going to do?" Libby shivered as a breeze pressed her damp nightgown against her skin.

She reached out to touch Shad's arm. "I'm worried about you."

His glance flickered to her pale hand on his sooty sleeve. The urge to kiss each of those delicate fingertips was strong. Shad ignored it by returning his attention to his muddy boots.

"If Hoyt's truly trying to murder you—"

"Then he's doing a lousy job," he said, cutting her off as he eased his arm from her warm touch. A minute more and he'd be kissing her for certain. "It's my life, Libby. You let me worry about it."

"All right."

She hugged her arms about herself a moment, chewing on her lip, looking vulnerable and reminding him of that sad little dark-haired girl of so many years ago. He was about to apologize for his abrupt remark when her chin snapped up and her eyes flared.

"Then I'll just worry about your boots instead. Sit down, Mr. Jones."

"What?"

"Sit down." She gave him a little push in the direction of Amos's big chair. "Sit."

He did, more out of surprise than obedience, and no sooner was he sitting than she was kneeling before him, using the hem of her gown to clean one mudencrusted boot.

"Aw, here now, Miss Libby. You hadn't ought to be doing that..."

"Hush."

And he did that, too. He hushed partly for a sudden lack of breath and partly because he didn't know what else to say to the beautiful and oddly determined woman at his feet. Her pretty mouth went taut with concentration, and as she worked, the lace neckline of her gown kept dipping to reveal just enough of her breasts to make Shad's mouth go bone-dry and his bloodstream go rushing south.

Without looking up, she whispered, "Thank you, Shad."

"For what?"

"For putting out the fire. For all the things you do around here that I'm not even aware of to keep the place going."

He mustered enough spit to answer "It's my job."

"Not for long."

"You planning on firing me again, Libby?" he teased.

She shook her head and her purposeful mouth relaxed into the smallest of grins. "Not a chance. I'm planning, just in case you've forgotten, to marry you."

By God, he *had* almost forgotten. But now her reminder, coupled with the enticing view down the neckline of her gown, nearly jolted him out of the chair. This woman was going to be his wife. His legal, signed-sealed-and-documented, God-blessed mate. Soon he would have legitimate, husbandly rights to the body that had been bewitching him incessantly. The knowledge brought a prickle of sweat to his skin and made his fingers tighten on the arms of the chair. Wanting her this way was one thing. Wanting her and having the right to take her was something else instead.

"Unless," she added quietly, her blue eyes searching his face, "you've reconsidered."

Shad was doing that right then. Reconsidering. Asking himself if his will was strong enough to resist the soft temptations of her body, day after married day, night after married night. They hadn't even tied the knot yet, and his resistance was already as thin as a string.

"I'm a man of my word, Miss Libby. I meant what I said." His voice roughened. The need to touch her was so strong he had to tighten his grip on the chair. "Only..."

Pride flashed in her eyes, just before hurt clouded them. She sat back on her heels. "I'd never hold you to a promise you didn't want to keep." Her shoulders stiffened. "Believe me, Mr. Jones, if I'd known you considered marrying me such a painful task, I'd never have consented."

Why did the woman persist in misunderstanding him? Shad wanted to shake her, but instead he stared out at the charred end of the bunkhouse, willing a patience he didn't particularly feel, along with a cool indifference he didn't know how to achieve.

Hell, maybe it was his own damn fault. He'd always accused ladies of being two-faced, of saying one thing and meaning another. Because she was a lady, and an inexperienced one to boot, it was he who was putting a polish on every word that came out of his mouth, sweetening every phrase, never saying exactly what he meant. By now his tongue felt sugarcoated and nearly stuck to the roof of his mouth.

He cleared his throat in an effort to get the words out plain.

"What's painful, Miss Libby, is wanting to take you to bed." He swallowed audibly, then added, for clarity's sake and just to be certain he wasn't misunderstood, "To make love to you, ma'am."

Chapter Seventeen

"Please do."

She spoke so softly with her head bowed and her eyes downcast that Shad wasn't sure he'd heard her right.

He swallowed. "Pardon?"

Then those blue eyes—wide and shining—came up to meet his while a shy smile flirted with the corners of her mouth. "Please do. Make love to me, Mr. Jones." She paused a second then and blinked before whispering, "*Shad.*"

He tried to swallow again, but now his throat seemed to have closed. He'd told her the truth—unvarnished—the naked truth—but now he realized he'd said it in order to scare the lady off. Not to coax her into his bed. She should have reacted to his statement by plucking up her gown and running away. She should have hauled off and left her handprint on his brazen face. She should have told him no, in no uncertain terms.

But the lady had just said yes. Yes, please.

Lord Almighty!

Shad was swamped by urges then. Nearly drowning

in desire and fear. His need to take ultimate, passion-ate possession of this beautiful woman was as great as his need to run away. Need battled fear, leaving him nearly paralyzed for a moment. But he had to do something, anything, so he stood up, coming to his feet so swiftly that he overturned the chair behind him and sent Libby sprawling in front of him. But then, instead of running away, he bent down, circled Libby with his arms and brought her to her feet.

She gasped in an effort to recapture the breath that had been knocked out of her, and the next thing Shad knew his mouth had covered hers and his breath was replenishing hers while his strength served to main-tain her upright.

"I want you, Libby. Tonight. Now."

He wasn't sure if he'd thought those words or ac-tually spoken them until she whispered back.

"Yes. Now."

She was cradled in his arms then, high against his chest, and Shad was kissing her as he carried her into the house and up the stairs. With each step, his heart beat harder and his breathing roughened, not from the exertion, but from his mounting desire. He'd never wanted a woman more.

For a moment his mind was blank of anything but that desire and the anticipation of its fulfillment. But then, just as he set Libby down in front of her bed-room door, old memories burned across his brain.

Wide-awake, but still that dream, that terrible nightmare started scrolling through his head. Scene after scene raced through his mind. Vivid. Almost real. The swish of his stepmother's gown. Her soft footsteps coming nearer to his bed. Then the scented heat of her body. And then the husky throb of her voice. *You want me, Shad. You know it.*

His guilt and shame felt as raw, as unhealed as if twenty years hadn't passed. Rage clawed at the back of his throat. *Get off me, you clumsy little half-breed.* Her laughter, the lady's laughter, was ringing painfully in his head. Right now.

No. Never again. Hadn't he sworn that no lady would ever have a chance to scar him that way again? Hadn't he made that solemn vow? He looked down at Libby now and swore that her features were becoming those of that other lady. Dark hair fading to light. Sweet features changing. Innocence in her eyes hardening to the glint of experience. Angel transforming into the devil's own daughter.

His heart caromed dangerously in his chest. A curse surged in his throat.

And then she spoke. Not in a husky tone, though. Softly. Uncertainly. She was Libby again—sad little Libby—leaning against the door frame for support while worry crumpled her forehead, while her hand fluttered up to her throat. "I'm afraid," she said. "I've never…"

"I won't hurt you, darlin', if that's what you're worried about."

Her reply was quick. "Oh, no. It isn't that." She forced a nervous little laugh. "It isn't that at all, my dear. I've seen you with Andy, don't forget. I know you're capable of great tenderness. It's just that… well…"

"What?" he whispered, cupping her chin and raising her gaze to his. "We don't have to do this, little Libby. Not now. Not tonight. Not ever, if that's what you want. You don't have to be afraid."

"I know I shouldn't be, but..."

"But what? What are you afraid of, Libby?"

She dragged in a breath and released it in a rush of words. "I'm twenty-five years old, Shad. Some would call me an old maid. You see, I've never...I don't...I'm afraid that...afraid that you'll laugh at me."

"Laugh at you!" Shad nearly did laugh as he echoed her words. Laugh at her! At *her!* She was a lady to the marrow of her bones and he was, in his worst dreams at least, a clumsy half-breed.

Or used to be. But no more, for Libby's outspoken fear suddenly seemed to obliterate his own. His heart, instead of freezing solid, felt as if it were melting along with all of his old, haunting memories.

Lady—yes. But this was his Libby, his sad little Libby who called forth every ounce of protectiveness he possessed. He needed her, not for the sake of Paradise, but for his own sake. And for the first time in his life, Shad felt filled, flooded, brimming over with love.

When he gazed down into her worried face, he was hard-pressed to control a lopsided grin.

"I'm an experienced man, Libby," he said softly, "but right now I feel like I'm just as new to this as you."

He brought his other hand up to cradle her face, tracing each thumb across a satiny cheek as he continued to speak. "I expect I'll shout for pure joy when we make love. Or I'll smile and sigh like some young and tender fool. I may even howl at the moon, darlin'. But I will never, ever laugh at you."

Libby stared up into the handsome face that once had seemed so hard, its planes sculpted in stone. But now the expression there was soft and absolutely sweet. She believed Shadrach Jones. Utterly. Completely. And she loved him with all her heart. The realization brought a happy little cry bursting forth from her throat.

"Shh." He glanced down the hall toward Andy's room while he pressed a finger against Libby's lips. "We don't want to get so carried away that we wake the little one."

"I nearly forgot," Libby said. "I confess I forgot for a moment there was anyone in the house, in the whole blessed world, but the two of us." She leaned away from his touch. "Maybe I should go check on her and make sure she's all right."

She barely had time to move a foot before Shad's solid arm circled her and locked her in place at his side. "Maybe you should just let her sleep." His voice had slipped a husky notch or two, and his dark eyes glittered in the dimly lit hall. "And come let me love you, Libby. Now."

After a last, fluttering glance down the hall, Libby gave in to the pull of his warm hand and let him lead her into the bedroom where he lit the lamp beside the bed, then turned down the wick until a fragile, almost magical gold illuminated the room and cast their shadows on the wall.

She watched then, wholly entranced, as the taller, broader shadow encompassed hers, consumed her as greedily as the real mouth that took possession of hers. She should have felt chilly, she thought, standing there in her damp nightgown, but Shad's big, warm hands supplied a heat that seared her skin and penetrated her flesh as they moved over her.

"Libby," he groaned, pulling away from her

mouth. "Climb into bed and keep warm while I wash up. You don't want to sleep with a man who smells like a burnt bunkhouse."

"I don't mind," she said.

"Well, I do." He turned her half circle, kissed her neck and gave her a gentle shove in the direction of the bed, then proceeded to unbutton his shirt and shrug out of it before walking to the washstand and pouring water from the pitcher to the bowl.

As he did, Shad noticed his hand was shaking. Damned if he'd ever been nervous about making love in the past two decades. But then it had never meant anything, he thought. And this meant everything. He'd meant what he'd said before, even if his intention had only been to reassure Libby. It was like his first time. Truly. It was like a second chance. A way to recapture his own lost—no, his stolen!—innocence by sharing this with the woman he loved. Funny, he thought. He hadn't washed up yet, but he already felt clean. Cleansed.

While he lathered his hands with a cake of soap that smelled like full-blown roses, Shad glanced in the mirror just in time to see Libby whisk her white gown over her head and stand beside the bed for a moment, naked as a goddess, while lamplight shimmered gold over her full breasts and her smooth hips and her long, lithe legs. She cast him a glance that caused his breath to jam in his chest—a glance of such pure seduction that he doubted she was even aware of the sensual set of her mouth or the heat radiating from her eyes—just before she scrambled under the covers.

She was Amos's daughter, no doubt about that. Having decided what she wanted, she knew just how to get it. A week or two ago, this knowledge along with that come-hither glance might have sent Shad running for his life in the opposite direction, but now he was glad, even proud, that he was the object of Libby's desire, that he was the man the lady wanted. He lathered up faster, rinsed off and barely dried off before he joined her in the bed.

"You smell like roses," she said with a sigh, fitting her smooth curves against him.

He chuckled. "Better than smelling like burnt pine or horse."

"Not better," she murmured. "Just different."

Libby took in another deep breath of him. Beneath the fragile fragrance of roses, there was the undiminished scent of male. She traced the tips of her fingers along the bunched muscles of his arm, across the sculpted planes of his chest, all the while amazed to find herself in bed with a man and astonished that she wasn't the least bit nervous or afraid. Not now.

Shad wouldn't laugh at her clumsiness or inexperience. He would teach her to make love, just as he'd taught her to waltz. He would lead her through the mysterious act of love the way he'd led her through that dance. With warm confidence. With patience. With tender care. Libby trusted him now. Completely.

Wanting to tell him, not knowing just how, the words suddenly seemed to tumble from her mouth. "Oh, Shad, I love you. I truly do. I never thought I'd say that. To anyone."

He was quiet for a moment then before he levered up on an elbow and gazed down at her. "I love you, too, Libby," he said, although the words came forth almost solemnly when he spoke them. "And I never thought I'd say those words either. Or feel what I'm feeling now.''

He gathered her hand and placed it against the hard curve of his chest. Beneath her palm, Libby felt the insistent drumming of his heart. The rhythm matched her own wild heartbeats.

"Here." She guided his hand toward her, wanting him to know just how gloriously their bodies were in tune. "Feel my heart. It's a perfect match."

But his hand only held flat and still a moment before it moved to curve gently beneath her breast. Then his mouth followed.

Libby was flooded with sensations she had never felt before. She was filled with a longing she had never known existed, much less one that could replace her blood with honey and turn all of her bones as limp as those of a rag doll. As Shad's hands moved over her, the heat inside her increased. Need rose up like a fever. Desire arced through her like a bolt of lightning, sizzling every muscle, shocking every nerve.

And when Shad's bronzed, lamp-lit body rose above her, when his warm weight covered her, when his firm hands urged her legs apart, and when he whispered, "Now, Libby. I have to have you now," that spoken need thundered through her and she met her lover—her love!—with a passion that was a perfect match for his.

Whatever Libby thought she understood about the coming together of men and women—the sparse details she had gleaned from books and Shula's melodramatic and highly unreliable descriptions—was inadequate if not completely wrong. There was a spiritual aspect of this physical union that Libby hadn't been prepared for, and when her whole body felt as if it were exploding, her soul felt as if it, too, were burning bright and fierce.

Later, lying in Shad's arms, letting her heart settle back to a normal pace, Libby wondered where she had been all her life never to have known this deepest desire, this highest ecstasy? The answer, of course, was that she had been in Saint Louis, a thousand miles away from Paradise. No. Not Paradise. A thousand miles away from Shadrach Jones.

She sighed and flattened her hand on the smooth, slick muscles of his back. "This is paradise," she said.

"Your daddy named it well," Shad replied, and placed a soft kiss on Libby's temple.

"No, I don't mean the place," Libby said. "I mean this. Us. It isn't about the ranch anymore, Shad, or my father's will. If I lost this place, it wouldn't matter. Not one bit. Not if I still had you."

His only reply was a rumble of appreciation deep in his throat while his hand smoothed along her arm and his lips drifted across her cheek.

"I spent fifteen long years in exile," she whispered. "So many years wishing so hard. To come back here. To be loved. And now..." Her voice faltered.

"Now what?"

"I didn't even know how to wish for *this*. It's too perfect. I'm not sure...well, I'm not altogether sure that I deserve it."

Shad raised up on an elbow and gazed down at her face, so lovely in its seriousness, so flushed still from their loving.

That loving—that passionate union of two bodies

and two souls—seemed to have taken him as much by surprise as it had Libby. In all his experience, Shad had never felt such searing pleasure. At the end, after he had come into her with a hot rush, he'd waited for the familiar chill to grip his heart and the urge to run to take possession of his every nerve as had always happened in the past. But it hadn't happened. Not this time.

And the lady hadn't laughed at him. He'd waited for that, too, but she had only sighed and melted more deeply into his arms.

"I truly don't deserve this," she said again, her breath warm against his neck and a small tremor resounding in her words.

Deserve it. Hell, Shad thought. If he'd gotten what he'd truly deserved, he'd have been shot dead by the Reverend Jones at the age of fourteen. And as for deserving this beautiful woman...

"Life's not about what you deserve, Libby," he told her quietly. "It's about what you get."

She smiled up at him. "That sounds like something my father would say."

"Amos would be the first to agree." He brushed a damp strand of hair from her forehead, then said, "God knows I don't deserve you. I've done some things...well, one thing in particular..."

"What?" she asked then when he appeared reluctant to continue.

"I probably should have told you before."

"Before?"

Shad dropped a kiss on the worried crease between her dark eyebrows. "Before loving you. Before I took what you can only give once, to one man."

"There's nothing you could tell me now that would

make me regret that, Shad. There's nothing you could say that would change my feelings for you.''

Shad wasn't so sure of that, so he riveted Libby with his gaze and moved his hand to her chin in order to prevent her from averting her eyes when he told her the truth. He thought he would be able to see instantly if her feelings changed. Expecting the worst, he spoke slowly and deliberately.

"What if I told you I'm probably wanted for murder in the Indian Territories?"

Libby didn't blink. Nothing on her face gave any indication of surprise or dismay or—as Shad had feared—disgust. Her reply came swiftly and with steely certainty.

"Then I'd say you'd been falsely accused."

A smile of undisguised relief spread across his lips. "I was."

"Tell me what happened, Shad."

In the twenty years since those disastrous events that had changed his life, the night that had scarred his soul and marked his dreams forever, Shad hadn't told a soul. He never thought he would, and yet he heard himself now, at Libby's behest, beginning to tell the story of his life. How an abandoned half-breed baby was given a name and a home, and then—after fourteen years—after his crime—after his shame— how that boy was thrown out of the only home he'd ever known.

He spoke quietly and calmly, and he didn't dwell overmuch on his stepmother's seductive behavior that last, long summer. Libby, after all, had only just surrendered her virginity and wasn't meant to hear such dark details. Still, he told her the truth about that night, and how the lady had laughed, and the brutal end when the Reverend Jones came up the stairs, shotgun cradled in his arms, and killed his unfaithful wife with a blast that instantly turned her white gown a bloody crimson.

And he told Libby how the preacher, his father, had stared at him then for the longest time while the gun barrels still smoked in his hand, and then Shad repeated, over the catch in his own voice, the last words he'd ever heard his father speak.

You run now. Before I change my mind and blow you to perdition, too. You run, Shadrach. And you run far, and keep on running, because when they come asking who killed this harlot, I plan to tell them it was you.

"I didn't kill the lady, Libby." He sighed roughly. "What I did was probably worse than murder. But you need to know this. I should have told you before."

Libby nestled more snugly against him. His body, so relaxed after they had made love, was coiled with tension now and slick with sweat. He didn't know what she was going to say, but he knew whatever it was would change his life forever. For better or for worse.

Her silence lengthened. It seemed interminable, and Shad could hear his own heart beating violently while he awaited her response.

"It wasn't your fault, Shad," she said at last. "That was no lady. Your stepmother was an evil creature. I'm glad she met a violent end. And I hurt, my dearest, for all the pain she caused you."

Her warm hand covered his heart then and her voice became soft and soothing as a lullaby. "You were a child, Shad. You were innocent. It wasn't your fault. Just like our little Andy. Perhaps if you imagine that your pain and suffering has helped you to understand hers, that might make it easier for you to bear. Something good has come out of all that evil.''

Hearing those softly spoken words caused something in Shad to let go. Some terrible weight seemed to lighten. The core of darkness in his soul seemed to brighten. He felt free all of a sudden, unfettered, for the first time in twenty long years. A hot sheen of tears burned his eyes.

Hell and damnation. It was one thing to confess his sins to Libby, but he didn't want her to see him cry. Ever.

''Speaking of little Andy,'' he said, using the first excuse that came to mind, ''maybe you ought to go check on her. Just in case.''

''All right,'' she replied without hesitation, as if she knew of his need to be alone.

Then, when Libby sat up and began to reach for her dressing gown, Shad caught her hand. He cleared his thick throat before he whispered, ''Come right back to me, Libby darlin'. We've got more loving to do before this night of ours is over.''

He lay there then, listening to Libby's soft footsteps going down the hall, letting his tears subside, thinking vaguely about ladies and little children and innocence both lost and found. Then he heard Libby cry out from Andy's room.

''She's gone! Andy's gone! Oh, my God! Somebody's stolen her away.''

Chapter Eighteen

Libby stood—her hand covering another scream lodged in the back of her throat—amid the shambles that had once been Andy's tidy room.

A primer lay open on the floor at the foot of the bed, torn copybook pages scattered all around it. At the window, one of the linen curtains dangled from its rod and one white sheer was ripped and went spilling over the sill and out the window like a waterfall. The bed linens were in wild disarray, but even so three small puppies slept there, snuggled in a heap.

It was the sight of those sleeping pups that terrified Libby and convinced her the child was gone. Andy would never leave her precious pets alone, unsupervised on the high bed. Not of her own volition, anyway.

Shad rushed past her, shirtless, still buttoning his pants. "Are you sure she's gone, Libby?" His eyes swept around the room. "Have you checked around the house? Downstairs?" he asked her before heading for the open window.

"No. I..."

"Never mind," Shad said then. "There's a ladder

down there." A curse ripped through his clenched teeth and his fist slammed into the sill. "He stole her right out from under our noses. Goddammit. I should have known."

"He? Who?" Libby blinked stupidly, unable to comprehend what had happened.

"Hoyt. That's who. Or one of his hired hooligans. They took her out the window."

"Oh, my God." Libby rushed to Shad's side now. She shoved the tattered curtain aside and stared down at the ladder on the ground below. "Andy," she wailed.

A tremor coursed through her. And guilt. Terrible guilt. It felt as if a leaden weight were pressing on her heart. Only moments ago she had felt so happy and so in love. Only moments ago she and Shad had been the only two people in the world. And during those moments Andy had been dragged from her innocent bed and wrenched out the window.

"It's my fault," Libby whispered. "I was selfish. Too swept away by my own happiness. I should have thought of Andy. I should have checked on her. It's all my fault."

"Hush." Shad's warm arms surrounded her then, and he pulled her solidly against himself. "You weren't selfish, Libby. It's not your fault."

Barely able to speak now, Libby just shook her head insistently.

"Listen to me." He shook her gently. "It wasn't your fault, Libby. I won't let you blame yourself, and I'm not going to let you blame me, either. Dammit, honey. Our loving was good and honest, not selfish. And Andy was already long gone by then."

"What?" She tipped her chin up. "What are you saying, Shad?"

"I'm telling you it didn't happen while we were making love, Libby. Don't you see? It was earlier. During the fire. Somebody set it to distract us."

"The...the fire?"

"Uh-huh. Whoever set that fire was the one who stole little Andy away."

Anger—a hot wave of it—replaced Libby's guilt. She pulled out of Shad's protective embrace and stepped back. "We've got to find her."

When she started for the door, Shad stopped her with a hand on each shoulder. "Settle down now. You won't find anybody out there in the dark, Libby." He glanced out the window toward the east. "It'll be first light in an hour or so. You can have all the hands saddle up then and head out. There's not a one of them who wouldn't ride twenty miles before breakfast to help you out, especially after last night."

Libby took what little comfort she could from that. "All right," she said. "I'll change into my riding clothes and be ready to go by sunup."

His grip tightened on her shoulders and his face darkened. "No," he said. "You won't. You're going to wait right here at the house where I know you'll be safe until I get back."

"I'll do no such thing," she answered. "If you're so worried about my safety, then you can ride with me."

"No, I can't." He let go of her shoulders in order to put on his shirt. "As soon as I get my boots on, I'm leaving."

"Leaving?"

"If I ride out right now, I can be at Hellfire just

after sunup, then one minute after that I'm going to be yanking Hoyt Backus out of his comfy bed and making him wish he'd never heard the word Paradise much less wanted a piece of it or stolen a sweet little girl to get it." Shad stabbed a final button through the placket of his shirt, then swore as he shoved the tails into his trousers. "And if he hurt even one hair on her head, by God, I swear I'll kill him."

Rage hardened every plane of his face. It frightened Libby just to see it. "Are you so sure it was Hoyt?"

"I don't know who the hell else it could have been, do you?"

No, she didn't. Libby shook her head and then she put a hand on Shad's arm. "Just be careful. Please."

"I'm always careful," he said. "Just see that you stay here so I don't have to be worrying about you, too."

Libby nodded, already thinking about which horse she'd ask Eb to saddle for her and in which direction she'd search first. East, probably. Yes, east. Out around the elbow bend of Caliente Creek.

"You needn't worry about me," she said. It wasn't a lie, exactly. "Just find Andy, Shad. Soon. Please."

Shad didn't have to drag that big old grizzled coyote out of bed, as it turned out. As he approached the main house at Hellfire, the first gold rays of the sun struck the portly lord of the manor as he stood on his front porch striking a match and lighting up his first cheroot of the day.

"'Mornin', Shad," he called through a small cloud of blue smoke. "What brings you over at the crack of dawn?"

Shad dismounted. "I'm looking for someone," he said as his boots connected with the ground.

On the porch, Hoyt dragged on his cigar and blew a hard stream of smoke from the side of his mouth. "If it's Miss Shula you're looking for, you can stop right there. This is where she wants to be. And with me."

Hoyt jabbed the cigar into a corner of his mouth before he added, "We sat up half the night making wedding plans so I expect she's plumb tuckered out. Anyone trying to wake her will have to get past me."

At the foot of the porch steps, Shad stood with one hand resting on his gun. "It's not Miss Shula I'm looking for, Hoyt. What did you do with Andy?"

"Andy?" The big man squinted against the rising smoke. "Who's that? What're you talking about?"

"I'm talking about the little girl you had snatched from her bed at Paradise. The little girl you're using to get to me. It's too late, Hoyt. Miss Libby and I are getting married. Whatever hope you had of taking over Paradise is gone. And whatever you thought you'd accomplish by stealing a child isn't going to work. Now tell me where she is so I don't have to kill you."

Hoyt dashed his cigar to the porch boards and ground it out with his heel before coming down the stairs. "You best remember where you are, Jones, before making threats like that."

"I know where I am," Shad growled. "And I know what I'm saying."

The two men would have been nose to nose then if it hadn't been for Hoyt's imposing belly. Still they glared across the space between them until the front door slammed and the tinkle of bracelets resounded in the morning air.

"What in the world is going on out here?" Shula's voice was still husky with sleep, and her red curls tumbled down the back of her dressing gown. "Oh, it's you, Shad. Well, if Libby sent you to fetch me back, you can just tell her—"

"I'm here looking for Andy," he said, cutting her off and keeping his eyes fixed hard on Hoyt. "Now what the hell have you done with her?"

"Andy!" Shula exclaimed, coming down the steps to stand beside Hoyt. "What's happened to Andy?"

"That's what I'm here to find out." Shad jerked a thumb at the big man. "Ask him."

Shula blinked up. "Hoyt, honey?"

He swore roughly then groped in his pockets for another cigar, and swore again when he came up empty-handed. "You're barking up the wrong tree here, Shad. Believe me. Once I got a look at this pretty little thing here, any notions I had about taking over Paradise just flew right out of my brain." Hoyt looped a beefy arm around Shula and pulled her closer. "This is all I want in the whole damn world."

Shula smiled and plastered herself closer to his side, her bracelets jingling happily. "Aren't you sweet?" she murmured. "Hoyt didn't have anything to do with Andy's being missing, Shad. He was with me." Her eyelashes fluttered coquettishly. "All night."

Amazingly enough, and to his total dismay, Shad believed them both. Hoyt was standing there looking like a sixteen-year-old boy in love for the first time in his life. And Shula Kingsland didn't seem all that far behind him in the heartstring department. Either that or the raspberry tart was a far better actress than he'd ever given her credit for.

But if they were telling the truth and it wasn't Hoyt or one of his men, then who...? His eyes snapped toward Shula then, meeting her wide eyes, and in that instant, it was as if they shared the same sudden and horrifying thought.

Shula's mouth dropped open in an astonished little *O.* "Andy's father," she whispered. "Maybe he did follow us. Maybe the poor little thing was telling the truth all along."

A cold fear gripped Shad's heart. He felt frozen with dread, barely able to speak.

"Can you spare me some men, Hoyt?" he asked.

"As many as you need," the big man replied immediately. "Just let me get my sidearm and I'll ride along with you, too."

Libby pulled back on the reins of the big roan mare. Her eyes hurt from squinting into the distance. Her head ached. The rest of her ached, too, but nothing so much as her heart.

Andy, Andy, where are you? Why did this have to happen just when everything looked as if it were going to work out fine for all of us? Shad and I were planning to marry, then make you our own little girl. Your wish was about to come true. My own wish, too.

The thought of Shad reminded Libby that he was going to be furious when he discovered she had donned a shirt and a pair of denims the moment he had left, then had set out on her own just after sunrise. But she didn't care about that now. Let him be mad. She'd deal with his anger later. All that mattered right now was finding Andy. Finding her soon. And safe. Please, God, let the child be safe.

The sun was well up now, already promising another day of relentless Texas heat. Its fierce rays lit the narrow stream of water in Caliente Creek, just to Libby's right. Why she'd chosen to search here first, she wasn't sure. Perhaps because this was the spot where she and Andy had been shot at not so long ago. Perhaps because it was her favorite spot at Paradise. Perhaps she'd had no reason at all. But she had to start someplace.

She gave a forlorn sigh, and then, suddenly, her gaze was drawn to a speck of white, bright against the green of a prickly pear. Libby nudged her knees into the mare and rode closer before dismounting. The speck turned out to be a piece of paper. A fresh piece, not an old weathered and yellowed scrap. She held it up to the light then and her heart jumped when she recognized the watermark. Andy's copybook!

Just then a second piece of paper caught her eyes, and then another several yards away. They were clues. Like Hansel and Gretel with their breadcrumbs, Andy was leaving a trail of paper scraps.

One by one, Libby collected them, searching each for further clues. But there was no writing, no secret code or arrows pointing hopefully. Still Libby was certain that Andy had been here and had left these papers in her wake. When was she here? And, more importantly, where, oh, where was she now?

Libby scanned the surrounding mesquite trees frantically, then dropped her gaze to the ground, trying to make some sense of patterns in the grass and marks in the dry dirt, wishing Shad were here now to detect more than mere crushed blades of grass and vague, meaningless swirls in the dirt. She needed help, she realized, but in the time it would take her to ride back to the house, Andy might be even farther away.

"Damn!" She slapped a fist into her palm and launched the toe of her riding boot at a squat prickly pear. "Damn, damn, damn!"

"Swear all you want, you child-stealing bitch. Go ahead. It ain't going to help you any now."

Libby whirled around, but she didn't have to see the dark, ugly features of the man standing behind her to know it was John Rowan. Just hearing that horrible voice had been enough. As Andy had said, he sounded as if he'd eaten gravel as a child.

In that instant, Libby comprehended that Andy had been right all along. It was her devil of a father who had been stalking her like some voracious beast. This had nothing to do with Paradise or Hoyt or Shad. Not with anyone or anything else. It had been John Rowan, Andy's father, all along.

"Where's Andy? What have you done with her?" Libby demanded, her eyes burning into his.

The man wasn't much taller than Libby. His chin and cheeks were pitted, as if he'd fallen face first into one of his gravelly meals and those rocks had left a lifelong impression. His lips were jagged, and they pulled back now in a cruel and sadistic grin. "Where's who? Oh, are you talking about my Amanda? My own, sweet, soft little girl?"

At the sound of those words, Libby felt her stomach clench, as if she were going to be sick. "You monster," she screamed. "Where's Andy? If you've touched her, I'll see that you hang for it."

There were several yards between them, and when John Rowan began to move toward her, Libby noticed he was limping badly. His face, already contorted with hate and rage, twisted even more with pain.

"You're hurt." Her tone was cold and held no sympathy. It was merely an observation, one she was more than a little happy to make, for although Andy's father wasn't tall, he appeared quite muscular. She knew she was no match for him in strength, so his every weakness proved to be to her advantage now.

"Yeah, well." Rowan snorted. "I busted my damn ankle falling off a ladder back at that highfalutin house of yours."

"It was you who set the fire," she said accusingly.

"Sure it was me. Wish I'd burned the whole place down, too. My foot hurts like hell, lady, but it'll heal and the pain ain't gonna stop me from taking my Amanda back where she belongs."

"Over my dead body, Rowan." Libby's spine snapped stiff. She widened her stance, prepared to stand her ground when the man lunged for her and grabbed her by the front of her shirt.

"Over your dead body, lady?" he growled. "I ain't decided about that yet. But it could be. Yes, indeed. It just could be." He tugged her roughly. "Now you shut up and come with me."

If the fire had been a diversion, then Shad figured little Andy had been gone at least ten hours. She could be miles away by now, especially if her father had a mount. If the man had been afoot, though, he might not have gotten all that far, especially with a reluctant little girl.

It made sense, then, to plot a big circle around Paradise and Hellfire and to begin searching at the farthest point, drawing the circle smaller and smaller in the hope that their quarry was still inside. Between them, the two ranches had come up with about forty riders, all of them eager to find the missing child.

Forty-two riders, if Shad counted himself and Hoyt. Forty-three, if he counted Libby, who had ignored his instructions to wait at the house. After confronting Hoyt, Shad had ridden back to Paradise to question Libby about Andy's father, since Shula didn't seem to know all that much about him, other than her description of the man as "worse than slime and lower than a snake." Libby was long gone, though. Eb told him she'd ridden out not ten minutes after Shad had left for Hellfire.

"And you just let her go?" he growled at the old man.

"Wasn't much I could do, Shad. Miss Libby had that Amos look about her. She was going, and that was that."

Forcing his temper to cool, Shad patted Eb's sagging shoulder. "It's not your fault, Eb. Which way did she ride? Do you recollect?"

Eb pointed east. "Guess that don't help much, but it's a start."

Not much of a start, Shad thought, as he caught up with Hoyt near the elbow bend of Caliente Creek. The big man had dismounted and was squatting beside a prickly pear, studying it thoughtfully.

"Take a look at this," he called to Shad, pointing to a piece of paper that was wedged into the cactus leaves. "Wouldn't surprise me if that little one tried to leave a trail. What do you think?"

Shad thought Hoyt Backus was a hell of a lot more optimistic than he was. Then his heart froze when he glanced down and saw the distinctive hoofprints of the big roan that Libby had been riding. Interspersed with those were the prints of a man's boots.

"I think," he said somberly, "we're looking for Libby now, too."

Chapter Nineteen

When the sun disappeared below the horizon, darkness came on fast. Thank God, Libby thought. If she deemed this one of the worst days of her life, she could only imagine how poor, terrified Andy was feeling. The child's eyes had been red rimmed and glassy with tears all day as she'd trudged along, her fearful gaze continually skittering toward her father, then away.

But John Rowan hadn't touched her yet. If there was anything to be grateful for, Libby knew it was that. Her presence was keeping the monster at bay. For the time being, anyway. And now she was grateful for the darkness, as well. Perhaps, just perhaps, she and Andy had a chance to escape.

Under John Rowan's constant, even frenzied vigilance, escape had been impossible. The man's wild, beady eyes had flashed from Andy to Libby and back all day long. Even more threatening than his gaze was the long-barreled pistol he clutched at all times, waving it crazily, mostly at Libby, and swearing again and again that he'd shoot her dead ''in the wink of a gnat's eye'' if she so much as lifted a finger to help his little Amanda get away. *His sweet, soft Amanda. His little love ever since her mama had passed away. His own in every sense.*

All day, there had been nothing Libby could do but keep walking, gnashing her teeth behind the gag she wore, thinking and plotting but doing nothing. Now, however, with darkness settling in all around them, she thought she might have a chance at least to loosen Andy's bonds and let the child make a run for it.

What she'd do after that to save herself, heaven only knows. Like Andy, her own wrists were tied behind her back and a strip of cloth was fastened hurtfully around her mouth to silence her. Not that screaming for help would have done any good. They had been forced to crouch down once to hide from a lone Paradise cowhand, but for several hours now, Libby had had the terrible feeling that there was no one within miles.

What baffled her was how very alone the three of them seemed when she was certain most of the hands at Paradise had been sent out in search of Andy. Surely if Libby had found John Rowan as quickly as she had this morning, even though it was quite by accident, the experienced men of Paradise could have tracked the three of them down by now.

Shad was surely on their trail with his keen, dark eyes and his intimate knowledge of every acre, every square inch of Paradise. Libby tried not to think about his intimate knowledge of her. This wasn't the time or place to savor the memories of their lovemaking. She would do that later, she vowed, after this ordeal was over.

She shifted her jaw now, easing the pressure of the cloth that bound her. Her lips felt numb and her tongue felt dry as leather, but Libby consoled herself with the thought that because of her presence, the monster hadn't yet been able to lay a filthy hand on his daughter. It was also some consolation that the monster appeared to be in excruciating pain from his injured ankle.

Earlier, he had ridden Libby's horse, cursing down at them while she and Andy stumbled along beside him. But the roan mare had bolted several hours ago—Libby had no idea why—and afterward Rowan had been forced to limp, slower and slower, until he stopped here, cursing, beside a gnarled old mesquite tree, sweat dripping off his brow, apparently in too much pain to go another step.

"C'mere, girl," he commanded Andy gruffly.

When she approached him, he pulled a wicked-looking knife from a sheath at his waist. "Turn around," he told her, and then proceeded to slice through the rope that bound her wrists.

"Build us a fire, and be quick about it." He sheathed the knife, then picked up his pistol again and pointed it menacingly at Libby. "Don't do anything stupid like trying to run away or I'll shoot your fairy godmother here right through her meddling heart."

Libby nodded to the clearly distressed child, angling her head toward a pile of dry brush to encourage her to do as she'd been ordered. Build him a fire, Andy, she was thinking. Go on and build the biggest, blazingest, brightest bonfire ever. One that can be seen for miles and miles.

"What the hell's he doing?" Hoyt rasped. The big man was hunkered down in the darkness, his ample belly flattened against the ground, his head close by Shad's shoulder, his eyes narrowed down the barrel of a rifle. "Don't that fool know that fire's nothing but a dead, dumb giveaway to his whereabouts?"

"He knows," Shad answered in a voice that was more growl than whisper.

The two men were concealed in the thick brush less than two hundred yards from their quarry's resting place. They'd been within a quarter mile all day, sometimes even closer. Close enough once for Shad to lob a rock at the big roan's flank and spook her so she'd bolt. Always near enough to see the ugly Navy Colt in John Rowan's jittery hand. Each time the bastard would jerk the long barrel in Libby's direction, Shad's heart would stop momentarily. That had happened so often today he thought he'd probably shaved at least a year off his life.

Hoyt wanted to plug Rowan right between the eyes. He'd been yammering about it for hours. "It don't make no sense," he kept saying, "trailing a man when all you have to do is shoot him and bring him down, for God's sake."

Easy enough for him to say, Shad kept thinking, when it wasn't his woman and his child in the line of fire. Maybe the ring wasn't on Libby's finger yet or Andy's adoption papers signed, but in his heart Shad already claimed them both as his own.

"We'll wait," he said each time Hoyt got trigger-happy. He had no idea how good a shot the big man was. Hell, if he fired a gun the way he talked, there'd be bullets spraying all over creation, and Libby or Andy might just get hit in the cross fire.

But that danger wasn't the only reason Shad was reluctant to end this nasty business with bullets. Part of his reluctance was Libby and the way she despised violence. He wasn't so sure she'd ever forgive him if he took John Rowan's life. Mostly, though, Shad was holding back because of the child.

He'd had ample time to consider his alternatives during this long day, and he had concluded that he didn't want young Andy to witness a murder that might cause her to spend the rest of her life in a stew of guilt and blame. The way Shad had spent his life after his stepmother's murder. By God, if he could spare the child that horror, he would. Whatever it took. Because Andy was innocent. Because twenty years ago he'd been innocent, too, only he hadn't known it then.

"We'll wait," Shad said again now.

Beside him, Hoyt swore harshly under his breath, all the while keeping his rifle in his arms and John Rowan in his sights.

"There." Rowan sliced through Libby's gag with one quick and brutal stroke of his knife, then he hobbled back to the other side of the fire where he'd ordered Andy to sit. He lowered himself beside the girl, cut away her gag, too, then reached into a canvas bag, extracted a metal flask and took a long drink from it.

"Go ahead and scream your fool head off if you want," he told Libby, pointing the knife at her, taking a second swig while dark liquid dribbled down his chin.

Scream! Libby couldn't even manage a whisper at first through her numb lips and bruised, dry mouth. What was the man up to? she wondered. At first when he'd ordered Andy to build a fire, Libby had thought he was simply stupid. Didn't he realize the light could be seen for miles? But now that he'd removed their gags and made it possible for them to cry out for help, even encouraged her to do it, she realized he wasn't stupid at all, but crafty. The man was obviously in too much pain to walk anymore. He was using his knife now to slice down the side of one boot.

"You want someone to find us," she said calmly, surprised that her voice, so long unused, was nearly as rough and gravelly as Rowan's.

"What I want is transportation," he replied, gingerly removing a sock while he grimaced with pain. His ankle was badly swollen, nearly twice what would have been its normal size, and darkly bruised. "I can't walk no more, so I might be willing to trade your worthless, child-stealing life for a horse or a wagon. Go ahead. Yell." He picked up his pistol and pointed it at her. "Yell real loud."

Libby's lips drew together in a tight, stubborn line. She'd wanted to cry out for help all day, but the gag had prevented it. Now she was free to scream, but since it was the monster who needed help, she'd be damned if she'd be the one to provide it.

"I said yell." He moved his thumb to pull back the hammer on the gun. "Now."

Libby merely glared at him through the flames of the fire.

''Yell, God damn you.''

She would have stubbornly crossed her arms if they hadn't been bound behind her. As it was, Libby battened down her lips even more and hardened her gaze. She wouldn't scream. She wouldn't yell for help when that was precisely what the monster wanted. If he traded her life for a horse, as he had threatened to do, then Andy would be alone with him. Libby wasn't going to let that happen.

''You'll scream, all right,'' John Rowan told her now. He swigged from the flask again, then his wet mouth slid into a leer as he reached toward Andy, his big hand flattening across the front of the little girl's shirt. Still staring at Libby, daring her to keep silent now, his hand began to slowly—slowly and insidiously—caress his daughter's chest.

Libby screamed, and kept screaming until her throat was raw and burning.

Hoyt Backus let out a long, low curse. ''Is that snake doing what I think he's doing?''

At first Shad didn't reply even though he was looking in the same direction as Hoyt, listening to Libby's screams and witnessing the shameful, deliberate violation of an innocent little girl. He was trying to take in deep, slow breaths, to force himself to do nothing when every nerve in his body was demanding immediate and violent action. He was trying not to explode when rage was burning through him like a wildfire.

Stick to your plan, he told himself. Don't let that bastard push you into making a mistake that might cost Andy her life if not the better part of her soul. Trust your instincts on this. Wait. Wait him out.

Hoyt swore again, then he elbowed Shad in the rib cage. "What the hell's the matter with you, Jones?"

"Nothing. I said don't shoot, Hoyt, and I meant it."

"What's wrong with your eyes, man? Can't you see what that son of a bitch—"

"I can see," Shad growled. "And I can see a man who probably hasn't eaten in a long time, who's hurting now and trying to drink himself into a pretty good stupor. After he polishes off that flask, he won't last long."

"Yeah, but..."

"We'll wait." Shad forced a grim smile in the darkness. "Hell, even the devil has to drop off to sleep now and then, Hoyt."

And then the devil called out into the dark, his voice like rough sandpaper. "I know somebody's out there. I can feel you. So listen up. I want a wagon. Tonight. Now. I'll trade the woman for it. You hear?"

Both Shad and Hoyt heard, though neither one replied. There would be no negotiations, they seemed to agree silently. No trades. No deals with the devil.

Every time Libby was certain John Rowan had finally fallen asleep, his chin would jerk up from his chest and his eyes would blink furiously for a moment while the gun twitched in his hand. Each time the monster snapped out of his alcoholic stupor, he would bellow into the dark beyond their fire about trading her for a wagon. Nobody answered him. Libby despaired that anybody even heard him except for herself and Andy.

"It's going to be all right, Andy," she kept saying quietly to the little girl. "I won't let him hurt you. Not ever again. Don't worry."

The child kept trying her best to summon up a brave smile in response. "It's not so much me I'm worried about right now, Miss Libby. It's...it's..." Her eyes brimmed with tears.

"What, honey?" Libby whispered.

"It's my puppies. Nobody fed them last night. And maybe not today, either." Tears coursed down her pale cheeks now, glistening in the firelight. Because her hands had been bound again, she couldn't wipe them away. "I'm awful worried about those pups, Miss Libby. Who'll take care of them? Who'll see that they get warm milk? What if...?"

"Shh. Hush now, Andy." Libby glanced at John Rowan, whose eyelids had begun to flag at half-mast again and whose chin was sagging once more toward his chest. Maybe this time, she thought, the monster would fall asleep and stay that way. Maybe—Lord willing—he would fall asleep before Libby and Andy succumbed to their own exhaustion.

At any other time, her instinct would have been to dissuade Andy from talking about anything that caused her such distress. But right now Libby was almost glad that the child was more concerned for the well being of her puppies than she was for herself.

"I expect Shad's taking good care of them, honey," she whispered reassuringly, at the same time that she hoped he wasn't, while she prayed that Shadrach Jones was nowhere near those pups but close by.

Shad edged closer to the campfire. On his belly, moving forward an inch at a time, silent as a snake. It was the first time in his life he wished he were a smaller, lighter man. Each time John Rowan called out about his wagon, Shad took the opportunity to move forward a little more.

He was about twenty feet away now, close enough to see that Rowan's hand had loosened some on his pistol and that the man wasn't all that long for consciousness. The sight of Libby tore at his heart at the same time it encouraged him. Just like him, she was watching, waiting for a chance to escape. His sad little Libby. No. That wasn't true anymore. She was his all right, but she wasn't sad. She was strong now and brave as any man he'd ever known. By God, he swore to himself, when this nightmare was over...

Suddenly the clatter of a fast-approaching wagon obliterated all Shad's thoughts. What the hell? He thought Hoyt had agreed with him that there would be no deals. No wagon. At his back then, he heard Hoyt shouting. "Whoa, now. Slow down there, honey." And then he barely had time to roll out of the way of two tons of horseflesh and a hundred pounds of redhead who was whipping their reins.

John Rowan's head snapped up at the sound of the horses' hooves and the squeak of the wagon wheels. He struggled to his feet. "'Bout time," he grunted.

Libby struggled up, too. No. This couldn't be, she thought. Did somebody actually believe that trading her for a wagon was any kind of solution? Didn't they know what would happen to Andy if her father carted her away? Alone?

She peered into the darkness, trying to see who was driving the wagon, but as it drew nearer, even though she couldn't see the driver, Libby could hear the distinct and familiar jangle of bracelets. Shula! What in the name of heaven did she think she was doing?

Libby was about to call out to her sister when John Rowan shoved roughly past her, knocking her to the ground.

The wagon screeched to a halt a few feet away. "Don't you dare hurt my sister!" Shula screamed. "And don't you touch that little girl again, you monster."

"Get outta that wagon," Rowan commanded.

"I will not."

"Get out or I'll shoot you, you damn interfering female." Rowan wasn't waving the pistol now, but rather pointing it directly between Shula's eyes.

For a moment Libby couldn't move. Her first instinct was to rush to her sister's aid, but now that Rowan was distracted, she realized it was the perfect time—now or never, she thought—for Andy to escape.

"Run," she told the child. "Run for all you're worth, Andy. Now."

Instead of taking flight, though, Andy stood there as if her feet were nailed to the ground, staring at her father and Shula.

"Scoot, Andy," Libby hissed. "Now. Run."

"Stand still, Andy." Shad's voice sounded calm and low as he stepped out of the darkness into the circle of campfire light. "Just stand still, honey." He thumbed back the hammer on his gun as if for emphasis.

Libby had never been so happy to see anybody in her whole life, but his gaze flicked past her. "Shoot that gun, Rowan, and it'll be the last move you ever make."

Now Hoyt Backus emerged like a huge grizzly from the dark on the opposite side of the fire, his rifle aimed at Rowan. "Like Shad said, you even twitch a finger, mister, and you're dead."

The next minute seemed to last an eternity to Libby. John Rowan kept his pistol trained on Shula while Shad and Hoyt kept Rowan in their sights. Other than a twig popping in the fire, everything and everyone was silent. Lethally silent. As much as she hated violence and guns, Libby thought she'd never been so glad to see two men with weapons. This was violence in the service of goodness, she thought. Somebody do something, please, she thought.

Shad, meanwhile, was hoping nobody would make a move, for there were no good moves in a standoff like this. There was only death. He had angled himself as much as possible between Libby and Andy and Rowan's pistol. If there was going to be shooting, he figured he could take a bullet or two and survive them well enough. Still, he prayed that hotheaded Hoyt would stay cool and they could somehow talk Rowan into putting down his weapon.

It was the hotheaded redhead, though, who upset the delicate balance of the standoff.

"Well, this is a pretty picture," she said from her perch on the wagon seat, adding a resonant little snort and a quick jangle of her bracelets for emphasis. "Three great big men all standing around, twiddling their guns. I'm getting tired of this. And I'm tired of being out in this chilly night air. I can feel my hair curling up like corkscrews.''

''Shula, honey,'' Hoyt pleaded.

But the words were hardly out of his mouth before Shula shrieked like a banshee and flung herself directly on top of John Rowan. With the firelight playing over her deep rose-colored silk dress and red satin petticoats and wild auburn curls, she looked like a ball of fire striking Rowan and knocking him to the ground. His pistol disappeared in the chaos of clothes between them.

Then, almost before anyone could comprehend what was happening, a muffled shot sounded and both Shula and John Rowan lay absolutely still.

''Dear God,'' Libby cried. She took a step forward, but Shad's hand on her arm restrained her.

''Stay back,'' he told her as he cautiously approached the tangled heap of clothes. With his gun pointed, Shad put a boot on Rowan's arm at the same time he reached to pull Shula away.

Libby shrieked again when she saw the blood that darkened the front of her sister's dress. Then Shula opened her eyes, looked down at her bodice and shrugged.

''Oh, for heaven's sake, Libby. It's not my blood. It's his.'' She sighed. ''Either way, I guess this dress is ruined.''

By now Hoyt had his arms around Shula, allowing Shad to bend down and roll Rowan onto his back.

''Shot right through the heart,'' Shad said softly, not wanting Andy to hear.

''Ha!'' Shula jangled her bracelets furiously. ''That's assuming he had one.'' She turned toward

Andy then. "Honey, I'm sorry. It was an accident," she said briskly. "I didn't mean to kill him, but I have to say I think you'll be a lot better off now that he won't be around to torment you anymore."

"Shula," Libby hissed. Good grief. Maybe she was even a little bit glad that John Rowan was dead and no longer a threat to his daughter, but that didn't mean this was going to be easy for Andy to endure. Despite everything the man had done, it was horrible that the little girl had had to witness his violent death.

She couldn't tell much from Andy's expression. Her face was pale and her eyes were glistening in the firelight, but she didn't appear to be crying. In fact, she looked almost calm. Much more than Libby would have anticipated under the circumstances.

Shad moved close to Andy. He squatted down and began loosening the bonds that held her wrists behind her. "Here. Let's get this rope off, honey, then we'll take you home." Slowly, almost subtly while he was untying her, he was also turning her so she wouldn't be looking at her father's corpse.

Andy turned back, rubbing her wrists. Then she took a tentative step forward, toward her father's lifeless body.

"Honey, don't," whispered Libby, reaching out to stop her.

Shad grasped Libby's hand. "It's all right, Libby. Let her do it her way."

They stood there watching as Andy slowly approached John Rowan's body, not knowing whether the child would inflict more violence on the man who had hurt her in so many ways or whether she would scream or faint dead away or simply stand there mute.

"It's not your fault, Miss Shula," Andy said, gazing down on the body. "And it's for the best. Now my papa is with my mama, where he always wanted to be."

She looked over her shoulder at Libby and Shad, her face oddly peaceful, eerily mature. "It wasn't my fault, either. It's just that he missed her terribly and I guess I reminded him of her so much."

Shad wouldn't have bet a plug nickel that John Rowan was anywhere near heaven, but if that helped his daughter accept his death, and the pain he'd inflicted on her, then so be it.

He wound his arm around Libby's waist, drawing her close. "It's over now," he said softly. "Let's take our daughter home."

Chapter Twenty

Libby slipped her hand through the crook of Shad's arm. They were standing at the rail of the side-wheeler, *Star of Texas,* as it steamed into the harbor at Corpus Christi. "Look. There's Eb," she said, pointing toward the big red-and-black coach parked near the dock. She waved happily. "Oh, it's so good to be home."

Shad slanted her a warm smile, one that made the butterflies flutter deep inside her. A smile that drew a soft sigh from her lips.

"Still, I hate to see our honeymoon end."

Her husband's smile hitched up a little more at the corners. "What makes you think it'll ever end, Mrs. Jones?"

Even after four weeks, the name startled Libby slightly. It still required a tiny mental shift to realize that Shad was referring to her. Elizabeth Kingsland Jones. Mrs. Shadrach Jones.

It hadn't been easy leaving Andy just two days after the death of her father. They had wanted to take her with them, first to Corpus Christi where they in-

tended to find a preacher and then meet with old Bob
Cleland about Amos's will. After that, they planned
to go on to Saint Louis to begin adoption proceedings
and to see to the disposition of Libby and Shula's
property there. *If* there was anything left after Shula's
mismanagement.

But Andy had refused to leave her puppies, and in
the end both Libby and Shad agreed that maybe it
was best for the child to remain behind with Shula at
Hellfire.

Heaven knows they'd enjoyed their time alone. On
more than one day in Saint Louis the honeymooners
hadn't even left their hotel room, not to mention the
big brass bed situated there. Why she'd ever dis-
dained marriage, Libby had no idea. But then being
married to a man as warm and gentle and generous
as Shad was far different, she supposed, from being
married to a man as cold and selfish as Amos Kingsland.

Her mother had chosen poorly twice. Libby knew
that now. She, on the other hand, had chosen once,
and well, and for always. That it happened to be because of her father's will didn't bother her. Shadrach
Jones was her destiny, her perfect mate. And now her
fondest hope was that Shula would find the same fulfillment in her marriage to Hoyt Backus. And then
Andy, when her time finally came.

She felt warm in a way that had nothing to do with
the August sun. Even Shad's complexion appeared a
deeper, warmer bronze, as if this love of theirs had
altered them physically, as well as emotionally.

Eb confirmed that when he greeted them. "I'll be
damned. If you two don't look happy, then I don't

know what happy looks like. Marriage suits you, Shad. You, too, Miss Libby.''

Once they had loaded all their luggage into the boot of the coach, along with the few boxes of mementos salvaged from the house in Saint Louis, Libby sighed. ''Take us home, Eb. I can't wait to get back to Paradise.''

''Well, you will, Miss Libby. You will,'' Eb said, then added almost as an afterthought, '''Cept just not today.''

Shad immediately raked the old man with a fierce glare. ''Is there something going on that I ought to know about, Eb?''

''What's wrong?'' Libby asked at the same time.

''Nothing's wrong, Miss Libby. But...well...I guess you could say there's definitely something going on.''

Shad continued to glare at Eb. ''At Paradise?''

''Nope. At Hellfire. Hoyt and Miss Shula are tying the knot today. Seems all the satin and lace and gewgaws she ordered from back East arrived last week. Then she commenced to keep half the women in the county sewing day and night. Soon as her dress was done, that little spitfire wasn't about to wait to wear it. So the wedding's today and I'm to get you two to Hellfire by five o'clock.'' He rolled his eyes. ''Or else.''

Libby nestled deep in the circle of Shad's arms as the coach sped north. ''It'll be so good to see Andy.'' She laughed softly. ''I expect she and your new sister-in-law have been irritating the daylights out of each other these past few weeks.''

"Wouldn't surprise me," Shad murmured, rubbing his cheek against Libby's temple. "You're about to get yourself a new brother-in-law. Maybe a slew of redheaded nieces and nephews, too."

"Oh, Lord. I hadn't thought about that." Libby laughed again, then tipped her chin up to meet her husband's gaze. "Speaking of breeding programs..." she said.

Shad's dark eyes glittered. "Are you referring to gentlemen cows now, Mrs. Jones, or are you expressing a fond desire to populate Paradise?"

"Both."

"My little Libby." His voice was soft as velvet. "We'll have beautiful, dark-haired babies."

She nodded, adding dreamily, "And beautiful, chocolate-colored cattle."

"Thousands of them."

"Babies or cows?" Libby asked.

"Both, darlin'. Both."

With the speeding coach rocking her like a cradle and Shad's warm arms curled around her, Libby drifted off to sleep, unfazed at the notion of having thousands of babies now that she'd discovered the thousands of pleasures in making them.

Eb pulled the horses to a stop in front of the big house at Hellfire at five o'clock sharp. No sooner had the coach stopped than Hoyt Backus—dressed in top hat and tails—loped down the front stairs.

"Hot damn," he called up to Eb. "We said five and durned if it isn't, right on the nose. Good job, Eb." After a few more "hot damns" and hoots of joy, he wrenched open the coach's door.

"Welcome home, honey. You, too, Shad. Step on out now. There's gonna be a wedding."

His giant paws lifted Libby to the ground, setting her on the ground as delicately as if she were a porcelain figurine. She was flustered, nevertheless.

"Now? Right this minute?" She batted at the wrinkles on the front of her traveling suit and then lifted her hands to fuss with her hair. "Shula will have a fit when she sees me looking like this. Surely there's time to freshen up a bit."

Hoyt grasped her elbow and began to usher her up the front stairs. "Sorry, honey. This wedding's set to go off right now. And besides..." He paused and winked down at her. "If you think my pretty little bride gives two cents what anybody looks like but her, then you've just got another think coming."

Just behind her, Libby could hear Shad's deep chuckle of agreement.

"You're absolutely right, Hoyt, honey," Libby said. "Let's get on with this wedding."

Hellfire's parlor was swagged with silks and scented with rose petals. There were at least fifty guests seated on small gilt chairs. Libby recognized several people from her father's funeral, including his attorney, Bob Cleland, whose eyes twinkled as she walked past him.

"There you go, honey." Hoyt gestured to a small chair near the fireplace.

Libby tucked her wrinkled skirt beneath her, sat, then immediately bobbed up again. "Isn't there time just to say a quick hello to Andy?"

"Andy?" Hoyt scratched his head.

"The little girl, Hoyt," Shad said, a note of irritation in his voice. "How is she? You been treating her all right?"

"Oh. Andy! I clean forgot. Have we been treating her all right? Hmm. Well, I guess you'll have to be the judge of that, Shad. Sit down. Go on. Sit. Take a load off." He winked at Libby, then grinned as he turned to leave. "You just sit tight, the both of you. Your Amanda'll be along in a minute."

"Amanda," Libby whispered to Shad as she settled in her chair. "If he calls her that, Hoyt probably hasn't paid much attention to her. And what with all her fussing over this wedding, I doubt if Shula's even looked at that poor little girl these past few weeks."

"Maybe we shouldn't have left her so soon after her father's death. Maybe we should have insisted she go along with us. Maybe..." Libby was half tempted then to bounce right out of her seat and go in search of Andy. She would have, too, if Shad hadn't grasped her hand in his.

He was looking toward the silk-swagged doorway to the parlor from the vestibule. His lips were curved in the gentlest of smiles. "Maybe you shouldn't fret so much," he said, gesturing for her to look in the same direction.

Libby turned to look and her breath caught in her throat. There, poised in the doorway, stood a little girl in a pink satin dress. Blond curls—short, but curls nevertheless—framed her sweet face. She was as feminine a creature as Libby had ever seen, and as beautiful as an angel, in spite of the tiny devilish grin on her lips when her bright eyes met Libby's stunned gaze.

"I don't believe it," Libby whispered. Blinking, she said it again. "I don't believe it."

As if on cue, the musicians seated at the back of the room began to play a kind of angelic music. Little Andy stepped forward in perfect timing with the soft strains. No, Libby thought. Not Andy. Not anymore. She was Amanda now. A little girl who was no longer afraid to look like one.

Clutching her bouquet of pink roses to her waist, the child came closer, and as she did her smile increased to a full-fledged grin.

"It's me, Miss Libby," she whispered as she passed. "Look, Shad. It's me."

Libby couldn't speak for the lump in her throat, so Shad spoke for both of them when he said, "You look downright fetchin', Miss Amanda."

"Why, thank you, kind sir," Andy replied.

A little tremor of panic coursed through Libby just then. It was all well and good for the child to have quit denying her femininity, but she seemed to have gone too far, too fast in the opposite direction. Good grief! She sounded almost like Shula.

Just then, though, as if sensing Libby's concerns, Andy's grin got even wider. "Just wait'll you see those pups of mine, Miss Libby. I'll be so glad to get them back to Paradise and away from crabby Miss Shula."

The volume of the music increased dramatically then. It was accompanied by an abrupt *psst* from the doorway, where the bride stood in all her satin glory, motioning her flower girl along.

"Oops," Andy gulped, then picked up her pace

toward the fireplace, where the minister and Hoyt were waiting.

In truth, Shula looked altogether queenly as she came down the aisle between the guests' chairs. Her eyes were fixed on Hoyt, for the most part, but they did stray occasionally to appraise the reactions of her audience.

Like Andy before her, Shula paused where Libby and Shad were sitting.

"Libby, Libby, Libby," she whispered, shaking her head slightly. "You look…"

For once in her life, Libby decided she'd beat her sister to the punch by insulting herself before Shula could do it.

"It's good to see you, too, Shula. And I look what?" she asked irritably. "Like I just got off a cattle train?"

Shula blinked. "Happy, Libby. I was going to say you look happier than I've ever seen you."

"Oh."

"You, too, Shad. You both look like marriage suits you perfectly."

"Much obliged, ma'am," Shad drawled.

Libby was nearly speechless. "Yes. Thank you, Shula. I suppose it does. Suit us, that is."

Shula cast a smile toward her eager groom. "Well, I only hope it suits me as well." She took a small step forward, then paused. "Oh, and Libby?"

"Yes?"

"Honey, you do look like you just got off a cattle train." Shula winked. "And it must've been one hell of a trip."

*   *   *   *   *

MEN at WORK

All work and no play?
Not these men!

July 1998

MACKENZIE'S LADY by Dallas Schulze

Undercover agent Mackenzie Donahue's
lazy smile and deep blue eyes were his best
weapons. But after rescuing—and kissing!—
damsel in distress Holly Reynolds, how could
he betray her by spying on her brother?

August 1998

MISS LIZ'S PASSION by Sherryl Woods

Todd Lewis could put up a building with ease,
but quailed at the sight of a classroom! Still,
Liz Gentry, his son's teacher, was no battle-ax,
and soon Todd started planning some
extracurricular activities of his own....

September 1998

A CLASSIC ENCOUNTER
by Emilie Richards

Doctor Chris Matthews was intelligent, sexy
and *very* good with his hands—which made
him all the more dangerous to single mom
Lizette St. Hilaire. So how long could she
resist Chris's special brand of TLC?

Available at your favorite retail outlet!

MEN AT WORK™

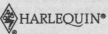

Look us up on-line at: http://www.romance.net   PMAW2

Take 2 bestselling love stories FREE

Plus get a FREE surprise gift!

Happy Birthday, Harlequin Historicals!

Now, after a decade of giving you the best in historical romance, **LET US TAKE YOU BACK...**

to a time when damsels gave their warriors something to fight for...ladies wooed dashing dukes from behind their fans...and cowgirls lassoed the hearts of rugged ranchers!

With novels from such talented authors as

Suzanne Barclay	Margaret Moore
Cheryl Reavis	Ruth Langan
Deborah Simmons	Cheryl St.John
Susan Spencer Paul	Theresa Michaels
Merline Lovelace	Gayle Wilson

Available at your favorite retail outlet.

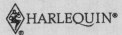

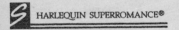

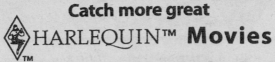 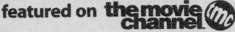

COMING NEXT MONTH FROM

HARLEQUIN HISTORICALS